A
PLACE
TO
— STAND —

allison astorino

"A wounded deer leaps the highest,"
- Emily Dickinson

1 — UNITED

It was something that rippled.

"You guys can all stay gone, seriously, no need to come back," Melrose huffed, kicking the heels of his boots into the dusty dirt that surrounded the car Sasha and Calliste were loading up. He wasn't helping. His eyes were covered with thick messy hair, to see better he said, against the sun. Sasha always suspected it was rather to see less, or let others see less.

"Some damn peace and quiet around here with you guys gone," he mumbled, looking out at the hills and valley that greeted the edge of Sasha's home property. She lived at the edge of town, closest to the sea and sky, rather than the highway or city vista. Calliste eyed him with annoyance for just a moment as he set the last of the old furniture going back to Sasha's grandparents' house in the back of the sedan. Laughter spilled out of an open window from the house. Both Sasha's and Melrose's parents were still having a good time inside, talking about the summers everyone was going to have – except Melrose.

"Ah, the boy will get a lot of work done this summer, a good start to the rest of his life. Whip him into shape, you know? The kid's too damn lazy, too damn into his own head. He's going to get a lot of work done this summer with those hands," his father was always repeating himself, "Yes, you're going to see in a few months, thick calluses all over his hands."

Melrose imitated his father well, but perhaps always added a thicker malice to his words than his father really had for him. The tone Melrose's father used most often, rather, was one of complete misunderstanding. And besides, Melrose did have thick calluses on his hands, from all the fighting.

"Mel, are you trying not to cry underneath all that hair? Huh, buddy? You going to miss us so much you just can't even stand it?" Calliste teased, coming a little closer to playfully tap his shoulder with a fist. He was such a small, delicate person. With lengthy blond hair, a perfect complexion, and baby blue eyes, many wondered how he had managed to live this long, and perhaps the answer was that he was surrounded by a monster, a witch, and a fool.

"You are coming tonight? Aren't you?" Sasha asked, her words cutting through the boys' teasing. Melrose was still deciding whether or not he finally wanted to let his fist make contact with Calliste's face, once and for all. He decided against it.

"Maybe," he replied gruffly, hands in pockets, expertly lounging against the garage's sturdy walls. Sasha's house was a thing of architectural beauty, but it was mostly horrifying in the night. Melrose loved it.

"Yeah, of course," Calliste replied happily. He, the most, was trying to forget where he was going that summer. His efforts so far had kept the idea at bay, but tomorrow morning at exactly six a.m. he would be off on a train to a place he wouldn't be able to easily escape. It was his father's idea.

"Where the hell is Davey? Kid too damn lazy to come and help pack up a car?" Melrose muttered, mocking his father some more. Melrose frequently compared himself to a dead horse; one his father was still beating relentlessly. Sasha always shuddered at the comparison.

"He's probably eating lunch with his Nonna or something, give him some time," Sasha mumbled as they finally closed the trunk of the car, then leaned against it, her hands tucked into the sides of her loose-fitting cotton pants. She was dark and light, all at the same time. Strange clothes, but a beautiful face. Thick dark hair always pulled back in massive, yet artful braids. Melrose almost hated her.

"Ah, the life of a church boy," he mocked, and Calliste snorted a little at the joke. Davey was the most put together out of any of them. He was the one they always pushed forward first to smooth things over when they inevitably got caught trying to pull one of their stunts. It was stunning to a lot of people that the four of them were still together. Of course, they had all found more similar circles of peers to surround themselves with in places such as school, late-night diners, parking lots, homecoming dances, and the like. But rather than call up these friends when going away for a summer, when fixing a broken car, finding out your mother had a stroke, or when you almost kill someone; instead, they called one another.

"You're just jealous that you weren't invited this time. Nonna Romano makes a mean ravioli," Calliste commented, doing a little dance around Melrose that caused him to violently roll his eyes before charging the kid, throwing him wailing over his shoulder, and pretending to dump him down the old well Sasha's home had out front. She looked on with the smallest grin playing at the corners of her mouth.

"It's not his fault you're not Italian, and no one's cooking authentic meals at your house," Sasha said after the two had settled down, sitting together along the edge of the nearly dried-up well. Sometimes animals would get stuck down there. Melrose was always the volunteer on every mission to save a poor baby bird or squirrel or something, climbing down the well with practiced expertise. He didn't mind small spaces.

"I really can't stand you sometimes, you know?" Melrose commented back, huffing a little. She shrugged, sitting down beside him, the three looking up at the vast porch of the house, all

3

in stone. They could hear the laughing tones of their parents' conversation. Calliste's parents didn't come around too much anymore.

"Rose, you'll write, won't you?" Sasha murmured, looking at him from the side of her eye. He shrugged harshly.

"Don't know if I can," he muttered.

"Might have too many damn calluses," he replied a few moments later, his voice louder, dismissing his lack of summer plans. He wasn't sure exactly what summer was to hold for him. Knowing his father, he had a small inclination about the extent of hard work that would plague him for three months, and possibly the rest of his life. He could already feel the heat racing through his body, the fire baking his skin. He certainly preferred his thoughts to damning basements.

"I'm glad we got together before the summer, we'll have to catch up, you know? Never mind the kids being away to so many different places. I'm sure it'll just be so great for them, all this new experience," Melrose's mother rambled on to Sasha's parents as they walked them out to their car. Calliste gave a little wave, vanishing off into the side lot, down the road, and off to his own house for a few hours until they were meeting up later that evening. He, the most, needed a goodbye.

"Daisy, really, I think it will all go just fine," Sasha's mother, Vivienne, replied, giving her a little hug at the car. The men shook hands, their voices gruff and cut up into short sentences.

"Oh, it'll be good. A little separation, a little bit of time to think on their toes, good stuff, all good," they repeated, over and over, saying the same things in a loop. Melrose rolled his eyes, standing up when Daisy looked at him, his cue.

"Sasha, I'm sure you'll have a lovely time with your grandparents up in the city, It'll be wonderful," Daisy said, so tipsy, as she gave Sasha the biggest, most engulfing hug. Sasha tried her best to return it, but couldn't as Melrose pretended to blow his brains out behind them. A firm hand grabbed him up by the shoulder, pulling him away from the women and into the men's small circle. His father, Bernard, was nearly the opposite of the petite Daisy. It was a hard dichotomy to live around most of the time. The strictness, yet the leniency. It was like pruning flowers. At least if he lived only under strictness, then he would just relinquish himself to not growing. Or if it were all leniencies, then he'd probably grow like a wildflower. But this in-between, where he could grow, and then be immediately hacked back, simply led to inner fury and quiet mumbling.

"Melrose, you going to work hard this summer?" Sasha's father, Frank, asked, voice loud and booming. Melrose nodded, mumbling his reply as always.

"Yes, sir."

"Couldn't think of anything better, might straighten you out, keep you on that right path. Could lead to a full-time position. That would be good. You know, I've known you since you were a kid. And we all want the best out of life for you," he continued. Sasha looked on, past their mothers' conversation, to study Melrose's face. It was so well constructed, so many places to hide his feelings. It was almost like he didn't have any until he was mad. Then you knew, but it was already too late. The rage, of course, was something Sasha's father was hinting towards.

"It'll be good," Melrose meekly replied, barely surviving the vigorous handshake to follow, only to be shuffled into the car in one fell swoop. As Daisy and Bernard drove off, Melrose looked out the back window, watching Sasha give a little wave in front of her chest. Thankfully, they were getting together that night, one last time.

2 – BROTHERHOOD

Davey hustled out of his Nonna's front yard. He'd only meant to get caught up for an hour or two, but of course all the cousins, aunts, and uncles had stopped by when they smelled the ravioli cooking and the deep tree smell of summer. It was both a pleasure and a calamity having the entire family occupy one block of the neighborhood.

"Now, you're going to call, aren't you? Not going to get caught up in the way those Bianchi live their lives, yeah? That lifestyle might be fun for the summer, but I know your mother and father raised you better," his Nonna had whispered in his ear after giving him a tight hug goodbye, as if he were going off to war or something of the violent, horrifying sort. Her words were often venom; she sliced others apart as the matriarch of her own flock. It was just how the Italian women were, gossip floating around through each branch of the family, trying to be the best, always excusing their own but never anyone else. Davey suspected it wasn't all about blood.

"Nonna, I promise I'll come back and keep cutting your grass and going to church on Sundays," he had whispered in the best most comforting tone he could muster. He loved the old woman, but she drove a lot of people mad. With a few pats on the head, he was out the door, scurrying away to finish packing for the ride to his mother's cousin's house. He remembered his Bianchi cousins from a long time ago. The idea entranced him. He wanted to get away, to see some deep forests, to live beside the lake. He wanted to eat fish by the fire every night, chucking bones out behind him into the brush. Mostly, he wanted to taste another flavor of wine. Perhaps he would choose white over red in the end. That thought alone would send old Nonna to the grave.

With enough tee shirts to stock him for a summer, Davey made peace with his parents before heading out the back door, taking the short cut through the woods to Calliste's property. While they lived in town, his family owned substantial acreage out in the countryside surrounding their small village. And conveniently, there was an old abandoned house from the last century, and it had housed the four happily over their decade-long friendship.

He didn't even make it off the street.

"Davey! Hey! Come here a second, would ya?" his uncle called out from his garage, wearing khaki pants and a tucked in undershirt, a cigarette blazing between his lips. His hands were greasy, and Davey rolled his eyes internally. Something was wrong with the car, again. He needed help, again. And again, he still knew nothing about an engine.

"Yeah, what do you need?" he asked, coming over, being the good nephew he knew himself to be. He had a reputation of true dependability within his family. All the aunts and uncles and cousins and grandparents knew that without a doubt, Davey would come running to fix so much as a leaky faucet. That was probably why his Nonna favored him so much.

"The transmission isn't shifting, again," his Uncle Giovanni complained, staring at the open hood of their family car. Davey hardly had the gumption to tell him that most fifteen-year-old cars just die. They don't live forever, and you can only make so many trips to the junkyard for the right parts.

"Well, we could try what we did last time, that seemed to set it right for at least a few months, until we can go and get the parts again?" Davey inquired, trying to speed up the process. Giovanni liked to talk, but most of it was incoherent mumblings.

"Yeah, yeah…we can do that again. Here," he said, handing a wrench over to Davey, who was already rolling up his shirt sleeves and sticking his hands into the depths of the complicated engine. They worked together for about an hour, and after that, covered in grease, Davey was finally free to go.

"You're heading out to your mother's family tomorrow, aren't you?" he said curiously, just as Davey took one step out of the garage and into the waning light of the evening. A yellow hue was cast over their entire street; it helped to hide the stains on his arms from the bargained work.

"Yeah, her cousin's place. I'll be there for the summer," he replied, sensing a little bit of judgment in his uncle's voice. As close-knit as everyone was, there were always secrets and family dramas, proving to be, what Davey thought, of the worst kind.

"Well, stay out of trouble," Giovanni reminded, waving him off as he finished yet another cigarette. Davey didn't spend too much time thinking about his uncle's words; he just quickly ran across the street, through a yard of a distant cousin, and hopped the fence into the woods, quickly finding the trail. The woods didn't scare Davey Romano, but they weren't exactly exciting, either. They just seemed like trees. His cousins, he knew, lived out in a house in the woods. He wondered what it would be like, and although he was excited to see these people he hadn't seen in so long, a part of him felt anxious. They were extremely different, so he thought.

"You're late, as usual," Melrose commented from his perch on the top of the old porch roof of the house, his words shocking Davey out of his thoughts as he reached the small clearing. Davey bit back his tongue to keep from telling him about how unsteady that old roof was.

"Is anyone else here?" he asked.

"No, you're the first," Melrose replied. Davey sighed.

"Then how are you giving me shit for being late?" he asked,

walking over and climbing the tree next to the porch. It was much sturdier. And if Davey got a scar, his family would notice.

"Well, they have actual things to do," Melrose said, laughing a little as he lit up a cigarette. He had stopped offering them to Davey long ago. He never asked Calliste. Sometimes, Sasha would take one and smoke half.

"Your sense of camaraderie is endearing," Davey said, leaning back against the trunk of the tree, appreciating how easy it was to be around people who expected nothing from him, neither in labor or crafty solutions. Melrose rolled his eyes at his comment, smoking the rest of his cigarette in silence. Neither Sasha nor Calliste showed up before he was done. He debated smoking another one in succession but decided against it if only to save Davey from chewing on his tongue longer to keep from telling him about lung cancer. He knew what he thought.

"So, you're going to the forbidden land tomorrow?" Melrose asked.

"Yeah, but it's not forbidden," Davey mumbled, looking over at his friend. They were the most at-odds with one another, but it never seemed to matter much.

"Oh, I bet if I ask your Nonna after a couple glasses of wine, she'd have plenty to say about forbidden land," Melrose said, chuckling a little, fixing his position on the top of the old porch. It creaked and groaned but still held him up. Davey's heart raced.

"All right, but she has ideas about families based on nothing but superstition," he replied, thinking back to the look his uncle had given him. She wasn't the only one.

"Well, if you ask me, which no one ever does, superstitions come from somewhere. She's worried you're going to ditch your shoes, or grow out your hair. Or, heaven forbid, start drinking white wine," he teased, and Davey huffed. He didn't think he'd ever choose the white over the red. He liked the bitter; avoided the sweet. It was too easy to drink, almost bubbly. His family had ideas about easy alcohol.

"Well, Mel, at least she'd have you to replace me with to drink all the red wine," Davey teased, and Melrose took it well, considering he was really trying to stop drinking. The Romanos were split down the middle about Davey's loner friend Melrose. Some of them found him charming and solid, while others found him dark and shifty. Regardless, wine was offered at every dinner, every visit. Melrose had to stop going around the Romanos' street so often if he was going to entertain the idea of staying sober.

"I don't know how all three of us can be here first when Calliste owns this place," Sasha shouted up, emerging from the wooded path. She was wearing a loose, long-sleeved white shirt that flowed in the faint breeze. She seemed the lightest thing there, even though her thickly braided hair was nearly black.

"He's small, give him some time," Melrose said, looking over the edge of the roof to peer down at the third member of their band. She didn't stay down on the ground long, instead climbing up to sit next to Davey on the tree branch. She didn't have as much anxiety in her chest as he did, but even she preferred not falling through hundred-year-old wood and nails.

"You're so mean to him, Rose," she said, using his nickname lightly. He shrugged. They all knew he wasn't.

"Are you already packed?" Sasha asked Davey, looking at his stained arms.

"Yeah, I have to be. I leave tomorrow morning early," he replied.

"What about you?"

"Not really. I don't know what to bring and what not to. My grandparents have... certain ideas about things. Most of my family does. It's easy to hide out here," she said, thinking.

"Must be hard, not knowing which bank account to put all the money in," Melrose said quickly. She let his words dangle in the air for a moment. They fell quickly, shattering on the dirty ground beneath them.

"You'll be making bank this summer. I guess you can catch up," Sasha said after a moment. He moaned, sinking down on the roof until he was lying down completely. He didn't want to think about it. The sun was sinking fast behind the tree line, and although their eyes were adjusting, it wouldn't be much longer before they'd need to start a fire.

"Hey, if you learn anything about transmissions, my uncle could really use a lesson," Davey added, retaliating for the talk about his forbidden land.

"I hope a machine falls on me and ends it all," Melrose finally replied, as Davey and Sasha laughed at how melodramatic he was being. He was careless sometimes, but they both felt he'd be fine.

"It would have been easier to find this place if you had started a fire," a small voice said, rising up from the path. The three looked down to find their forth and final member, small as could be, heaving after most likely running the whole way.

"Oh, but you're so good at it," Davey said, jumping down off the branch quickly and wandering over to the fire pit with Calliste, ready to do whatever work he could. Sasha and Melrose stayed up high for a moment, looking down at the two hardest workers, the ones eager to please.

"You don't actually want a giant machine to crush you, do you?" Sasha asked as soon as she finally started to see small flames at the base of the fire, just begging to grow larger and consume the bigger branches.

"Being shot with a pistol would also be satisfying," he replied with a sly grin, pushing himself to the edge of the roof, the whole structure swaying a little as he finally jumped down. He waited for Sasha to climb down. She wasn't as good at jumping and landing on her feet. He grabbed her hand, spun her around a few times, and let go as they made their way to the fire that was now roaring. The sun was officially gone; leaving a darkness that surrounded them but couldn't invade their circle.

"Record timing," Sasha said as she perched herself on one of the logs that surrounded the fire, much too big to ever burn.

"I have a very specific skill set," Calliste said, setting more wood onto the flame as Davey fanned it with an old piece of cardboard. It was Davey who could truly engineer a fire, but they liked to give the credit to Calliste every time. Eventually, they felt confident enough to let the fire tend itself.

"Look what I found," Melrose said, coming out of the old house. He had chocolate, marshmallows, and crackers, things he had raided from the cooler they kept inside. He hated to wait for the treats to be brought out every time they came to the old house. He wasn't greedy, though, and passed them out before taking some for himself. Everyone was quiet for a moment, feeling content. It was, of course, Davey who broke the silence with his worry.

"What are we going to do all summer?"

Nobody knew. If asked by anyone else, Sasha would say spending time with her grandparents, Davey would talk about experiencing the lake, Calliste would mumble something about building up himself through exercise and discipline with no sarcasm in his voice, and Melrose would spout some speech about being alive just to work until death. But there was a feeling over all of them that suggested something else. When one of their own asked the question, the answers didn't come as quickly. Most were lying to themselves. They'd never gone months without being able to knock on one another's front door and demand proof of life. There were times when each of them had gone away for a little while, needed a break. It was never forced, not like this, and not all at once. Davey felt anxious. Calliste felt fear. Sasha was curious. And Melrose felt trapped.

"Well, you'll probably get a sunburn," Melrose finally said, breaking through everyone's silent thoughts. Davey laughed, thinking about it.

"My skin doesn't burn," he reminded. Melrose shook his head, almost annoyed.

"That's what you think because you live in a cloudy place. Wait 'til you see some real sun, you damn American," he said, stripping away the always-mentioned Italian.

"You're going to be getting the sunburn," Davey said, leaning back a little and tucking his hands into his pockets, his legs separated and outstretched in from of him. He always took up the most room.

"No, I got in at the assembly plant. So I'm never going to see the light of day ever again," he added, for dramatic flair. Sasha rolled her eyes.

"Maybe I'll get so strong I'll be able to take you on," Calliste quietly mentioned, trying to sound hopeful. He flexed both his arms, kissing each side that held no muscle.

"Yeah, man, maybe," Davey replied, equally hopeful.

"It'll be good," Melrose agreed.

"Definitely," Sasha said, without thinking. She was distracted by her own worries, but wasn't completely shut off from her friends'. She'd never spent so much time away from her parents. It wasn't exactly homesickness that she was worried about, but no one else in the Raskova family thought quite like her three-person family. Cast out of the quiet acceptance her parents offered and their country home, Sasha wasn't sure how to fit in as effortlessly as she did everywhere else.

"You sound so convinced," Melrose said, picking on Sasha. He either made things easy for her or very hard. His moods and attitudes shifted easily. She didn't blame him for it, though.

"Calliste, you have all my confidence that you will come back able to knock this guy in the face in a few months," Sasha said directly to the littlest and palest member of their group. He smiled at her confidence but knew absolutely it would never happen. Davey stood up quickly and came back with some more supplies to make s'mores. He was the only one with any trace of true excitement about what his summer would hold.

The four spent a few hours sitting by the fire, talking about the summers they'd have, their excitements and their curiosities, the things they liked and the things that worried them the most. Together, they finished off the last of the treat supplies at the old *Chateau*, as Calliste liked to call it. The name had stuck. It got to be about midnight when the fire died down, and it was finally time to leave. They hugged, said their goodbyes, and promised to write to each other. With that promise, they knew that Davey would write the most frequently, Calliste would write if he really needed something, Sasha would write when she thought about them, and Melrose would read everything. As they departed, Melrose and Davey in one direction, Calliste and Sasha in two different directions, Sasha looked back one last time and watched as Melrose did the same, looking at the same log he did every time, the one that remained empty each meeting they had under the stars.

3 – STRENGTH

He was never quite sure what he'd be walking into. It was always a toss – his father's views of the world directly tied to how his mother was feeling that day. Was she nauseous? Or did she enjoy the food he cooked for her? Was she depressed? Did she smile when the sun came out? Did seeing her son make her proud? Did it just remind her she was an inadequate fixture in his life? Calliste never thought the latter, but truth is not always the basis of other's emotions.

Stepping inside, he was greeted by silence. That was the most unsettling, because he was never sure what it meant. Things could be truly good or horribly wrong. Noise meant life was happening, or at the very least, he knew where the problem was and could avoid it. He often, now, tried not to ever inspect – just avoid. He couldn't that evening.

"Are you packed?" his father asked, glaring down over the railing of the upstairs balcony. Calliste nodded. He did everything by the book out of dread. And of course, he packed before he was asked to.

"You have everything on the list?" he asked, peering down which such doubt. Life had played a cruel joke on Adam, but

Calliste hadn't. It was something he needed his father to know.

"Your mother is sleeping. Say your goodbye early tomorrow morning. Do not forget. Do not wake up late," his father said, and Calliste quickly nodded. He did not roll his eyes or make any kind of snide remark. It was a true skill, although some likened it to being a coward. Satisfied with his son's single nod, he retreated to the back office, the closest room to his wife. He had no doubt she was actually sleeping. She was starting to feel better these days, and that meant more restful nights and better mornings.

Climbing the steps carefully, Calliste walked down the long hall that led to the back room he called his own. It was far away from the rest of the house, occupying the far corner. It looked back over the wooded back yard, and sometimes from the roof, he could see the small clearing where the *Chateau* was. His mother had taught him some of her native tongue before she started to slip away.

For an average-sized house, Calliste had a large room, and it held a lot of things. As a child, he had spent a great deal of time alone in his room, creating magic kingdoms and wild stories within the four walls. What he liked was too whimsical for many others to understand, or empathize with.

The military camp had been very specific in what they allowed into the dorms. They had also been extremely explicit that anything not mentioned on the official list was prohibited. It wasn't that Calliste didn't care about that rule, but he couldn't possibly go somewhere without a book or two, leaves pressed into the pages he favored the most. He also couldn't fathom how harsh a place it could be. He thought he'd seen enough, experienced enough, to be able to go through a few months of yelling and running. He couldn't possibly have known.

That night he slept fitfully, his dreams filled with dark monsters prowling through tall grasses by a deep creek. He could only feel their shapes as they treaded through the grass, pushing him to the bank of the creek so they could pounce. Black shadows jumped out at him, pushing him down, forcing him to look up at the sky, brilliantly lit up with green shimmering shapes. He woke promptly at five-thirty with a start; breathing heavily and thinking about how Sasha and he would sometimes sit up on the roof and watch the Northern Lights entertain the sky. His alarm went off a minute later.

He got up, stretched, and went to shower. He used shampoo that smelled like strawberries. After drying off, he wiped the fog off the mirror and looked at himself for a long time. He was short, and small. His features were more boyish than that of a sixteen-year-old. Bright blue eyes sat wide in his face, and he worked to comb back his translucent blond hair. He'd had to shave the sides; nothing could touch his ears, but he had kept the top a little longer, combing it back and securing it with gel. It didn't look half bad. He got dressed and crept out into the hall, towards the stairs.

"Calliste," his mother whispered softly from her room, able to see him through the crack in the door. He turned around quickly.

Come see me," she asked, waving him in. She was still in bed and would need her husband's help if she wanted to get up and dressed. He moved forward, the hall still dark in the early morning. His mother's room was mostly dark anytime of day. Carefully, he sat down on the bed next to her, cross-legged. She looked up and studied his face for a long time. Sometimes, it took her awhile to collect her thoughts and speak.

"*J'amour tu*," she whispered through her teeth. He repeated it back to her, grabbing her hand only after she reached out for his.

"Will you be okay, for the summer?" she asked, opening her eyes and looking back into his. Calliste always felt uncomfortable looking her in the eyes, because they were exactly his, staring back, just in a much different person.

"*Oui*, don't worry about me," he quickly replied, trying to assure her. She didn't seem convinced, wasn't sure of the plan.

"And this place is a, well, a camp or something?" she asked, confused by it.

"Yeah, like a summer camp. It'll be fun. I'll write to you, even call if they have a phone," he replied, knowing already that there was only one phone call allowed for the first three weeks, and that was reserved for when you first arrived. She squeezed his hand. He wondered briefly, again, what it would have been like to be raised by her through it all.

"Do you want to go?" she asked. She seemed sad, upset that he didn't want to stay. He knew she couldn't possibly know much, trapped in that room all the time.

"It's not that I want to go. I just think it'll be nice to try something new," he offered, so stupidly he couldn't believe she even bought it. Maybe that wasn't the right word; she seemed less sad but more confused. Her grip tightened.

"You'll write?" she asked, eyes begging.

"Of course," he promised. Her hand loosened up; it was too early for her to have much strength. He let it fall gently to her side, then stood up and quietly left while she was half asleep and half awake. It was a weird dimension to be stuck in.

Adam was already up and making eggs when Calliste came down. Part of that annoyed him, but he stayed indifferent on the outside.

"Good morning, Dad," he murmured as he went to pour himself a bowl of cereal. The eggs were never for him, sometimes for his mom, but never him. His father murmured a good morning and continued to cook. He disappeared for a while, probably talking to Alice about where he'd be that morning, if she wanted any breakfast, and of course he'd have his cell phone on him if she needed anything. After their conversation, he seemed more stressed than relaxed. She had put in a good word for Calliste, he was sure of it.

"Put your bags in the car," he said, coming back down the steps, dressed and ready to take Calliste to the train station. He didn't have the heart to tell his dad they were already in the trunk, so instead he calmly walked out to the garage and waited for his dad to come out to drive him. The radio was never on during their rides together. Calliste looked out the window for the half an hour drive to the train station in the next town over. He already missed the trees that lined his driveway, the rolling hills where Sasha's large home was nestled. He watched as they drove past the dirty, packed streets of working family homes, Melrose probably sleeping on the roof of his own house or doing something equally as ridiculous. When they drove past the downtown full of shops and restaurants, he caught a whiff of bread cooking and thought about Davey's Nonna's homemade pasta. He already missed everyone.

His father parked the car carefully in the lot, taking a moment before getting out and walking Calliste to his platform. It was a moment of thought, careful consideration. Calliste had never told him he'd rather not go. His father never really considered the possibility. Somewhere down the line, he'd forgotten his son felt things differently than he did. He truly did love him. It was just hardened now, like a diamond, after dealing with so much pressure over so much time. Adam did think this would be good for him.

"Are you ready?" he asked, a little softer than before. Calliste almost choked but nodded anyway. Anxiety was starting to take over, and he felt his hands shake as he carried his two duffle bags to the right platform, waiting for the train to pull up so he could board.

"Your mother would really appreciate it if you'd write," Adam commented, not looking down at Calliste, who looked paler than usual.

"Yeah, I'll write," he promised quickly, his words mixing together. The sun was just starting to peak over the top of the hills and trees that surrounded the little towns scattered in between country and city. Calliste felt cold. The train pulled up, whooshing dirty air into everyone's faces on the platform. Most people got on wordlessly, others gave big hugs to family and friends and waved excitedly as they boarded. Adam just nodded at his son as he picked up the bags from the ground and boarded the train, taking a seat in the middle of the car. He stayed until the train started to move forward, watching, but didn't wave.

4 – RICHES

Sasha always felt out of place at family functions. It wasn't her own doing. The blame, rather, rested on her parents' shoulders. But she didn't blame them. The Raskova family was full of old money; her concept of cost was almost nothing. Her parents took that information with a grain of salt, and so they crafted her outcast life before she was even born.

Her father was a painter, painting canvases bigger than he was. They were magnificent depictions, and the art world had always validated these creations. He was far from unacknowledged. Sasha's mother was a writer and often spent long, tortured hours deciding whose fate it would be to live and die. Her books ranged up to a thousand pages. She was heavily criticized. Her parents' lives had left Sasha with a very quiet childhood. She was their creation together, words and looks. She was a completed work, or so everyone felt, and so she often did foolish things to try to break the mold and find some part of herself that wasn't carefully constructed or completely solid. She loved her parents but had grown to hate the silence. So, she took up the violin, and her parents opened their doors when working to let her haunting melodies inside. It was a way of communication, and they could always tell when she was happy or upset.

So, at family gatherings, they had always sat in the back, quietly eating their food, unable to pretend to care about all the boastful conversations happening around them. They appreciated the money they had and were grateful that it allowed them to pursue the things they wanted to do without having to entertain the idea of having a job specifically to pay the bills. The lifestyle had given Sasha a lot, and she wasn't blind to that.

Spending the summer with her grandparents would be an interesting change of pace. Her grandmother had suggested it. When Vivienne told her daughter, she had been expecting her to laugh, wave it off, and continue eating her cereal. Instead, Sasha had looked her dead in the eye and asked when she could go. She'd finally have to act the part a little, dress like she meant it, and maybe see some sights the countryside couldn't possibly offer her. Also, she was curious to see how her mother's childhood must have been. She was already promised the room her mother grew up in; it had been barely touched. She had seen it a few times in passing but never was left alone in it, to look around, explore, stare out the window that faced the ocean, or sleep. If anything, she was nervously excited. Her mother, on the other hand, was just nervous.

"Are you sure you want to be gone that long? It's almost three full months. That's such a long time," Vivienne reminded, sitting on her daughter's bed as she watched her finish packing. They'd loaded the heavy stuff earlier, things her mother was giving back to her parents. Now, she was just finishing up. Sasha kept asking her mother for advice on what to bring and what not to bring, and so far, it looked like she might have to go shopping. Her clothes weren't up to the standard her grandmother would demand.

"It's two months and a few weeks. And yes, I think it'll be fun. Normally you advocate for new experiences," Sasha said, folding up a few tee shirts and tucking them neatly into her open suitcase. Her windows were wide open even though it was late at night; it was one of the many good things Sasha liked about living out in the country.

21

"Yeah, but not from my mother," Vivienne whined, laying back on the bed. She often felt like her mother had tried to suffocate her in her sleep dozens of times and blamed the suffocating presence her mother had as the reason why she felt the need to marry at eighteen and have her only child at eighteen and a half.

"Besides where her values lie, she seems like a fine person," Sasha argued, looking up at her mother. Her face was turned towards her daughter, giving her a look that pronounced insanity upon her.

"That hardly makes any sense," Vivienne replied, huffing. Sasha shrugged.

"My girls, how is all this packing going?" Frank asked, coming into the room with two mugs of hot chocolate. Everyone was trying to get off the caffeine for various reasons, mostly work-related, and not wanting to try Adderall.

"Mom thinks Grandma is going to turn me into an evil, chiffon-wearing, prototype of a sophisticated brat. I might demand servants when I get back," Sasha teased, and her father shared her laugh while her mother just groaned from the bed. She'd closed her eyes, unable to even entertain such ideas.

"Honey, I think we've raised a stable daughter. She'll be just fine. You turned out alright," Frank reminded, sitting down next to his wife on the bed. He looked over at her, and she could feel his gaze digging into her. They loved each other.

"Did I, though? Some say I'm completely deranged. And if you ask the New York Times…" she started but trailed off as her husband put his finger over her lips.

"Who here is asking a magazine about your mental status?" Sasha asked, pretending to be bewildered. Her father and herself were often on the receiving end of a lot of rants about criticism. So had a few plates, one window, and occasionally the old cat. Vivienne sighed again.

"But if you ask me, it is kind of bullshit that Joslyn had to die like that," Sasha teased, and her mother sat up quickly, looking at her daughter for answers. It kept her up at night, if her character rightfully died, and her daughter almost never talked about her work, or even mentioned if she read it.

"Did you…?" she started to ask, but Sasha cut her question short.

"Is this skirt too short for gallivanting around the beach?"

"No, it's fine," her mother replied, sinking back on the bed. Frank rubbed her shoulders tenderly as they watched their daughter move back and forth getting clothes out of the closet, the dresser, and occasionally off the floor.

"Are you going to miss your friends?" her father asked, breaking the silence.

"Not as much as I'll miss you two," Sasha replied with a silly smile. Her mother waved her comment off, but it made her happy anyway. They really were very proud of the person Sasha was turning out to be, even though sometimes they questioned if their parenting style was really conducive to raising a child.

"How's Melrose going to be, with everyone gone?" her mother asked. Sasha stiffened slightly but didn't let it break her careful packing decisions.

"He's the same. He'll be just fine. We all promised to write," Sasha said, her back to her parents for the first time all evening. They seemed to think about her answer.

"He's not really the same though, is he?" Frank asked.

"He is," Sasha said, needing that to be the end of it.

"Bernard seems really happy to get that kid to work," Frank continued, though taking a different path, one Sasha could talk about a little easier. Two years was two years too short.

"Yeah, and Rose is just thrilled with that," she replied, turning back around to hold up two different pairs of shoes for her mother to look over. She silently pointed to a pair, and those were the ones Sasha tossed into her bag. They weren't the ones her grandmother would like best, but Vivienne knew Sasha liked them more.

"Oh, he seems like it. Bernard seems to think he's going to get into some serious trouble otherwise," he said, wondering what his daughter thought about it. The three of them were always able to have very open conversations. There seemed to be only one topic where Sasha closed the door and preferred the silence she so often fought.

"I don't think so. He's the same old Rose, making the same old decisions. They might not all be good ones, but none of them are going to land him in any kind of real trouble," Sasha said, believing that to be true. Of course, she knew he smoked more than anyone thought, he fought more than anyone realized, but friends are gatekeepers, and Melrose had good ones.

"I tried to tell Daisy that, but I think she already knows. It's not her who necessarily needs the convincing," Vivienne added, thinking about her most recent conversation with the two. Vivienne was often comparing her marriage to others', and her most recent comparisons rested with the Bartletts. She was having the hardest time with it, however, because she couldn't even begin to fathom putting herself in their situation.

"Yeah, probably not," Sasha said, putting one last dress into her suitcase before zipping it up. She took a sip of her hot chocolate; smoke still rising from the top.

"Are there baby marshmallows in this?" she asked.

"Of course, how else do you make a good cup?" her dad replied, and smiling, she took another big sip. She wondered if her grandparents had hot chocolate in their kitchen. She glanced down at her full name, scribbled on a nametag attached to the handle of her bag. *Sasha Raskova*, only owning her mother's name because her parents had thought it would be a wild social experiment. Her father had quickly changed his last name to match his daughter's and also to join in on their wild social experiment. She always laughed at their telling of her birth.

"What are you two going to do when I'm gone?" Sasha asked, although she already knew their answers before they could offer them up.

"Finish *Blue Day*," her mom chipped in right as her father mentioned, "Finish my third installment in *Monarch*."

"So more of the same?" Sasha asked and they both nodded, unable to say it aloud.

"You both have to promise me you'll go outside at least twice a day, preferably for a walk around the back if you can manage to fit it in," Sasha said. Often, Vivienne and Frank got so wrapped up in their work that they lost track of the time, sometimes for days. Now that Sasha was older, she forced her parents to sleep at normal hours, eat breakfast, and go on much-needed walks in the sun. "Your vitamin D, I'm sure, has plummeted," she was always reminding them, and because they loved her, and they loved each other, they welcomed her reminders. Their walks and omelets in the mornings courtesy of the chickens Sasha had insisted they get as part of an incentive to get outside and care for something other than their art was the best part of their days. "Art isn't everything, and it only comes from you caring about something else first," she also always reminded.

"We will, we promise. I'll send you pictures of it," her mother promised her, smiling with a little sadness, already missing her daughter's company.

"And do not let Freckles die," Sasha demanded, looking both of them in the face.

"We solemnly swear," her father replied, holding up one hand. Freckles was her favorite, and the matriarch of the flock. Her mother had asked if maybe the poor hen deserved a name with more power, and her father suggested a few famous artists, but Sasha had demanded Freckles. It was a chicken; she didn't need to be revolutionary.

"Well, get some sleep, okay? We have to leave bright and early tomorrow. I think your grandparents already planned a lunch to show you off at," Vivienne said, trying to entice Sasha to just stay home for the summer.

"Sounds like fun," Sasha replied sweetly, hugging both of her parents tightly before they left, leaving her alone to change into one of her father's old tee shirts, and unbraid all of her hair. It was long and thick, and she always twisted complicated braids together to keep it out of her face and not have too much weight in one place. It wasn't even that she liked her hair long; she just didn't like the thought of hair salons.

She looked out her open window from her bed, able to see everything lit up by moonlight once her eyes adjusted. She'd miss the country, her friends, her violin, and her parents' quirky lifestyle. But she was ready for a little change, and a little voluntary discomfort.

5 – Church Boy

Everyone acted as if Davey was leaving for war. All the cousins and uncles and aunts crowded around the Romanos' driveway as Davey and his mother tried to pack the car with some sense of haste. Of course, they were all Romanos, so the thought was it was everyone's driveway to walk and crowd on. Davey liked the closeness, though; it was all he had ever known. Growing up on a street that consisted almost exclusively of family was an interesting way of living. Sometimes, his mother got a little claustrophobic. She wasn't from city life. Instead she grew up out by small wooded towns and around many lakes. Her son didn't know what a lake summer was like; she thought perhaps it was time he got a taste of what it was like to live as a Bianchi. He had that blood in him too, after all.

"Oh, he'll be fine! I'm sure you can get any number of your grandsons to cut the grass, Mama," Vince announced loudly as he stood around with his brothers and mother, waiting for the car to be packed and his family to take off. He was a big, strong man who was always cracking jokes, his loud voice sure to catch everyone's attention. He wasn't worried about anything. He lived contently with all his family and enjoyed summer grilling and evening wine drinking up and down the street.

"That's not the point," Nonna replied, a little quieter, but not so quietly so that Marie couldn't hear her. No one was ever good enough, except Davey.

"You're going to miss a lot," his cousin Joel commented as Davey slammed the trunk shut. His cousins surrounded him; they had always made him feel like anything but an only child. Davey shrugged, his fingers gently touching the gold crucifix around his neck, and beside it, the bull's horn.

"You mean fixing your dad's car and cutting Nonna's grass?" he asked, teasing, and Joel pushed him back. For a second they gently tossed each other around, fighting a little until Nonna screamed for them to stop. She was never pleased with roughhousing.

"Okay, ready?" his mother whispered, and Davey nodded.

"*Ciao*, everyone, I'll write!" Davey yelled out across the crowd of people. Most would miss him, some just wanted to make sure he came back the same way he was leaving, and some worried about his impressionability.

At that rate, they wouldn't arrive at the cottage until after lunchtime, the sun already well overhead. There were many hugs to give, lots of cheek kisses, too. Finally, he reached his dad, who gave him a heavy handshake and a big engulfing hug.

"You'd better behave out there," Vince said, messing up his son's perfectly combed hair for a moment. Davey was so good at it, though, it was quickly fixed.

"Yeah, of course," he replied. He didn't sense any danger; it was just a vacation.

"You always are," Vince replied, equally unworried. Nonna gave him one more tight hug before he climbed into the front seat of the car. Marie carefully backed up, concentrating on not running over any small children. He waved until he couldn't see anyone anymore, then sat back and looked out the window at the passing houses, the end of his street. It was, without a doubt, his street.

They would be traveling across the state. It took a few hours before Davey and his mother were able to talk – her from finally getting the space to breathe again, and her son from adjusting to the quiet and lack of immediate need that was always thrown his way. He didn't even need to navigate. His mother knew exactly where she was going.

"So you grew up out here, in the woods?" Davey asked, the highway turning into an uncensored two-lane road. All that surrounded them were open fields and open skies. He'd seen it before. After all, Sasha lived in a beautiful country house. There was something different about these views, however, but he didn't quite notice.

"Well, not quite where we're going, but my cousins and I would spend our summers there. It would be nice to stay. But it's also nice that Sidney keeps coming out here, bringing her kids," his mother said, thinking back to her own childhood adventures of the sun warming her skin and living with a fear of lake monsters that could drag you down. Her imagination had run rampant those summers of her youth.

"So a big family, like Dad's?" he asked. She shook her head.

"Not big, but close," she replied. She was struck by how little her son knew about her own family and how she had grown up. It surprised her, but she instantly knew all the reasons why and how it had happened, remembering the way her husband's mother looked her over and spoke, ever-so passive aggressively.

"How did you and Dad meet again?" Davey asked, trying to piece a story together he hadn't even realized he was missing.

"At college. I was the first in my family to go, even out of my cousins. I didn't even really do it for the education, though that's important," she added, looking over at her son for a moment before continuing.

"I just felt like I needed to get out for a little while," she said.

"Seems like it's been a long while," Davey said, so quietly.

"Seems like it," she said, her tone closing off their talk for another hour, at least. His mother was always quiet, always moving around in the background. He was starting to realize that more and more as they drove, wondering how it had happened. Davey loved his mother very much, and they got along well. He had great memories of her telling wild ghost stories when he was a kid or making amazing ice cream sundaes at midnight when he couldn't sleep because of a storm. And as he got older, she was very good at giving advice or sensing when he needed to talk about something. He was starting to realize she was best at this when they were alone.

"Do you think they remember me?" Davey asked suddenly. His mother scoffed.

"Of course. I know you don't see them often, but you have seen them a few times. Having second thoughts about going?" she asked; ready to turn the car around if he didn't want to go. She wanted him to want this, not just her. He shook his head. He wanted to go more than anything, but he didn't know why. He just felt a push, even with all the anxiety drowning him.

"No, I do. I think it'll be a good time," he replied, running his hand over his dark brown hair to smooth it back a bit. His mother grinned to herself. His hair was bound to get roughed up out there in the woods and on the lake. She was ready for that change.

"Well, you can always call and write, you know that. Sidney and I had a really good time together, growing up. I know you haven't seen her kids in awhile, but I really think you guys will get along," she said, trying to reassure him. He accepted that. The ride was just another hour longer, before they finally exited the highway and drove another forty minutes on unpaved back roads. The trees seemed much different on that side of the state. They were taller, and more space was beneath them. Davey looked out through the woods and felt he could see their entire expanse, except for when a small hill would hinder his sight.

"We're here," Marie said quietly as the car crunched over the gravel in the driveway of the old cottage. Davey looked up at it, never having seen it before. It was two stories, small, but with a big porch. It was a weathered mint green and wooden. The lake was just behind it, a small piece of it, anyway, that got bigger the farther out you went. It glistened, beckoned to him. He turned away. A few kids were running around barefoot in the back, and for a moment, they looked over at the car, and then turned back to their games.

"Marie!" a woman yelled out, excited. She was tall and beautiful, her blonde hair pulled back artfully in a ponytail. Davey thought of Sasha's braids when he saw it.

"Sid!" she called back, getting out of the car and running up to give her a big hug. Davey had never seen his mother so animated in front of other people.

"And you remember Davey," Marie said, waving him over as he got out of the car slowly. Sidney gave him a huge hug, as if it hadn't been years since she'd seen him last.

"Oh my, how old are you now?" she asked, sizing him up. The way she did so made him blush.

"Uh, seventeen now," he replied, a little gruffly.

"Seventeen? So it's been five years, then. Whoa, Marie. How did that happen?" Sidney asked, giving her favorite cousin another tight embrace. They held it for a moment, unable to let go.

"Well, come on in. You guys hungry? Here, Davey, let's introduce you to the kids, or reintroduce you, I don't know how that works, exactly. Five years…my god," Sidney rambled as she led everyone inside the house. It was one big room, the kitchen to the left and the living room to the right. It was cluttered with everyone's clothes, bags, old shoes and misplaced furniture. Suitcases were sprawled around, there were four couches packed into the small living room and a big blue dining room table that took up most of the kitchen. In the very center of the space was a sliding glass door, and the view from it was breathtaking. Davey felt very much like a fish out of water. In the solitary armchair sat an older man, reading a newspaper with small glasses perched on his long nose.

"Nick! Look who's here!" Sidney said, her voice intrinsically loud. Nick looked up from his newspaper and smiled warmly at Marie.

"Well, if it isn't the old troublemaker," he said, his gaze resting on her for a minute before moving over to look at Davey. He felt like he was under a microscope.

"You sure raised a church boy, didn't you, Marie?" he commented, but instead of taking offense, she just wrapped one arm around her son's shoulders for a moment and laughed.

"He turned out to be one of the good ones. What have you been doing? Rotting away in that chair?" she said, and with that he set the old newspaper down and tried to stand up, but it took him a second try.

"Oh, still recovering from the incident back in '93," he said, and as he wobbled to the kitchen on a bum leg, he seemed to enjoy the memory of that moment in that year. Marie even chuckled. Davey didn't know what to think. He was used to taking things more seriously. Nick's humbled walk seemed painful, and he winced a little as he watched him move.

"Stop flirting with my cousin," Sidney said, right before she yelled out the back door for all the kids to come in. Nick gave her a kiss on the cheek before continuing to wobble to the refrigerator and set out cheese and lunch meats.

"You two hungry for lunch?" Nick asked, looking over at them.

"Sure," Marie replied, easily going to the fridge to help him bring out leftovers. Davey looked up at the clock, noting it was three in the afternoon.

"We just eat when we're hungry around here, son. There isn't exactly time when you're at the lake house all summer," Nick said, not looking up from the plates he was setting. Davey didn't have time to reply before the small herd of kids came running in, hungry, and curious as to whom their visitors were.

"Davey, you remember my kids? Jimmy and Karen?" Sidney asked, pointing to the two oldest kids. They looked at one another for a moment before nodding. Jimmy was Davey's age, but he looked wild. His sandy blonde hair was long and loose, his blue eyes piercing from underneath his dark brows. He was shirtless and barefoot, and his body was lean and appeared overworked. Karen was a smaller frame, a lighter blonde, but also barefoot and wearing cut off shorts and a loose tank top. Her legs were bruised and dirty, having trampled through the woods. She had the same eyes as her older brother.

"Yeah, it's been years, man," Jimmy said after their moment of taking each other in, and as he walked by, he clapped Davey's hand. Davey nodded, a little shy.

"You two are so big now," Marie said, giving both of them a big hug that they retuned. It was as if everyone had switched places. After being introduced to some of the other kids, Sidney's nephews and nieces who would come and go all summer, they sat down around the blue dining room table to eat the leftovers and lunchmeats. It was a free-for-all, kids grabbing bread, meats, cheeses, lettuce, and tomato and building their own kinds of sandwiches. There were days-old hard-boiled eggs, some calzone, and prosciutto sitting on the table as well. It was all served cold, and although that was something new for Davey, he found it exciting how easy it was to eat. He watched as his mother laughed openly, eating rolls of crackers with her prosciutto and ricotta. As his eyes scanned the room, they caught sight of two opened wine bottles sitting on the counter, the light hue of the white wine shining brilliantly in the bottle as the sun touched their surfaces through the open window.

6 – CALLUSES

It always started with not doing anything. That was Bernard's biggest complaint when it came to Melrose. He just didn't do anything. He perceived his son as lazy, unmotivated, and unfazed by the bigger picture around him. That was another phrase Melrose often mocked his father about – the *bigger* picture.

He'd gotten home late the night before his job was to start. All of his real friends were gone; he was stuck with the crowd from the high school, the leather jackets and switchblade carriers. And even though he was really trying to stop drinking, he got wicked drunk the night before his first day. Daisy teetered around the house nervously the next morning as she made breakfast for her boys. She wasn't sure how the morning would go.

With ten minutes until they had to leave, Melrose stumbled into the kitchen, half dressed, hair a mess, and with a dull look in his eyes. He carefully poured himself a large mug of black coffee, unable to even entertain the idea of eggs or bacon. Instead, he buttered some toast. Bernard was almost on fire.

"What were you doing last night?" he asked, struggling to keep his voice calm. Melrose always took it as a challenge, a fun little game. It made everything worse.

"Bible study. You know the Methodist place up the street is a lot more welcoming than the Catholic one we used to go to?" he replied, so evenly that Daisy wanted to believe that was what her son had truly been doing all night. But Bible study didn't get out at two in the morning.

"Is that so? You're just filled with the Spirit all of a sudden?" Bernard mocked, arms crossed over his thick chest. He looked a lot younger than he was. He was a workingman, and it kept him in shape. Besides, they'd had Melrose young, too.

"Certainly am, sir. Figured I'd recite the rosary while I screw something onto a car for eight hours today. And tomorrow. And the next day…" he would've continued, but he could tell that he had almost reached Bernard's threshold. Next there would be a broken dish or two, and he cared too much about his mom to let that happen on that particular morning.

With a gruff goodbye, Melrose pulled up the top half of his blue trousers, already full of grease and grime. They were from his dad, an older pair. He kissed his mom on the cheek before he followed his dad out to the truck, watching her as she watched them pull out of the drive and go a little too fast down the street. She'd be home alone, all day, all summer. *Probably looking through the picture albums again*, Melrose thought. It irked him that she did that so often. He didn't need pictures. It was all in his head, all the time.

The first fifteen minutes of the ride were in silence. Melrose watched as the sun rose over the multitude of small houses that dotted his heavily populated neighborhood. Old, sick trees and phone wires interfered with his view, but the sun always rose higher than all the garbage that could possibly get in his way. An old country singer drawled on from the radio, and it took all his force inside of him to not reach out and smack the thing off. He hated that kind of music.

"Now, what you're going to want to do is go to the overhead's office first; get a punch card. Don't fucking lose it either, understand? The machine is pretty easy to use. They got you in with the axles and tires. Think you can mange that? I got some friends… Doug and Tom…they'll help you out and show you the ropes. Kid, are you even listening to me? I'm trying to help you," Bernard rambled, his voice growing louder at the end. Melrose nodded. Contrary to popular belief, he was always listening. His father continued with some advice and small talk about the factory, but Melrose kept his eyes and attention focused on the sun and the colors it was creating in the sky. He learned to dread cloudy mornings.

Finally, they pulled up into the cracked parking lot, other men and a few women leaving their cars, some with lunches in their hands, as they headed into the plant. Melrose had only driven past the place; had never come up to it so closely. Soon, he'd be inside. The vastness of the grey and brown hues almost killed him. It was stuffy, and the smell burned his nose for a moment and made his eyes water.

"There, that's the office. Go there and get your card. He'll tell you where to go. Do you think you can handle that? Can you mange to do something, for once?" Bernard asked, exasperated by his son's silence as they stood on one of the many balconies, looking down at the assembly line beneath them. Melrose took a deep breath before answering.

"Yeah, Dad. I can do something," he answered honestly. Bernard paused a moment, not used to any sentence leaving his son's mouth that didn't drip in sarcasm. He mumbled something, huffing a little.

"Well, well that's good. You'll do good here. Make some money. Get some calluses on those hands. It'll be good," he replied, looking his son up and down for a moment. He clapped his son's shoulder for a brief second, then headed with purpose to his locker, and then later his own station assembling engines. Melrose looked down one last time at the pit, as he would later call it, before walking over to the office to meet the overhead and ask for his time card. He found his locker soon enough. His station, a little later on. And just like his dad had said, Doug and Tom were right there, introducing themselves briefly before showing him exactly what he'd be doing for a very long time.

"You see, it ain't hard, just a little borin' sometimes. We talk a lot of the times to keep our minds occupied. Don't we, Tommy?" Doug called out, over the sound of scraping metal as Tom soldered something together. He looked up after a moment, grinning with a little too much enthusiasm. It was fake.

"Yeah, whatever he said. Good to get some fresh meat around here. You got any good stories about some girls?" he asked as Melrose's eyebrows shot up, amazed at how quickly he was being asked to give them up.

"He's jokin'. Tom, how many daughters you got again?" Doug called out. Tom pretended to take a moment to think about it and count; Melrose wasn't sure how to take him.

"I have four daughters, as far as I know," he finally replied.

"See, he jokin'. What you say your name was again?" Doug asked.

"Melrose," he introduced himself, and Tom laughed.

"What kind of name is that?" he asked, curious. He was rough, but there was something honest about him, and Melrose found himself attracted to it.

"I don't really know. It's a band, or a street name, or something my mom liked. My parents were young and stupid when they had me," he replied, shrugging it off. Tom let out a loud, booming laugh. It was genuine.

"Aren't you Bartlett's kid? You just call Bartlett young an' stupid? Oh man," Doug said, like he couldn't believe the gall Melrose had. He shrugged again. He didn't have much to say about it. The proof was already there.

"Come around here, I'll show you what we have to be doing. We all have to work on this together, so don't start slacking. Understand?" Tom said, waving him over, suddenly serious. He sounded just like a father. Melrose came over quickly and watched intently as Tom showed him how to attach the axles underneath the car, how to work the machinery to lift the car up and down, and how to send it on its way when finished.

"You'll pick it up as we go. This time tomorrow, you'll be a pro," Tom assured, and Melrose wasn't sure how he felt about that.

"You good?" Doug asked. Melrose quickly nodded, worried he'd zoned out.

"Yeah, this'll be fine," he replied quickly. Tom laughed again.

"I don't know if this will be good, but it sure pays the bills," Tom stated as he pressed a button, starting up the line. They got to work. Melrose worked a nine-hour shift with two fifteen-minute breaks and a thirty-minute lunch. By the first fifteen-minute break, his hands were black, and his back ached from so much leaning over. By lunch, he felt exhausted, and a peanut butter sandwich had never tasted so good in his life. He gobbled the whole thing down in record time, swallowing most of his water at the same time. The lunchroom was full and rowdy, but he just couldn't sit and listen to the conversations anymore. He instead wandered out on the balcony and watched the engines get assembled. He knew so little about how they were constructed, how all the different devices worked together. Out there, Bernard maneuvered everything with ease, gave orders with true leadership. As Melrose sat, legs dangling, arms on the mid bar he was also resting his face on, he could hardly believe he was looking at the same man who would take him home that evening and ask how much he had finally done.

"C'mon, kid, you can't be a minute late with these kinds of things," Doug said as he walked back, already heading down the metal steps with urgency. Melrose hated that he didn't care, but for the sake of the first day, he got up quickly and headed back down to the pit. His back already ached at the thought of four more hours.

"You go to school?" Tom asked after the first hour back into the work. Melrose shook his head, not offering any words.

"This works better when you use your voice, man," Tom replied, a little darkly.

"I just graduated in June," Melrose replied, not lifting his head but raising his eyes to look at Tom. His face was clouded for a second, but it quickly shifted back to the Tom who laughed too loudly at jokes.

"My daughter Sara will be a senior this year. Did you go to East?" he continued, working on the opposite axle from Melrose.

"Nah, I was up at West. I have some friends still there, though, seniors this year, like your daughter," he replied. Tom didn't say anything for a long moment.

"How did you do?"

"Alright."

"I did al'ight, too," Doug said, from the front of the frame. He let a few seconds go by before laughing. Tom rolled his eyes before going back to his work. They had a time limit for every car. It was for the sake of efficiency.

"I hope you did better than alright," Tom said, a little quieter. Melrose didn't reply, and it was left at that. He worked the rest of the hours trying to keep up, learn just where all the parts went, and listening to Doug and Tom banter back and forth and make crude jokes. When it was finally time to clock out, Melrose felt a wave of relief wash through him. He had been starting to feel a little lightheaded from so much concentration and a lack of water to aid his hangover. It wasn't too bad of one, though, because so far, he really was trying to give up drinking.

"See you tomorrow, Melrose," Tom said as they finished up the last car. Doug threw him an old rag to wipe off some of the grease, but it didn't do much.

"Yeah, 'til tomorrow," Melrose replied, giving them a half hearted wave before ascending up the metal stairs to the balcony, punching out on his time card, and heading to the truck to wait for Bernard. It was about ten minutes before he spotted his dad walking out of the factory, shaking another man's hand before walking to the truck. Melrose quickly snuffed out his cigarette and ground it into the pavement with his boot. The sun reigned hot overhead, but it felt good to him to be somewhere so bright after being in such a dismal place for so long.

"You couldn't wash any more grease off you than that? Damn, c'mon," Bernard greeted, as he looked his son over after nine hours of manual work. He liked what he saw, for the most part. Melrose almost couldn't take the criticism.

"Work hard out there?" he asked as they got into the cab. Melrose nodded, not wanting to really say anything. Bernard didn't mind.

"Good. You're finally doing something. Feel good to be doing something?" his father asked, pulling out onto the road, the same country song drawling on softly. Melrose didn't mind it as much this time around, just looked out at the vast fields they passed before entering the thick neighborhoods once again. He nodded again in reply. Bernard seemed pleased enough with that.

"If your hands hurt, don't worry. You'll get some calluses built up and then everything will be easy," he said, his words hanging in the air for a while. Melrose looked down at his hands, feeling them with a thumb and index finger. They were the only things on his body that didn't hurt.

They were already full of calluses.

7 – TUCKED

His first week had been a hard adjustment. Devastatingly hard. But what Calliste found the most shocking about the place was that after a week, it was all strangely easy. There was no need to wonder if the sergeants would yell because the answer was always yes. There was no need to wonder if the showers would be cold, if the dinner meal would be hot, if the exercises would be challenging, because the answer was always yes. Everything was structured for Calliste to not think, not wonder, and especially not feel. Well, feel nothing but anger. Anger and commitment to the task were encouraged. That was the only thing Calliste found hard about this place. He didn't have that kind of anger in him.

"Tuck those corners in, Martin," Sergeant Adams demanded as he walked around Hall B for room inspections. Calliste did a better job next time, making sure nothing was left hanging off the side of the bed. He had almost laughed when he found out his sergeant's last name was Adams. It had worked out too well.

"Yes, sir," Calliste was quick to reply. Sergeant Adams hardly waited for his reply as he kept walking to correct other boy's poorly made beds. There was a certain standard, and no slacking was allowed.

The sun was rising as Calliste made his way out of the dorms and to the mess hall. Breakfast was usually just oatmeal and some fruit with toast. He didn't mind it. He was small and didn't eat a lot at home anyway. He had yet to call home, but hadn't seen the need to yet. His mother had probably been asleep more than she was awake and doubtfully knew it had been a week's time since he left. Instead, he took his breakfast out to the back patio and ate on the hill, near the flagpole. He decided to write Melrose a letter; he felt he the most might understand this.

His letter was short. He had wanted to start it out by asking Mel about his time at the factory, how the town was, and the woods. He wanted to ask how he was doing. But he couldn't ask so many questions. He just wrote how the first week had been, pretending to be someone else. He tried to write his letter the way he thought Davey would write one to Melrose. He had thought about their relationship a lot that first week of camp, surrounded only by boys. They were like brothers, tied together in ways that seemed extraordinary. Melrose was always dragging Davey into some kind of trouble; Davey was always pushing Melrose to stand straighter. They seemed an odd fit, but at the end of each day, Davey went home having enjoyed the thrill, and Melrose felt the structure and used it to keep growing upwards, towards the sun.

Calliste hadn't talked to anyone. So far, all he had done was tried his best to make good times during all the drills. He wasn't making good times, but that was what the whole summer was for, apparently.

"Hey, can I sit with you?" a timid voice asked as Calliste looked up from his letter to meet the face of a boy as equally small and petit as himself. He seemed to tremble at the possible rejection Calliste could hand off.

"Yeah, sure. I don't own this hill," Calliste joked gently, and the boy grinned a little as he sat down with his remaining breakfast.

"It's just too loud in there sometimes," he said. Calliste knew exactly what he meant, but the loudness wasn't the issue. It was more how big everyone else was, and how much space they took up. There was always a struggle.

"I'm Calliste. You?" he said, offering his hand for a shake.

"Lukas," he replied, taking his hand in his. It was cold and clammy; he was nervous. Calliste looked him over for a second. They appeared to be the same kind of person on the outside, but Calliste knew they were different. He just felt it.

"What brought you here?" Calliste asked. They still had ten minutes before their first set of drills. He wondered what bunk hall he was staying in.

"Ah, my family thought it would be good for me, or something like that," he replied quickly, not wanting to talk too deeply about it. He was a twitchy kid. Calliste thought he might include him in his letter to Melrose. He knew Mel would get a kick out of someone even smaller and more flustered than himself.

"Yeah, my dad thought the same thing," Calliste replied, trying to encourage him.

"I think everyone else here either has to be, or this is their career choice," Lukas commented, as both boys watched a group of what seemed like men walk across the bottom of the hill over to the flag pole, wrestling with each other as they walked. They certainly were intimidating. A few looked up at the two boys, and their eyes rested on them longer than Calliste preferred.

"Probably, but that's okay. They'll take this whole thing seriously, and in a few months, it'll be over for us," Calliste said, standing up and tucking the half-written letter into his pocket. He'd finish it later.

"Three months is a long time," Lukas replied quietly. Calliste helped him up, and together they walked down to the accumulating crowd, ready for drills. He shrugged. It was a long time, but he knew soon enough it would be over. It had to be. It was one of the only things allowing the mindlessness of it all to be okay. There was an end, and it was in sight, however far away it seemed in that moment.

Drills that Monday were an obstacle course of sorts, attempted in short spurts over and over again. There were mud, wires, tires, a giant wall, and a rope swing. Calliste tried so hard to care about it, to try to beat his opponent, to get a better time. The drill sergeants barked their commentary as he tried again and again to make a better time, but nothing seemed to work. He let his squad down, but again, he didn't really care, just wanted the day to be over with already. He wanted to sleep.

"Martin! Push through, c'mon, c'mon. You have men waiting on you! Depending on you! Is this how you show them respect? Pick up the pace, Martin. Let's go!" Sergeant Adams yelled time and time again. It went on for hours, only a small window of time allotted for some sandwiches and an apple for lunch. Everything was testing their endurance. Calliste wasn't sure how much he had. At the end of the segment, he'd only improved by five seconds. Others had shed whole minutes.

"Hit the showers," Adams yelled, throwing his hands up as if entirely embarrassed by the performances that day. He looked mostly at Calliste. It was ineffective; he was already very used to being the reason for disappointment. None of the other boys said anything as the group walked to the showers before dinner, but they kept looking back at the smallest of them, the one with the palest skin, the bluest eyes, and the blondest hair. He heard it as he finished his shower; nearly the last to leave the stall.

"*Gay*," it was whispered, an innocent whisper. Calliste pretended he didn't hear it; hoped it would stay just a whisper. He wandered out to his bunk to put his towel and deodorant away, to find Sergeant Adams waiting for him, examining his bed once again.

"Hello, sir," he said, pausing before getting too close. The man didn't say anything for a moment, just looked at the bed, then finally at Calliste. It was as if for the first time he was noticing how small he was.

"I've never seen someone so careless before. I've seen kids hate this place. I've seen them think it's the worst place to be. But I've never had such an apathetic cadet before," he said calmly. It was the first time he hadn't yelled in Calliste's presence, and it was a little off-putting. For the first time in a week, Calliste wasn't sure of what was to happen, and he felt he'd suddenly been whisked back home to deal with his own father, his mother's bedroom door shut. He felt his eyes widen a little, even though he didn't mean for them to. Adams almost smiled.

"You think you have it figured out here, but I promise you, you better start trying, or things are going to go from in your pocket, to very much out of your grasp," he advised. It didn't come off as a threat. It was as if he had been in the showers, too, hearing the small whisper Calliste had heard.

"Of course, sir," Calliste quickly replied, almost patronizing him. He thought of Melrose again and how he would react to a place like this, to a man like this. Sergeant Adams wasn't anything like Bernard Bartlett, but he wasn't anything like Adam Martin either. The Sergeant stayed a few moments longer, looking at Calliste, and then the bed once more. He couldn't see anything wrong with it.

"Make sure you're always tucking in those corners, son," he finally said, then walked away, leaving Calliste with some things to think about. Mostly, he wanted to know what kind of man Sergeant Adams was. That felt like the thing he needed to figure out the most.

He went out to get dinner – the staple items of meat, potatoes, carrots and green beans, and a cup of water. He took it outside to eat again, somewhat surprised to see Lukas already sitting beside the only tree on the top of the hill, just outside the patio. He walked up slowly, his body aching from the day. Lukas looked just the same, his face a bit more weathered than before, perhaps.

"How was your day?" Calliste greeted, sitting down next to him so he too could rest his back against the tree as he ate his food. It was hot, as always.

"Alright, better than the first, I guess," he replied, his voice tired. They ate a lot of their meal in silence, neither knowing what to say. Calliste missed his old house, the view from the back room, how sometimes he and Sasha would climb out and watch the sunset together and eat candy. He missed Melrose throwing him around but always setting him down gently. He thought about Davey, how uptight he was, yet compassionate, and mostly, how much food he always brought for everyone. Calliste started to think about their last summer together, how much fun they had, each day doing something different since they were all so different. He wasn't blind to that, but it had been too long to turn back. They knew everything there was to know about one another; their parents were good friends, for the most part. Things had drifted in the past two years, but they had stayed strong. The four of them could always count on one another. That much they knew.

He didn't know if anyone else was missing home as much as he was. Probably not, he thought. Sasha and Davey had both wanted to go out on their adventures. Even though they claimed different reasons, Calliste suspected it was all a common cause. Melrose hated them for it, but Calliste couldn't blame them. Everyone had their reasons.

"Who was your letter to?" Lukas asked, breaking Calliste from his thoughts.

"What letter?" he asked, confused for a moment.

"The one from this morning. At least, I thought it was a letter," Lukas said, his voice drifting a little. He seemed bound to fall asleep right there on top of the hill.

"Oh, yeah. That was a letter. To my friend Melrose back home. He'd hate this place," Calliste replied, surveying the camp a little. There would be too much space around here for him. He wouldn't be able to hide anywhere.

"Sounds like a cool guy," Lukas replied, not really continuing. Calliste was almost annoyed with how passive he was being. He, too, was feeling those things, but it wasn't doing anyone any good to wallow on top of the hill.

"We have some free time. Want to walk along the creek or something?" Calliste suggested, chewing on the last piece of meat on his tray. He'd eaten everything. Lukas merely played with his food a little, and without asking, Calliste took a few pieces of meat off his tray to eat. He didn't protest.

"I guess, can we?" he asked, unsure.

"Hell, why not?" Calliste said, standing up and leaving his tray under the tree. He walked down the other side of the hill, towards the woods that led down to the bank and the meadow. He had studied a map of the grounds for a long time during the train ride there; he thought he already knew everything about the land.

They made it down to the woods and ventured on a few of the trails for a moment, before Calliste decided to cut across the woods a bit to find a quicker way to the meadow he knew was hiding out there, somewhere. It rested on the far edge of the camp's property, a place hardly visited, he thought. They wandered for a bit; Calliste had a natural talent for finding his direction and sticking to it. He could feel Lukas getting a little happier, out there in the woods, walking around without so many eyes on him, without the need for a dress code. Their green tees and tan pants would never have been either of their first choice.

"It's beautiful out here," Lukas said after they were about half a mile out into the woods. He never asked if they were lost. He didn't care. It was beautiful out there; he enjoyed the fresh air and uncut grass.

"This is more beautiful," Calliste said, pulling some branches out of the way as he finally stepped into the meadow. It was a stunning little place with tall grasses that bent over in large patches, moss and rocks covering a lot of the spaces in between. There was a creek that ran along the edge of the meadow, and some parts of it were pretty deep. Fish swam through the clear water, and Calliste knew in the spring there were probably many fawns that hid in the tall grasses.

"We can come here sometimes; hang out. This makes it better, doesn't it?" Calliste asked, looking at Lukas who finally had a small smile on his face. His day was already brighter.

"Yeah, we can. This is a good place."

8 – DIRT

Davey had never been without an alarm clock. He always set a time to wake up. Always. For church, for school, for breakfast with his grandparents, for small jobs with his father or uncles, for everything. He used each day for something. It was a skill of his, making time for everything, doing anything with full dedication. It was his reputation – how he'd been raised. His room at the cottage didn't have an alarm clock, let alone any kind of clock. His cell phone didn't really have service, so he just turned it off. When he woke up the next morning, he was startled to find the sun high up in the sky. He felt like he'd missed out on something, that his day was already gone, and he jumped out of bed as soon as he realized just how high in the sky the sun really was.

"Dude, where's the fire?" Jimmy mumbled from where he slept, a few feet away. The place was small, and there were several beds to a room. Davey slowed for a moment, realizing other people were still sleeping, too. Maybe he hadn't missed anything.

"Uh, there isn't. It's just kind of late," Davey muttered as he changed out of an old tee and put on a clean shirt. Jimmy rolled over to look at him, shirtless, hair a mess. He tried to rub the sleep out of his eyes but was having a hard time.

"It's, like, ten o'clock at the most. Dude, you can really slow down," Jimmy tried to reason, but Davey couldn't help himself. He grabbed his toiletry bag and headed off to the bathroom, feeling how his own hair was a mess and his face needed to be washed with soap and cold water. He brushed his teeth, threw water on his face, and combed back his dark brown hair that was longer on the top than the sides. He briefly touched the crucifix that rested around his neck on a gold chain, with the bull's horn right beside it. He wasn't sure why he was there. Everyone had different ideas. In that moment, he thought he was doing this for his mother.

He wandered down the wooden steps to the first floor, each board creaking under the pressure of his foot. Nobody was in the large room, but he heard some voices outside and saw Sidney and her husband out on the dock, sitting on beach chairs. The windows in the kitchen and living room were all open, letting in fresh air from the lake and woods around the property. With each wave that hit the metal barrier wall by the dock, he felt that force inside his chest. He wanted to someday look at the water and not feel that. Davey took a deep breath and it calmed him down for a moment, assuring him that he really hadn't missed anything. Everything was fine, for once.

"I guess I'll make some eggs," he said aloud to himself, an old dog the only one who could hear him, sitting on a rug in the living room that was all couches and nothing more. A small wood-burning stove sat in the corner, but Davey felt it had to be a safety hazard of some kind, around so many flammable things.

Sifting through the refrigerator, he found that there was an abundance of food but it was overcrowding the fridge and some of it was very old. Finally, he found the eggs and a pack of bacon and decided to cook it all. There were about five other kids sleeping upstairs, all Bianchi cousins, somehow. While Sidney's family lived there all summer, she welcomed her other cousins, nephews, and nieces to spend as much time as they wanted up at the lake house. It wasn't until the food was almost done that most of the kids came tumbling down the steps, in varying outfits and varying degrees being awake. Jimmy was still shirtless, still tired.

"This smells good. Damn, what're you making?" he asked,

looking over everything. Davey shrugged; it was just breakfast.

"Breakfast food, found it in the fridge. There's enough for everyone; I used the rest of the eggs in the carton," he replied, handing out plates and setting the two platters of eggs and bacon onto the kitchen table.

"Well, don't mind if I do," Jimmy replied with a little laugh as he helped himself to a scoop of eggs and several pieces of bacon. He set his dish down next to his sister and then scooped some eggs onto her plate as well. He poured her a glass of orange juice, then himself, and then looked up to see if Davey wanted any. He waited for a simple nod before pouring him a glass.

"Knew there was a good reason to have you here," Jimmy said after a few bites, teasing Davey lightly. The other kids started conversations about what to do that day, but Jimmy quickly jumped in with his vote, which seemed to be the only vote that mattered by the end.

"Let's take the boats over to the island. Show your distant cousin here the best part about this place," he stated, pointing his fork at Davey across the table from himself. Some of the others weren't as sure about Davey as Jimmy seemed to be, but it had been quite a few years since he had seen most of them. There were the twins, Henry and Alex, the youngest of the group at thirteen, and Sidney's nephews by her only brother. Karen was Jimmy's sister, younger than he was by only a year. And lastly was Sidney's sister's only child, Celia, who was the middle at fourteen, and her friend, Hannah. They seemed tight-knit, close in age, and like they had always spent all their time together.

They quickly agreed that they'd take the paddleboats out to the island. Davey had no idea what he was in for. Everyone tossed their dishes into the sink and left, most going outside without really changing out of the clothes they had slept in. Davey wanted to wash the dishes and put them all away, but fought the urge. That was what he was here for, anyway, to loosen up, to learn that not everything was going to be in his control. He'd already learned that once, especially about the water.

"Davey made breakfast. Can you believe that?" Karen said to her father as everyone walked out on the dock to see Nick and Sidney. He was smoking a cigar while Sidney was tanning her legs in the morning sun. Nick looked up at Davey, covering his forehead with his hand against the sun to see better.

"Marie used to make us breakfast around here," he said, laughing a little at the memory. Sidney snorted from under her shades.

"She burned it more often than not but still tried. That always counts for something, especially around here," she said, moving a little to the side and looking up at Davey from her low-rise chair. He felt hot under her stare but didn't know why.

"How'd you sleep, kiddo?" she asked.

"Well, thank you," he replied a little stiffly. Jimmy laughed from where he was crouched on the side of the dock, untying one of the paddleboats from the pole.

"He slept in and woke up like he thought the house was on fire," Jimmy teased as he threw the rope into the boat, standing in it, holding it to the dock with just his hands on the pole. The twins were already in the other boat with Celia and Hannah and were trying to get at a good angle to take off.

"Ah, Romanos don't sleep in?" Sidney asked and Davey shrugged.

"Not really," he replied as he walked over to where Jimmy was, jumping in without a hand. He offered his hand to Karen, and she took it as she walked into the boat, a little wobbly on two legs, like a colt learning to walk. He took notice of her legs when they all sat down in the boat, seeing how they bowed to either side.

"Maybe now you will," Sidney said, waving to them as they drifted off from the dock and made their way to open water. He could hear Sidney and Nick laughing for a while about something, but soon enough they were too far out of earshot.

"You going to make me do all the paddling around here?" Jimmy asked, pushing Davey with a soft toss. They picked up speed as the two of them paddled together. The boat was small, just a little plastic thing with two front seats and even two smaller back seats. It was dirty, with algae growing on the sides, and old leaves and bugs crawling around under what had been covered with an old canvas.

"We have to catch up to them," Karen said, pointing at the small speck that was Henry, Alex, Hannah, and Celia. They had a much larger head start, but their legs weren't nearly as long or powerful as Jimmy and Davey's legs. They were used to work.

"Says the one not contributing," Jimmy replied, looking back at her. She shrugged her shoulders, but smiled.

"I'm much better at raising morale; you know that," she replied. Davey tried not to glance down at her legs again. He was curious about them, but knew he'd get a chance to see her walk soon enough, and that would fill up his curiosity. He almost felt like a bully for wondering about it so much.

"Oh, I nearly forgot just how helpful that was," Jimmy replied lightly, paddling a little harder. Together, they worked to catch up to the rest of their cousins, Karen calling out cheers the whole time, especially when they got close. Alex and Henry caught on after Celia started to jump up and down in the back, pointing at their approaching vessel. She almost caused the boat to tip with her excitement, and the boys quickly pulled her down as they tried to pick up speed. Davey was invested in winning, for some reason. He got wrapped up in the cheers and banter between the boats and thought it was hilarious when Karen pulled a bucket from under one of the seats and dumped water into their competition's boat.

Davey watched as the water glided past the boat effortlessly. How it swirled around in various shades of blue, small white bubbles popping up here and there. He dipped his fingers into it for a moment, thinking about it. Normally around large bodies of water he shuddered, but there was something about how carefree the Bianchis were that afternoon that made him smile when thinking about jumping into it and becoming fully submerged. It was something he hadn't felt in a long time.

"There's the island," Karen said, sticking her face between the two boys as she pointed for Davey to see exactly where they were headed. It seemed like a small island, in danger of being swept away within a few years. Half of it was wooded; the other half a mixture of sand and grass. An old doghouse stood proudly at one end of it, and there was a broken-down picnic table that came into view as they got closer. No one won the race; they landed on shore at the same exact time, the tide favoring no man.

The sun beat on the kids as they pulled the boats up onto the beach, a safe distance from any water. No one wanted to be stranded. The sky was cloudless and bright, and Davey watched as Jimmy pulled off his shirt and threw it in the boat, extending his hand to Karen who hopped out of the boat easily but uniquely. He suspected he would never see him in a shirt longer than an hour all summer long.

"We're building a fort over here," Karen said, waving Davey over to follow her down the side of the island and through some of the trees. It was a small place, but the two got lost in the woods for a moment, unable to hear the others. He followed her careful steps through the small grove of trees to a clearing only a few feet wide, and sure enough, a fort was up inside the biggest pine tree on the island. The lower branches served as a ladder, others carefully pruned out of the way. Davey didn't understand how great the fort was in that moment. To him, it was just a haphazard mess in a tree. But he did find it interesting that they had been able to build something out on the island.

"It's a work in progress, but if you're going to be here all summer, I would want you to know about it," Karen said, almost reading his thoughts. Jimmy had told her Davey was okay, but she wasn't sure yet. He didn't seem to think for himself, and that bothered Karen the most. She crossed her arms and watched as he walked around the tree, looking up at the fort, waiting for his judgment.

"You guys plan on finishing it this summer?" he finally asked. She nodded. That's what they all said every summer they stood gathered around the tree, looking up.

"You're going to help, aren't you?" she asked, arching an eyebrow. He quickly nodded in agreement, suddenly feeling like he was on trial.

"Hey! Where are you guys?" Jimmy called out through the woods, his footsteps echoing in the trees as he crashed through the brush almost violently, without care.

"Showing Davey the fort we built!" Karen called back, her voice piercing rather than expansive. Jimmy showed up soon enough, peeking through the trees, a wide smile on his face. He took a second look up at the tree house before he spoke.

"It's gonna be beautiful. C'mon, I already pushed Celia in the water," he said, changing thoughts quickly, waving them to follow, then letting the tree branches snap back together. He was gone, just the sound of him jumping through the brush letting the two know he was still around. Karen laughed and followed her brother, Davey trailing behind. Things seemed easy on the island.

He wandered back onto the beach with Karen, everyone else already swimming. She took off her clothes, a bathing suit hidden underneath, and wadded into the shallow part to her waist before diving in. Her legs were skinny and bowed, but it certainly didn't stop her. Davey took off his own shirt, his gold chain glittering in the bright sun. The water was glistening, each small bump in the surface a bright white contrasted by the light blue undertones. The air was so warm; the water pleasantly chilled. They spent hours out in the lake, swimming around the island, jumping off the rocks that were gathered to one side. They had races to see who could swim out to the buoy the fastest; who could stay under the longest. Karen won those competitions. Jimmy was the fastest swimmer but couldn't beat Alex when it came to artful dives. They ran the same races again and again, but they were always entertaining, and nobody realized how tired they were until they finally wandered back onto the beach, lying out in the sun, exhausted. Jimmy's chest heaved with every breath as he stretched out as long as he could, not caring how dirty he got. His hair seemed already lighter than what it had been yesterday.

"We didn't bring any food, did we?" Henry asked, also lying down in the sand. Davey was sitting back under a tree. His skin was starting to feel too hot, like it was burning. He noticed his shoulders looked incredibly red, and when he pressed one finger down on his skin it turned very white, but the red color quickly resurfaced again.

"Did you bring any food out here?" Celia replied sarcastically, Karen snickered a little in suspense of their conversation.

"I ate such a big breakfast I forgot to," Henry complained, though Davey couldn't see how that made any sense. It wasn't an excuse he was used to. Karen threw some sand in Davey's direction, laughing.

"Sorry your mama isn't here to pack you a lunch and cut off the crust," Celia shot back, looking for a fight. The tone pushed Davey close to the edge, but he could sense he was the only one. He watched and let it slide.

"Least my mama buys groceries," Henry replied, firing back at something Davey knew nothing about. Celia huffed, then grabbed a handful of sand and threw it at her cousin, hitting him dead on. He quickly sat up, wiped it from his face, and threw a fistful at her. It took them a few moments to finally have enough.

"There's some chocolate and graham crackers in the fort, maybe even a bag of chips," Jimmy said sleepily, eyes closed, after their fight had died down. Henry huffed.

"Now you tell me," he said, standing up and heading into the woods to get it. Alex was snoring down the beach a way, a baseball hat over his face.

"Do you guys make s'mores out here?" Davey quickly asked.

"Yeah, we try, but someone keeps eating all of the chocolate," Jimmy replied, opening his eyes for just a moment to cast a look at his sister. She shrugged as she kept drawing small circles and lines in the sand around her.

"We do a similar thing," Davey mumbled, remembering something, resting back against the tree once again.

"We?" Jimmy asked curiously, opening his eyes again to look

at Davey, this time not shutting them until he answered.

"My friends back home. We have an old house in the woods and we keep a cooler of things like that for when we have fires and stuff," he replied, trying to minimize just what that old house meant to him and everyone else. He didn't know why he felt he had to, but he did.

"That's cool. You better put some aloe on when we get back home. You're wicked burned," Jimmy commented, laughing a little as he saw just how red his cousin was. Jimmy, however, was a beautiful bronze. Davey had never burned before and didn't know why he was now. He thought about it until they got back in the boats when the sun started to fade.

Everyone stayed up late that night, having a big fire in the backyard that a lot of the neighbors came down to join. Davey got the impression that late-night fires were a usual thing and that who had to host was a rotating responsibility. A lot of the adults drank, and even Jimmy had a few glasses. Sidney offered Davey a glass of wine, but he declined, looking through the transparent bottle of white wine. He didn't have a taste for it. He sat quietly in one of the chairs, listening to the lively stories. He was used to loud, Italians were loud, but there was a different eminence to how everyone at the lake was using with their voices. There was a certain kind of excitement he'd never really felt before.

When he finally stumbled into bed around one in the morning, the moon was full. Jimmy and Karen were already snoring in their beds so Davey sat by the window and wrote Sasha a letter. He felt like she'd understand being with family that you weren't used to. She was doing the same thing, after all, except she was traveling to riches instead of wandering barefoot through the woods. He wondered if she was enjoying it. He wasn't sure if he was yet. There was a lot he didn't like, didn't think he could like. He didn't write much, and kept it upbeat, as always. Licking the envelope, he tucked the letter into the drawer at the table by his bed and lay on the sheets for a while, unable to sleep, feeling his skin burn from so much bright sun.

9 – GIRL

The thing that persisted the most, so far, was boredom. There wasn't much to do because everything was always being done for them. Sasha didn't even have to make her bed in the mornings; there was a girl for that. Cooking? Meals? There was a girl for that. Cleaning? Of course, there was a girl for that. Mostly, it made Sasha feel shameful, like they were judging her deeply for not doing these things herself. She didn't actually feel that vibe coming from them, but more so from within herself. She talked to her mother about it over the phone, late at night when her grandparents were already asleep and all the girls had gone home. The room she was in was beautiful, with a large king bed facing a set of double doors that opened up to overlook a small piece of the city, but most noticeably, that overlooked the sea the mansion stood so close to. The home was on a hill, so it seemed much larger than everything else below, even though it was all a short distance away. Something about the height, too, bothered Sasha. Her mother assured her it was just the newness of it all.

"Of course, though, there's a reason we don't have any help, or girls, as you keep calling them," Vivienne reminded, sitting in her own room looking out her own window with a view of the valley down the hill her own house was on.

"I mean, they are girls. Well, some are more adult than others,"

Sasha replied, slouching in her solitary chair on her small balcony. She liked the black metal railing it had; it was beautifully molded. The chair, of course, matched the metal.

"They used to have a doorman. Can you imagine?" Vivienne chuckled, thinking about how absurd the whole thing seemed. Sasha laughed.

"I can, actually, because they still have one," she replied, and her mother gasped over the other line.

"It's so damn pretentious. I mean, how many people are really coming to the door that you can't bother to go answer it?" Vivienne asked, outraged. She'd had a couple notable fights with her parents over the years, but they always seemed to overshadow her, never hearing her words, just looking at their daughter's distorting face with disdain.

"I think he does more than answer the door, but I don't know what just yet," Sasha replied, eyes focused on the moon over the sea. She could almost smell the water, but it was just a little too far away. She was okay with that.

"You can come home anytime," her mother reminded. She missed her daughter, and even though Sasha felt invisible to them sometimes, Vivienne always knew when she was home and when she wasn't.

"I'm okay, really. It's kind of cool here. Your room is beautiful, just so you know. I found some posters packed in the back of the closet...." She started to tease, and her mother laughed at the thought, not wanting to admit whose faces were plastered on that paper.

"Yeah, my room was always the nicest part about living in that place. How're the grandparents treating you?" Vivienne masked real concern. She wanted more for Sasha than to be influenced by people who thought status and being polite were the most important things a person could have, let alone a young woman.

"Good, honestly. It's a little awkward still, living with them. We're going to some lunch tomorrow. It's at like, two or something," Sasha replied, picking at more of her nail polish and waving her feet in the air as they rested upon the metal fencing of the balcony.

"Well, I'm glad to hear that. They're not very warm people, but you're not really into that, anyway. Just stay yourself, and you'll get along with them comfortably in no time. They do love you, after all," Vivienne assured, and even though Sasha didn't doubt it, it was still a nice thing to hear, especially from her mother.

"Did you figure out yet if Jo's daughter is going to get revenge on Christopher?" Sasha asked, teasing her mother just a little, asking about her story.

"I mean, yes, she has to. Right?" her mother asked, desperately wanting to talk about her novel's plot with her only child who would never talk about it.

"I mean, probably. I'd avenge you," Sasha promised sweetly.

"I appreciate that, so you don't think it's weird if..." Vivienne started, but Sasha yawned, which halted the conversation about the book once again.

"I'm really tired, Ma. I'll talk to you tomorrow or the next day?" Sasha asked. Her mother was a little hesitant to continue, always upset when she was shut out of what her daughter was thinking, especially creatively.

"Of course, get some sleep, love. Talk to you soon," Vivienne replied as she waited for Sasha to hang up first. It was her ritual; she always waited for the other person to hang up the phone first. Sasha always waited a few seconds in silence before she did. They both liked to hear each other breathe for a few moments before ending the call.

Sasha slept soundly in her mother's old bed. It was huge, feathery, and filled with pillows and soft blankets. She was someone who usually slept fitfully, but for the many days she'd been at her grandparents' house, each night had been spent in a single, eight-hour haul. Every morning she woke up refreshed, but it was always met with the boredom again. Then, it changed.

When she woke up the sun was streaming in through the open doors, a small breeze wafting in and rolling over her sleeping frame on the bed. She woke up slowly, stretching each of her limbs before opening her eyes and pushing the hair out of her face. There was so much of it. She breathed deeply for a few minutes, looking out the open doors, watching the soft, transparent white curtains blow in the breeze for a few moments before standing up. She walked over to the vanity mirror, brushing her hair and braiding it artfully as she always did. It was the one thing about her appearance her grandparents couldn't decide if it was beautiful, or rebellious.

She walked carelessly in her pajamas down to the kitchen to rummage through the refrigerator for something to eat for breakfast. Sasha was surprised, however, when she walked in and two women were already in the kitchen, sitting on barstools, one nearly half the age of the other. She looked Sasha over for a moment, her eyebrows arching. Sasha felt butterflies in her stomach but couldn't place why.

"Good morning," Sasha mumbled as the older woman stood up, nodded, and headed to a different room of the house. Sasha was left alone with the younger girl, who had a wicked smiled on her face. She was a stunning person, strong jaw, dark hair, and eyes that conveyed so much of the depth inside her.

"Hey, how're you?" the girl replied, not moving from her perch on the barstool. There were always people in and out of the house that Sasha didn't know, and she didn't know how to ask the girl who she was. It was unsettling. Sasha never thought she'd get used to it.

"I'm Gillian. My mom works here," the girl finally said after a few moments of uncomfortable silence that she seemed to enjoy infinitely more than Sasha, who was starting to wish she'd gotten dressed before coming down to eat.

"Want me to boil you an egg or something? I help out every so often. For the summer," she added, a little arrogantly. Sasha snorted at her offer, and not even wanting an egg, grabbed the smallest pot from the cupboard and an egg from the refrigerator.

"No, thanks. I'll boil it myself," she replied, just as smugly.

Gillian's smile reached only one side of her face, but it was an attractive look under her eyes.

"Touché," Gillian said, flipping back through the magazine in front of her at the marble island. There was something about the girl that caused Sasha to watch her as she carefully flipped the pages of her magazine, watch how she tucked some of her flowing hair behind her ear, crossed her legs repetitively. It was all a show, and Sasha realized it almost too late.

"Salt and pepper?" Sasha asked as Gillian looked up, her eyebrows pushed together in confusion and then went up in surprised realization as she watched Sasha hand her a plate with a boiled egg cut perfectly down the middle, a small green leaf decorating it, plucked from a plant in the windowsill. She gave Sasha a daring look.

"I just go for the salt," she replied. Sasha handed her the salt.

"I usually have both," Sasha commented.

"Enjoy."

Sasha walked slowly out of the kitchen and headed towards the stairs to her room to get dressed. She'd eat something later.

"I will," Gillian promised, and even though she didn't know why, Sasha smiled as she walked back up the staircase to her mother's old room. Sasha couldn't get Gillian out of her head as she picked a sundress to wear for the day, very strappy in the back, but it fit her slender frame well. She even sat down and put on some makeup, a new thing she was picking up now that she had so much time on her hands. She tried to create eyebrows like the girl in the kitchen, dark and strong, a vital part of her expression.

"Sasha, are you awake?" Ann Raskova's muffled voice asked, knocking on her granddaughter's door a little tentatively. She didn't want to scare her, but at the same time, she didn't know how to not be an intimidating force. Instead of answering, Sasha stood up, ready for the day, and opened the door to greet her.

"Good morning," she replied, smiling openly at her grandmother, who was impressed that she was already dressed and ready. She was already so different from her own daughter,

Vivienne. She thought.

"Oh, you look nice. I was going to ask if you wanted to go to the beach for a little walk before the lunch. Are you up for it?" she asked, already dressed and ready for the day herself. Her husband had left early, attending business meetings before noon. They were both retired now but still had a lot of investments and stocks to tend. It was a hobby, they liked to joke.

"Yeah, that would be great," Sasha replied, grabbing a hat and sandals out of the room and following her grandmother down the steps. She kept her eyes open for Gillian but didn't see her. They even stopped momentarily in the kitchen for a couple of apples to take with them. Ann always brought some kind of fruit with her on a walk.

"We'll meet your grandfather at the lunch. Are you excited to meet more of your family? It's been ages since you've been out here. They've all missed watching you grow up, you know that?" she asked as they walked out to the front hall and to the door.

"It has been awhile," Sasha replied, not knowing what to say, not even sure these people knew who she was apart from the image her grandmother had created of her to present to them. Walking down the sidewalk, Sasha looked up one last time at the old house, in all its well-kept and rich beauty, and noticed a familiar face in the front window, looking out at her. Gillian waved, and Sasha blushed, smiling, but turned away. She tried to focus her attention on where she was walking.

"Have you talked to your mother recently?" Ann asked, curious.

"Yeah, last night actually. She's well," Sasha replied, anticipating the next question. Ann knew she was fine, but wasn't sure why her daughter never called her.

"Oh, that's nice you two talked," Ann replied, not wanting to dive into her feelings on the matter to its depth. Especially not for a morning walk to the beach, her favorite thing to do. She often opted to put things off, sweep them under the rug, or dismiss them completely. It was much easier.

"Yeah, she's really missing me back home I guess," Sasha replied, her thoughts drifting off a bit. She couldn't believe her parents were missing her as much as they seemed to be. She didn't feel this much commitment when she was actually there, a few steps down the hall, playing the violin or feeding chickens or just lying on the couch in the living room screaming obscenities to see if they could hear her, or if they would listen.

"Well, she loves you very much. Of course she'd miss you," Ann replied, just as the two crossed the small street together outside of the neighborhood, finally on the sandy shores of the sea. Ann had purposely picked out their house all those years ago just because of its proximity to the beach and all the green trees.

"Do you feel like you're settling in all right here? Getting comfortable? I know we haven't done much this past week, but I'd like to start doing more with you if you're up for it. There's some really excellent productions we can see, a couple dinners your grandfather and I have been invited to, a benefit in just a month…" Ann continued to chatter on and on about her extensive summer list of events and banquets she had to attend, so many different social functions Sasha could barely keep up. She nodded at the right times, only paying strict attention again when her grandmother stopped talking.

"Unless you had other ideas…" she said, but it wasn't so much an offer of choice, rather a kind of condemnation. Sasha quickly shook her head. She didn't want to do any of those things, but that was why she was here.

"No, that all sounds fantastic. I can't wait," she quickly replied, with such vigor even Ann believed her for a moment. Sasha was trying to get away from things she knew. Those things hadn't served her well in the past. There was a sadness inside of her that no amount of comfort from home seemed able to cure. For two years, she had stayed. Now, she was trying to see how far she could run. A wave crashed against her ankles, waking her up from her thoughts of home. She shook her head. There was a reason she wasn't there.

"There's a lunch today, right? What's it for?" Sasha asked, submerging herself in the kinds of things her grandmother did. She'd realize later how they implemented similar tactics when trying to get away from things.

"Yes, it's just a family thing. We're in business with a lot of the cousins. I don't know if you knew that. It's at a great restaurant, and they reserved the whole back wall for us, right by the balcony. It's Italian, do you like Italian?" she asked, walking slowly beside her granddaughter as the waves lapped playfully at their ankles, the sun warming their skin, and the sky was so bright blue it blinded Sasha every time she looked up.

"I do," she replied, thinking of dinners at Davey's, his Nonna cooking and offering bountiful amounts of food to all of them, never satisfied until they'd had several plates and wiped away all the sauce with a piece of bread.

"Good, then you'll like this place. It's authentic," she said, smiling a little with the anticipation of the food. Going out to eat was one of her favorite things. Sasha almost laughed at the word *authentic*. She didn't think Ann really knew what that was. They chatted a bit longer, walking down to the pier and then turned around to walk back home, staying beach side as long as they could. They paused for a moment by the street watching the cars drive by, lacing up their sandals before crossing.

Everyone at the lunch talked to Sasha and introduced themselves with some relation to Vivienne, but Sasha neither knew of nor remembered any of them. Soon enough, Ann was talking to everyone's wives, and the men were just talking business. The table, as promised, did sit by the balcony, and looked out at the bright sky and over the ocean beautifully. Sasha spent her time eating her lasagna and salad, staring out the window at the seascape, and writing a letter to Calliste on a napkin telling him just how amazing she thought the colors in the sky at sunset would be here, of all places.

10 —WALL

"Man, you've gotten good at this!" Doug called out over the sound of banging metal as Melrose hooked up another axle and wheel jack to the car they were working on, finishing before the allotted time, and gaining another small water break.

"Just what I've always wanted to hear," Melrose said sweetly, and Doug laughed, then Tom muttered loudly enough for everyone to hear under his breath, "What a smartass."

"Tommy, why you always gotta be so damn cynical?" Doug asked, looking down at the man he considered to be his best friend. He didn't get out much other than work.

"Cynical? Where are you picking up such big words?" Tom asked, looking up with a bit of playfulness in his eyes. He never meant to be hard on Doug. It just happened most of the time. Melrose laughed at their bickering, wiping his brow with the back of his arm to avoid smearing the grease from his hands all over his face. He was getting good at keeping the grease contained but wasn't sure how he felt about having a skill like that.

"I pay attention, man. I pay attention," Doug insisted as he finished with his tire, pressing the button that lowered the car and sent it along its way to the next station. A few moments passed before another car appeared, and Melrose used it to take a big gulp of water, some of it dripping down his cheeks and wetting the collar of his jumpsuit. A crashing sound interrupted his bit of peace as another car rolled down the belt and stopped at their station, needing four axles and tires, just like the car before it, and the car before that one. The consistency was what bothered Melrose the most. He couldn't believe how efficiently the plant worked, how all of these people could come together and make the exact thing happen over and over again. He wanted to disrupt the system, cause some kind of delay, make someone have to think about anything different than the same small task for eight hours.

"Pass me the wrench, would you?" Tom asked, nodding his head to where the tool sat on the bench behind Melrose. He walked over quickly to grab it, holding the solid metal in his hand before turning it over. He thought about banging it into the car but quickly shook the idea from his mind.

"You took to this pretty easily," Tom commented as he fixed a bent piece within the car, looking up at Melrose for a response after it was fixed and secured again. It was something that happened about every thirty cars.

"Yeah?" Melrose replied, not sure he cared.

"Yeah, most kids around here don't make it past a week. What was the name of the last kid in here, Dougie?" Tom asked, turning his head to face Doug, who always took care of the front axle. The wheels turned together, so it was quicker for one man to tackle the job rather than two.

"Uh, Connor, or somethin' like that. He was here just a few days. Didn't like the smell, he said. Though, I can't really smell nothing, you know?" Doug replied, shrugging. Tom nodded.

"Exactly my point," he said, looking back up at Melrose. He shrugged. That wouldn't be his issue.

"Good for me, I guess," Melrose replied.

"Yeah, well, don't get comfortable around here," Tom said suddenly, a little darkly. Melrose didn't know what to say or how to take his words. This happened from time to time. Tom would turn dark and mean for a few minutes, and then lighten back up for the rest of the day. He was by no means a jolly man, but he had mood swings that made even Melrose feel uneasy. He had never imagined someone possessing a darker darkness than what was in his own thoughts.

"No problem, man. Don't think I could," Melrose finally replied, needing to say something. It was a pet peeve of Tom's; a silent answer was no answer to him.

"Oh, everyone gets comfortable around here," Tom said, leaning back after finishing yet another axle. He stretched his arms over his head a bit, drinking his own water in the few minutes he had before the next car came sliding down. Melrose was seconds behind; it had gotten to be some kind of competition. Melrose knew, though, he only won when Tom wasn't racing.

"Going through the motions," Tom murmured, and Melrose wasn't quite sure what he had said. Doug huffed loudly, annoyed with their conversation.

"I can't hear y'all up here, and it gets borin' as hell. C'mon now," Doug asked as he finished up the front axle, hitting the button again to send the car through. It was only thirty seconds later that another car came and they all set to work on it. Another hour passed before lunch came, and Melrose waved to his coworkers as he headed up the metal stairs straight to the sinks to wash as much grease as he could in a minute's time. He hated to waste valuable freedom at the sinks, with everyone else laughing and pushing one another around. He got in and out quickly, walking up another flight of metal stairs to his locker. On his way, a couple of guys said hello, or clapped him on the back. He waved to all of them but didn't start a conversation. He finally found a spot, up on the roof outside where he didn't have to smell the burning metal or look at all the grey. He had no idea how people got comfortable in there.

He ate his first sandwich in just a few moments, gulping it down with the coke that his mom had packed him. She always made her husband lunch; it was natural for her to make her son's as well. He ate the second sandwich a bit slower, able to look out over the fields surrounding the plant. He unzipped the top half of his jumpsuit, taking his arms out of the sleeves and letting the sun hit his bare arms. He liked sitting in just his pants and a sleeveless undershirt. It was freeing.

Carefully, he un-tucked the letter he'd gotten from Calliste and read it over slowly, then more quickly the second time. He didn't feel much sympathy for the kid, but he was curious about what Calliste had written. The letter didn't make it seem like he was very happy at the camp, but who would be? Melrose knew the letter was a cover for something else. It had the tone of being fine even when you weren't. Melrose knew that feeling well enough. He folded it back up and stuck it into his pocket. He ate his sandwich slowly, munched on the pretzels and orange, and looked out over the barrier at the grass swooshing in the wind. It was hotter on the roof than inside the plant, but Melrose didn't care. He liked to sweat, liked to feel the salty water drip down his spine. He thought more about Calliste, his thoughts shifting from dismissive to more or less apprehensive. He really did hope he was okay out there, doing drills every day. He could only imagine how awful that would be, but knew if anyone could handle it, Calliste could. He made so many things work out in favor of his old man, why couldn't he do this?

He was back at his station promptly thirty minutes later, shirt back on and zipped up, water bottle refilled. He was ready for four more hours of the same task. The consistency was driving him crazy, but he kept wiping the sweat from his brow, kept getting his fingers blacker and blacker with grease, uncomfortable as ever. When the bell rang at five o'clock, he leaned back and sighed heavily. Freedom.

"Same time t'morrow," Doug called out as Tom and Melrose stood up almost at the same time, doing the same stretch to get the kinks out of their backs. They nodded.

"Never changes," Tom said, laughing a little as he cleaned up his workstation.

"Never does," Melrose mumbled, quickly stacking his set of

tools away and bounding up the metal steps quickly. He hated looking down as he did so. He didn't want to look through the grates and see just how high up he was. As usual, he beat his father to the truck, enjoying a single cigarette before Bernard made his way over. He couldn't give up both – the drinking and the smoking. He figured since the drinking got him into the most trouble, he'd try that first. But now he was wondering if maybe the lack of drinking would be the first to catch up with him.

"Good day down there?" Bernard asked as he walked over, unlocking the truck, both of them getting in slowly. It felt good to sit down.

"Yeah, same as always," Melrose replied. It was the most they spoke the entire ride home. The music was still the same terrible country music that Melrose hated, but the volume had gotten quieter. He was thankful for that much. Bernard asked a few things once they drove past the fields, into town, into the dense and dirty streets of their neighborhood. He mostly talked to himself; not noticing that Melrose didn't reply and only nodded at inappropriate times. He only cared sometimes, but after a long day at the plant, his son visibly dirty from hard work, he could sit in the driver's seat content.

"Wash up," Bernard said as he pulled the old trunk into the driveway, facing the dingy, aging house. The yard was tightly maintained, the porch swept, the roof not leaking anymore. But no matter how much work went into maintaining a good presentation, something was off; something about the house was calmly astray. Melrose headed inside, right to his bedroom, allowing his mother to kiss him on the cheek quickly before he cleaned up. He was holding his pants up, having already unzipped the top half of his work suit and taken his arms out of the sleeves.

"Did you have a good day?" Daisy asked hopefully. She twisted the rings on her fingers nervously as she waited for him to reply. Melrose got caught up watching her wring her hands that he almost forgot she'd asked something.

"Oh, yeah. Nothing bad happened," he commented, heading

back to change and take a shower. That was his only measurement of good days.

Often, Daisy made a wide spread of ordinary dishes. She wasn't the greatest cook, and they couldn't afford the biggest selection at the grocery store, but she put a lot of effort into cooking the meat Bernard got during the hunting season and mixing it with vegetables from her garden or things she got from her mother's garden. She waited anxiously by her seat at the table, all the plates laid down perfectly, napkins and forks in place. It took her boys twenty minutes to come back to eat, but she stood there at her chair all that time, just waiting.

They said a prayer before they ate, even though no one was terribly religious, especially not anymore. For most of dinner, it was quiet, just the small noises of forks hitting the plates softly, or someone chewing an especially tender piece of meat.

"So, what did you guys do today?" Daisy asked, moving her small portion of food around her plate rather than eating it. She'd gotten terribly thin over the past couple years. No one had seemed to notice.

"Work," Melrose mumbled, not sure how she couldn't have answered that question herself. Sometimes, he was hard on her. It was just how he was now. Daisy nodded, accepting his answer.

"On what?" she continued, eager for anything.

"Uh, cars?" Melrose responded, the faintest bit of sarcasm in his voice. It barely snuck past Bernard, but Daisy swallowed it whole.

"Right, but what did you say you do again?" she asked, wanting to talk so desperately. She felt sometimes that she might lose her voice entirely.

"I put the axles and tires on the bottom of cars," Melrose replied, looking back down at his plate, almost sorry he'd gotten angry at her questions. He was having just as hard of a time as she was, and no one seemed to see that, either.

"Meat's good," Bernard said after a few moments of silence, not seeming to have heard the small interaction Melrose and his mother had moments earlier. He mumbled his words with a full mouth, gulping down water to swallow as if in some haste. Daisy continued to move her food around, wanting dinner to last much longer then it actually would.

"I cooked it how you like it," she replied, looking over at her husband. He nodded his head, acknowledging her words, but didn't say anything more. Daisy wanted to speak up again but couldn't think of anything to say. She hadn't done much with her day, and what she had done; she didn't want to talk about.

"Melrose, you going to save your first check, aren't you?" Bernard asked suddenly, looking over at his son. He nodded, though he wasn't sure just how much he'd actually save. He knew his father wanted him to spread his paycheck around the house, and save the rest for his own house someday, but he wasn't sure how he felt about that.

"Nah, I think I'll spend it all in one go," he replied, stuffing his mouth with a big piece of potato. Daisy braced herself. Bernard stopped for a moment, looking up.

"That's not very funny."

"Wasn't supposed to be," Melrose said, looking up.

"Don't get an attitude now, and ruin your mother's dinner," Bernard replied, his face tightening as did his fists. He never understood why his son was always giving him an attitude, always jerking him around, always making the wrong decisions.

"But not your dinner?" he was quick to reply.

"All of our dinner," his father said.

"I'm pretty much done," Melrose shot back, scooping the last bit of food into his mouth and chewing it loudly. Bernard sighed heavily, tired and annoyed. He rubbed the fork and knife in his hands with his fingers, almost bending the metal a little. Daisy sipped on her water but choked on it.

Melrose couldn't stand the silence any longer. The air was tense, and maybe that was his fault. In fact, he knew it was his fault. It was always his fault when tensions rose, and that was often. Even when things seemed fine, he always made some comment he knew would cause Bernard to erupt. It was just something to break the quiet, the silence, and the apathy. Everything worked entirely too smoothly at his house, and he needed something bad to happen to liven things up. He felt he deserved as much.

Almost violently, he pushed his chair back and stood up to toss his plate into the sink. Bernard watched with careful eyes, only speaking up when he noticed his son heading for the back door, not his chair at the wooden table.

"Where do you think you're going?" he yelled, louder than he needed to.

"Out this door, obviously," Melrose replied, almost singing his words. Bernard stood up, and even though they were far apart, Melrose felt the threat.

"Dinner isn't finished," he said, his voice low, but engulfing. Melrose almost laughed, but chose to save it for a different moment.

"Well, I'm finished," he replied, looking in his father's eyes.

"I don't care. Sit down," Bernard commanded. Daisy jumped a little at his words, as they came out harshly, and with more volume than before. Melrose felt he was the only one who noticed her jump, and that fueled his anger, but not for all the right reasons. He wanted to get away from her, too. He had a hard time looking at her, a hard time listening to her ask questions she already knew the answers to. Those were safe questions. Melrose was tired of being safe.

"No, I can't. I'm done. I'm going out, alright? Don't wait up," Melrose said, waving him off as he took a few more steps towards the back screen door. He only stopped when he heard Bernard pound his fists on the wooden table, shaking the ceramic plates. Melrose turned around slowly, his own anger rising.

"I wouldn't wait up. You don't ever come home. You stay out all night with the trash," Bernard yelled, his words dripping with what Melrose considered the truth. He couldn't believe how easily his dad could bring it up.

"Does it matter? I'll be at work alright."

"The fuck it does matter," his father yelled, banging his hands on the table again. Daisy let out a small cry, trying to keep it in, but she couldn't.

"Oh, nice one," Melrose mocked, waving his hand at his mother who was trying to make herself even smaller than she already was. Her dinner was ruined; she had been given no conversations. She'd wash the dishes in silence, smelling lavender in the soap. It was the only thing she spent money on without finding a coupon.

"I'm fucking stuck here, remember? I got left alone this summer," Melrose yelled back, hitting the doorframe as he ran out the back door, letting the screen door slam. Bernard yelled something out the screen, but Melrose hardly heard it, just figured it was his father berating him once again. He knew he deserved it.

Melrose headed down his street, kicking bits of stone as he walked, hands stuffed in the pockets of his jeans. He waved at a couple of the neighbors; they were friendly enough. He headed a couple of blocks down before cutting through an abandoned lot and then jumping into the woods, finding the narrow deer trail within moments. He followed it though the thick brush for a few minutes until it met up with the main trail. Then, he could walk without branches slapping his face, small leaves and thorns cutting at his neck and arms. He pushed his dark hair off his forehead; there wasn't anyone that could see him out there.

Carefully, he made his way down the trail to another cross trail and took a left. After about ten minutes, he came to a stone wall, crumbling in many places, only about waist high, if that. It was covered in moss and small weeds and mushrooms, and he carefully sat down on a small patch of grass and leaned up against it. He wasn't sure how far the wall ran, but he knew it was as old as the wooden shack on Calliste's family property. The woods seemed empty now, void of both animals and people. That was why Melrose liked the wall – it seemed to separate something far greater than simple farm land, even though it was crumbling.

Melrose sat there for a long time, his arms resting over the tops of his knees, just looking out into the trees, watching as the sun lowered in the sky. Some birds chirped in the air, but generally, he never saw much wander around those parts of the woods. Especially never a deer. Finally, he got the small pieces of paper out of his pocket and the pencil that he always kept at the bottom of his jeans. He wrote on little pieces of paper, not to Calliste, and stuck them into the cracks of the old stone wall.

They were for someone else to read.

He headed out shortly, smoking a cigarette with a shaky hand, thinking about where he could go to get some liquor.

11 – DRILLS

The mirrors weren't very reflective, but he could still see the light purple bruising on his arm from where he'd fallen on the tile floor in the bathroom. Carefully, he pulled at the skin, poking and prodding the dark contusions, trying to look at it from all angles. He believed that the other guy had really just slipped on a wet spot, pushing into Calliste so he fell. He believed it. Almost.

Quickly, he realized he'd spent too much time examining something that would be gone in a few days and put his shirt on hastily so he wouldn't be late for the morning meeting and drill assignments. Camp wasn't getting any easier, but his body was finally starting to hurt less from Sergeant Adams's assignments.

After rushing through the breakfast line, waving hello to Lukas from afar, he scarfed down his oatmeal and toast and made his way to the stone circle around the flagpole, for assignments and reporting duties. As they said the pledge of allegiance, Calliste kept thinking about how he used to be one of the last in the showers, but now, there were more guys out in the locker room halls than there used to be. He shook his head to keep the thoughts of those evenings out, wishing he could do the same to break up the tension he felt as he put his clothes on and exited the shared bathroom.

"Martin! You're in group C over there," Sergeant Adams called out, reading off the list to direct people to their stations for the day. Calliste heard a few sneers from the other boys, but again, he chose to just shake his head and hope it went away or to think that it really wasn't as loud as he thought it was. Once everyone was assigned, the groups marched off to their stations. Group C was destined to complete the obstacle course training in the morning and then a field practice after lunch.

While the sergeant went over the rules of the course, and gave the same speech that was always given about working together and how to make it through with the fastest time and least amount of injuries, Calliste's mind continued to wander. He told himself he couldn't stay focused because this whole place wasn't exactly his thing, that at this stage of the summer, it was more or less autopilot. But the part of him grounded in reality kept reminding him that the tension he felt around the other boys wasn't all in his head and that it absolutely was growing in momentum.

"Alright, divide yourselves evenly. Ten and ten per team. Let's start this thing," Adams yelled out. Quickly, people separated, and Calliste didn't imagine the eye rolls his team gave him when he wandered to the very end of the line. Briefly, before the whistle blew and the two boys at the start of the line began the course, Calliste thought about how Sergeant Adams was always with the group he ended up in. He didn't mind anymore; he had realized quite a few things about him.

The race was usually always neck-and-neck. Most of the boys had matched up evenly, so every so often someone would pull ahead, but then the opposite would happen when the next boy lurched from the line and on to the course. Calliste began to feel a kind of dread building up within him, feeling the need to do the best he'd ever done, but also feeling uneasy about being at the end of the line, the one to end the race.

The boy he stood next to eyed him as they walked up closer to the start line. Calliste pretended not to notice, instead focusing on just how to get through the course quickly and efficiently. The boy he would be racing kept leaning back and forth, swaying side to side, putting his shoulders back and standing up straighter. He didn't have to. Everyone here was bigger than Calliste. There was no need to size up.

Climbing the wall was the last obstacle in the course; everyone who had already finished was standing at the top, cheering their team on and helping pull up teammates as they approached the wooden barrier. The sun beat down heavily on the boys, warming the dirt they all stood on, and making the kicked-up dust almost unbearable. Sweat trickled down Calliste's brow as he took his position, ready to head off when he was signaled, when his teammate was finally at the top of the wall with everyone else. He noticed Lukas already on top of the wall with the other team, totally focused on the other boy.

It didn't matter.

The whistle blew.

Calliste took off, not faster than the other boy, but smaller. He jumped the hurdles quickly, using up a lot of energy to get the height he needed. Then the two raced to the tires, where again Calliste wasn't the best with his short legs, but made it through only a second or two behind his competitor. When he crawled under the wire through the mud, Calliste gained seconds, having a much easier time sneaking through than the other boy.

"You little snake," the boy hissed through gritted teeth just as Calliste made it through and went to climb over the small bridge, then another round of tires. By the time the two boys made it to the rope swing over another pit of mud, they were essentially at even times once again. As Calliste sailed over, he noticed that the mud was drying up, leaving deep grooves over the pit. He heard the voices of both teams over the top of the wall, but something was different about the way each team was cheering. One team sounded encouraging, another sounded threatening.

His lungs ached as he ran as fast as he could for the last stretch to the wall. Something inside forced him to feel that this was life or death, and although his energy was waning, he used everything he had left. The facts were that the other boy had longer legs, and Calliste hadn't been eating very much. Calliste's competitor hit the wall first, jumping as high as he could, grabbing the hands of his comrades as they helped him climb up the wall and make it to the top. Calliste hit the wall while he was still climbing and took a running jump but didn't hit high enough for his teammates to help pull him up. By his second jump, the other boy was just making it over the top.

Calliste took another running leap, pushing air into his lungs, stretching up his arms to grab onto the hands that waited for him. He gave it his all, and as he reached up to grab onto someone, suddenly, there were no open hands waiting for him.

He fell.

He didn't make a noise but felt for sure he had twisted an ankle or bruised the side of his knee. The pain rippled through his leg and hip in waves, breaking up his gasping breath, lungs begging for air, sweat pouring from his brow, wetting down the dirt he laid on. He couldn't hear anything for a moment, didn't listen to any of the voices. Just sat there, on his side, turned away from all the others, trying to breathe.

"What was that? What the hell was that?" Sergeant Adams yelled out, not looking at Calliste, not even acknowledging him, but instead looking up at his team who all had the same look on their faces. No one said anything. The boy with sandy blond hair and different-colored eyes spoke up after the quietness in the air that felt so heavy started to become unbearable.

"He just didn't jump high enough," the boy replied, his hands out, seemingly trying to make up for not grabbing Calliste's hand in the right moment. Sergeant Adams shook his head, more annoyed with the situation than anything else.

"You figure it out. You don't leave someone behind, do you hear me, Turner?" Adams demanded, using the boy's last name. Calliste didn't care to know it.

"Yes, sir," the boy replied, not a single syllable coated with attitude.

"And Martin, jump higher. You always have to jump higher," Sergeant Adams said, a bit quieter, looking down at Calliste who had not gotten up yet. He waited for a nod to acknowledge what he'd said, but Calliste made him wait a very long moment before he gave in.

"Yes, sir," he replied quietly, sarcasm dripping. Adams let it go; no one else had heard his reply. He looked down at Calliste for a moment longer, deciding he was fine, before walking off and waving at the boys to get off the damn wall. No one helped Calliste stand up, but Lukas at least gave him a sympathetic look.

Instructions and the course had taken up hours, and Calliste sat alone under a shady tree eating his turkey sandwich and apple for lunch at exactly noon. He listened as the other boys talked and laughed, watched as they poured water over their faces to cool off and un-tucked their shirts for a few moments. Lukas didn't come up and sit by Calliste; rather, he sat in some strange middle ground, not in the circle, but not exactly outside of the circle. Calliste watched him, happy that he finally seemed to find a niche he could be okay in, or at least, survive.

He ate half the sandwich, tearing the rest up for the birds, but he did eat the whole apple. When the whistle blew, he stood up slowly, stretching out his leg carefully. He was okay; his knee was a little bruised, but his ankle was doing just fine. He could walk, and Sergeant Adams was relieved when he watched Calliste stand up from afar. The last thing he needed was the scrawny blond kid getting hurt.

They marched to their next destination for the afternoon. They were doing field practice, which most likely meant airsoft or paintball guns. They'd done a couple of smaller versions back at the camp, but Calliste wasn't sure where they were marching off to that particular afternoon. His thoughts about the wall clouded his mind, so he didn't realize the direction they were taking until they reached the meadow.

Calliste looked around, sad to see all those boys walking

around in the grassy field, sad to see that the camp did use that place for something, but mostly sad because he thought he'd found one place to be alone, and now it all felt ripped away from him with a withdrawn hand. He wandered over to the meeting point, where again instructions were given out, and teams were divided. It was no surprise that the teams were newly made.

Calliste didn't listen. Instead, he looked up at the sky. The sun had moved from its position at high noon to a much less intense place in the sky. It had eased up on the heat for a while, hidden behind some small clouds and the tops of the trees that they were all surrounded by. He didn't have it with him, but he thought about the napkin Sasha had written her letter to him on, sitting back at his bunk. She seemed to be having a good time at her grandparents, or at least, the ocean and sky were beautiful where she was. That, she had conveyed well. He felt like she was keeping something to herself, however. He wasn't sure what that could be.

He chose to forget about that feeling; he was sure her next letter would tell him more. For now, he thought about the sun over the ocean, and how beautiful she said the sunsets were on the beach, or even outside of her balcony. Calliste closed his eyes for a moment as he sat in the thick grass, pretending to listen to instructions. He envisioned he was on the beach in the evening, alone, with just the simple waves hitting his feet and the sun exploding with color in the sky.

"Alright, come grab your weapons," Adams called out, motioning for them to hurry. He hated to stand around, always preferring for the activity to start quickly. He knew most boys were eager to start the game, anyway.

"Going to do better this time?" he asked Calliste as he picked up the airsoft gun reserved for him and the goggles to protect his eyes. He simply nodded, already making up his mind about what he was going to do with the time they had to spend here, in his meadow, trampling the grass and shooting at one another.

Once the game started, everyone scattered, but Calliste did so with a certain tree in mind. He looped around the field and then crawled carefully through the brush. Once he was sure no one had seen him do so, he began to climb the biggest oak tree existing in those woods. He did so quickly and easily, his small frame moving through the branches almost perfectly. Finding a decent perch, he settled onto the branch comfortably and watched as the boys shot one another. Sergeant Adams looked on intently as he smoked a cigarette, reminiscent of the way Melrose smoked.

Others found hideouts as well, but no one found a place to hide that was as clever as where Calliste sat. He almost fell asleep up there, away from the noise, away from pounding feet and heavy breathing. He turned his eyes up and looked at the sun as it changed positions in the sky, and felt the breeze on his face, and for a moment, pretended he was up in a tree at home waiting for his friends to meet him.

He couldn't stay up there forever. He wanted to.

"Martin! Where are you?" Sergeant Adams yelled out after most of the game had wrapped up, and everyone became aware that he was one of the very last remaining soldiers in the field. Only the boy he'd called Turner was still in, searching for the last person he had to take down before the game could finally finish. Calliste had picked that tree for a reason.

Carefully, he took up his aim, breathed in heavily thinking he knew the consequences, and pulled the trigger of his airsoft gun. The small plastic bullet hit the boy square in the chest, knocking the breath out of him for a minute. Calliste started his descent.

No one said anything. The others stared at Calliste with some kind of awe that wasn't complimentary. Sergeant Adams looked on as if he couldn't possibly believe this was how his day was going. Lukas smiled lightly, hiding most of his face from the other boys. And Jack Turner, well, his eyes were daggers.

"March out. Dinner," Adams said curtly, and the boys silently put away their cheap guns, got back into their lines, and headed out of the meadow and into the woods back to camp. Calliste stayed at the end, listening intently for any words directed his way. No one said anything.

The sun was fading behind the buildings that made up the camp as they arrived around dinner time. Calliste carefully collected his food and headed past all the tables to the back lawn to eat alone. He passed Lukas, who was now sitting at an actual table with a few others from his group that day. He didn't say anything to Calliste as he walked by.

Again, he didn't eat much. He just had no appetite, even after working so hard everyday to keep up and quicken his times during drills. Calliste felt like he wanted to write a letter to someone but couldn't think of who to address it to or what he would say. He didn't want to worry anyone or bring anyone else's day down. He could handle the rest of his time in this place, even if the homesickness was beginning to creep in, and he couldn't even believe that it was.

He decided to call home.

"Hey, Dad, it's me. How're you?" Calliste said into the phone, his heart pounding. He felt nervous to be talking to his dad, especially over the phone. So much of their communication was nonverbal.

"I'm good, I'm good. Everything's fine here. How's the camp been? Learning a lot?" Adam asked, not sure what else to say. He wasn't sure what he was feeling after answering the phone only to realize it was his son. He was feeling a lot, but he never knew quite how to handle that.

"Yeah, it's not bad here. Food's good," Calliste commented, gripping the phone a little tighter as he spoke. There were four phone stations for public use, but no one was using the other ones, and Calliste finally felt alone for the first time.

"And how are the activities?" Adam asked.

"Ah, well, don't know if I'd quite call them that..." Calliste replied, being honest but then quickly regretting it.

"They're, uh, they're fine, though. Good, actually. I'm improving, they say," he quickly added. In that moment, he could not have taken any kind of reprimanding from his father. He just couldn't hear it.

"I knew it would work out for you. Stick with it, alright? I told you it wouldn't be so bad," his father said. There was a bit of silence for a moment, but Calliste wasn't ready to hang up, so he kept talking.

"Yeah, I actually sort of won this field practice we did today. I was the last man standing," he said quickly, almost rambling, as he leaned against the wall where the phone station was mounted. He kicked his boots into the cement beneath him a little, irked that they were still as solid as the day he got them. They were giving him blisters.

"Wow, I can't even believe it," Adam said. Calliste sighed heavily but covered the mouthpiece so his father couldn't hear it.

"Have you heard anything about Melrose? Or Davey or Sasha?" Calliste asked quickly, wanting desperately to hear their voices right then but somehow knew he couldn't call them, for fear of something.

"Ah, no. I haven't," Adam replied.

"Of course you haven't," Calliste mumbled under his breath, moving the phone away from his mouth a little too late.

"What was that?" Adam asked as Calliste shook his head, clearing his thoughts.

"Uh, nothing. I have to get going, okay?" Calliste replied, banging his foot harder against the brick of the wall. Finally, a scuffmark appeared at the top of the boot, and it felt bittersweet to him.

"Okay. Your mom misses you," Adam reminded, in case his son had forgotten about her. He felt like he often did, or at the very least, forgot how challenging it was to deal with her all on his own. Calliste felt his eyes water.

"Yeah, I miss you guys, too. How is she?" Calliste said quietly.

"She's doing good, hanging in there. We're back at physical therapy," he added and Calliste was a little shocked to hear it, but it gave him some hope. He felt he might be able to carry on, if she could.

"That's good, I'm really glad to hear it," Calliste replied.

"Yeah, she's working hard," Adam said, his own voice softening. At that, Calliste almost couldn't take it anymore.

"I really have to go," he stammered into the phone.

"Okay," his father replied.

"*Au revoir*," he added, then hung up before Adam could say anything more.

12 – PERFORMANCE

The tickets had been on the refrigerator for weeks already. At dinner, Ann Raskova could not stop rambling about how excited she was to finally see this play and just how long she had been waiting for it to come to town. There was a small theatre troupe doing a rendition of an old Renaissance play called *Masque of Blackness*. She'd heard about it from some of the wives in her husband's circle, and they only used whispers and strangled giggles when they talked about it. Ann's husband nodded when appropriate and smiled genuinely at her excitement, but more often than not, he was more concerned with reading through The Wall Street Journal during their four-course meal than hearing about anyone's day.

Sasha played with her food as she listened to her grandmother talk. She, too, was excited for the play but was caught up in the amount of focus about what she'd have to wear, who she'd meet at the theatre, and just how long the show would go. She wasn't opposed to going, but it seemed a lot less about the show and a lot more about appearances. Sasha hadn't been there long enough to get used to that part of their lifestyle.

As they ate, Sasha's mind kept focusing on Gillian, the strange and confident girl who roamed the halls of the house all in the name of dusting and cleaning, or so she said. There was something unsettling about that thought to Sasha, but at the same time, in the deepest pit of her stomach, she felt an untamed excitement. They'd only seen each other a few other times since the hard-boiled egg at breakfast, and each time, Gillian smiled warmly at Sasha and threw out some kind of sarcastic remark. Sasha could never think of an equally creative comeback, instead too entranced by her dark eyes and sharp jaw line.

"Sasha, do you have something to wear for the show tomorrow?" Ann asked, bringing her out of her daydreams. She dropped her fork abruptly, letting it clang against her plate. Ann didn't appear to notice, but Sasha's grandfather looked up with a bit of disdain before moving his eyes down to peer through his small glasses at the fine print of the newspaper. Sasha sighed but looked at her grandmother.

"Well, I have that black-and-gold dress I wore to the benefit last week..." Sasha replied, trailing off a little as Ann immediately reacted.

"Oh, that's all, dear? Well, you need something new for this. Can't wear the same dress to everything, you know that, don't you?" Ann asked, thinking back to Vivienne for a moment and how her daughter wore the same red-and-green dress to every event she had to force her to attend, right until the end. She only stopped wearing the dress when it would no longer fit over her swollen belly, Sasha growing relentlessly inside of her. That was the end for Ann, because after that, Frank got her. And together, they set up a home in the hills of a town hours away, perhaps on purpose.

"Right, I guess I did. I just didn't have anything else to really bring, so..." Sasha said, trailing off again. Her grandmother waved her hand, as if Sasha's words were all too silly for her to even listen to the rest of her sentence.

"We'll go shopping tomorrow morning. You wake up early, yes? We can get lunch, too, out at the beach. I've noticed how fond you are of walking there. The sea is beautiful, isn't it?" Ann asked eagerly, hoping to see the same excitement she held within her also within her granddaughter. There was nothing vindictive about Ann. What made her happy made her happy. She only wanted others to share in that happiness of late lunches and expensive orchestra tickets for foreign plays.

"Yeah, we can do that, of course. Sounds great," Sasha replied, almost honestly. Ann nodded, pleased with the response, and took another bite of her steak. Sasha looked back down at her own plate, having eaten half of everything so far. She was almost enjoying her time there with her grandparents, although everything they did outside of the house was wildly uncomfortable. She was beginning to pick up on the culture her grandparents lived in; the lifestyle her mother came from. It was different and seemed scary on the outside, but so far, she didn't feel devoured as she was becoming a part of it.

Following the steak and asparagus was a small bowl of fruit accompanied by a kind of ice cream creation Sasha couldn't name and couldn't help but enjoy. After eating the cherry on top and tying the stem with her tongue, she spit it out onto her plate, noting again the disapproving look her grandfather seemed to permanently have on his face. She normally would have said something but recently had stopped. A part of her felt like maybe she wasn't thinking for herself anymore because she quickly hid the tied stem and watched as it seemed to make all the difference.

After dinner, Sasha called Vivienne from the balcony in her room. She liked talking to her mom while she watched the sun set over the water, hearing the seagulls sing and the waves beat down on the sandy beaches.

"She's buying you a new dress? I'm surprised she didn't do it sooner," Vivienne commented after her daughter had rehashed her entire day over the phone. She was bitterly surprised Sasha was still at her grandparents' house, having been sure that her daughter wasn't going to last a week with her parents.

"Ah, well, she's buying me one now. Also, she doesn't seem too bad. Like, I get what you mean; they are kind of wrapped up in this weird life. But Ann is really nice," Sasha said, hanging her legs through the bars of the black twisted metal railing, looking down at the garden that laid beneath her.

"You're calling her Ann?" Vivienne asked, surprised.

"Not to her face," Sasha teased, but Vivienne wasn't sure she believed that.

"You're going to get smacked if you aren't careful," Vivienne mumbled, her husband looking at her curiously from the kitchen table where he was carving an apple.

"Ma, she isn't that bad. You worry a lot for nothing, you know that?" Sasha said, never censoring her thoughts when talking to her mother. Though she never listened. Neither woman knew whose fault that was.

"Listen, Sasha. I'm glad she's being so nice to you. I've never said the woman was evil, okay, I just–" she tried to finish, but Sasha cut in.

"I swear you've said the word evil before,"

"Okay, maybe I have. In haste, though. Or for lack of a better word. The point here is, I know she isn't. But don't be fooled, she won't be there for you when you need her, okay? She just isn't... she isn't like you or me," Vivienne tried to explain but was at a loss for words. She knew her daughter wasn't listening. Sasha often felt like she was always right, and Vivienne knew that was partially her fault, for allowing her to be an adult when she was actually just a child. Not having the right words for her daughter made her feel worthless. Especially as a writer.

"Ma, I get it, okay? I'm not losing my head over here. I'm just telling you how everything's going. How are things at home, huh? How's Freckles? And Dad?" Sasha asked, trying to get off the topic of Ann and her richness. The topic was beginning to make her feel uncomfortable, and not voluntarily.

"Oh, Freckles comes before your father now?" Vivienne laughed, looking over at her husband sitting at the kitchen table. He cut into the apple he was eating a little too harshly after hearing that remark. He pretended to be appalled but flashed a grin that let his wife know he too thought it was funny.

"Oh, never," Sasha teased.

"Well, both bird and father are alive and well. I think Freckles misses you, though," her mother replied, looking out the back door at the hen house that all the chickens were already packed in for the night. Coyotes were relentless.

"Oh, but not my father?" Sasha replied.

"He might miss you just as much, if not a little bit more," Vivienne promised, and it made Sasha happy to hear it. She hated that she had to hear the words, couldn't just know it, but she had to hear them.

"Have you heard anything about the boys?"

"Well, sort of. I talked to Daisy on the phone a few days ago. She says Melrose is doing great at work, but he and Bernard have been fighting a lot again. Do you know what that's all about? She doesn't say much," Vivienne asked, knowing Sasha would deny any knowledge. Vivienne had her fears about the situation but had decided to let Sasha make the call. She hoped she would come back to them. Not everything was black and white.

"No, I don't. Just boys being boys, I guess," she replied.

"You hate that excuse."

"Yeah."

"Well, I also ran into Davey's grandmother at the bakery a week or so ago. She's worried her poor boy's been corrupted and wants to know when you're coming over for dinner," Vivienne replied, moving forward. Sasha laughed.

"I'll see Nonna when I'm home, I'm sure. I don't know if Davey's been corrupted by swimming in a lake, though," Sasha replied, thinking back to his letter to her. She was happy to hear from him, thinking he was probably having the easiest summer out of everyone. She worried about Melrose. He hadn't written her at all, and she thought he would, at least once.

"Nothing from Calliste?"

"No, nothing. I never see his mother anymore, you know," Vivienne replied, her voice getting a little quiet as she spoke of Alice Martin.

"He hasn't written me back in awhile. I hope that camp is treating him okay," Sasha said, not sure what kind of place he was truly in. Vivienne had no answers for her, even less sure of what was happening to Calliste those days.

"Give it a few more days, I'm sure he'll write you back," Vivienne replied, meaning every word. She, of all their parents, loved the friends Sasha had. Vivienne felt like she could have really benefitted from friends like that when she was seventeen. They talked a bit longer, before eventually hanging up and going to bed. Sasha dreamt about her friends, at the old *Chateau*, each of them doing something ridiculous or dangerous. Davey was running around trying to protect everyone while Melrose followed trying to ruin everything. Calliste just laughed. Sasha kept feeling like she was supposed to do something, or say something, but couldn't find the words. She woke up a little confused and with a deep ache in her chest. She missed them. They'd all laugh if they saw her now.

As promised, Ann took Sasha to a couple of her favorite boutique designers and bought much more than just one dress for one show. Ann paid for everything, and Sasha couldn't help but note how easily she had allowed Sasha to pick what she liked over the designs even Ann seemed to favor. As she paid for the last item, Vivienne's words crept into her mind, and Sasha felt unsure for a moment. Unsure about what, she didn't know. But anxiety crept into her chest, again, and Sasha bitterly tried to push it away. Anxiety had lived in her chest far too long, and there was no way she was going back. She was trying to get rid of those situations. The whole reason she was there was to get rid of it, not feel it come in waves like the water that beat down the beaches.

They took a private car with a driver to the theatre. Other than get ready, Sasha hadn't done much with her day and couldn't believe she was watching the sunset as the car drove with ease to the theatre. A gentleman came up and opened the door before Sasha could even undo her seat belt. Nervously, she began to wring her hands, and fixing the placement of her rings over and over again.

There were people everywhere, fancily dressed, chattering away loudly and enjoying a drink or two before being escorted to their seats and quieting down for the production to begin. Ann introduced Sasha to many people, and Sasha took every introduction in strides but found herself often falling silent, her eyes fading into the background, noticing the crowd with a different set of eyes, especially after her conversation with her mother. She didn't think anyone looked like a barracuda, but perhaps there was a little sting in people's eyes and venom in their words.

Someone handed her a glass of champagne, and she drank it almost too quickly, feeling the warmth flow down her body and dull her nerves just a little, enough to let her say a few words at a time without feeling awkward or uncommon. People asked her about school, about her mother, sometimes even about her father. They asked about what college she had her eyes set on and if she preferred red or white. She felt a bit, in that crowd, like a piece of silver amongst a gold field. It was too early for her to know that if you can afford diamonds, you only buy diamonds.

As the lights dimmed, she followed her grandparents to their seats and watched the show with mesmerized eyes. It was humorous in the beginning, and then it took a dramatic shift to tragedy throughout the end. The ending almost had Sasha sobbing, and she couldn't believe how invested she'd become in the story. When the lights rose up again, everyone else around her seemed to be critical of the storyline, of the character arcs, of why the lead chose what she did. Sasha didn't know all the answers, either, but something was stirring deeper in her soul than in those around her.

"Thanks for coming with us, Sasha. You had a good time, yes?" Ann asked. Sasha smiled in the darkness of the car and nodded. Her grandfather seemed pleased enough with the answer but stayed quiet as ever. She wondered when he would finally speak to her and what it would be about.

Up in her room, the night still young but the sky only lit up by the moon, she took down her hair and brushed it out on the balcony. Usually she'd call her mom, but she was feeling distant that night. The feelings of loss from the play, coupled with the crashing sounds of the waves, the immensity of all that water – Sasha tried desperately not to cry. She was over crying, over feeling gutted and mangled. She missed her friend. To her, the waves sometimes sounded like wailing, but it's impossible to wail while drowning.

"Hey! You awake up there?" a strong voice called up from the darkness of the garden, only some moonlight hitting a few shrubs and the gazebo. Sasha was jolted from her thoughts, and throwing her hair back over her shoulder, leaned over the metal railing and tried to spot who was calling up to her. It was Gillian, and she wasn't alone.

"What?" Sasha replied, feeling a little guarded, her voice tentative.

"I asked, 'Are you awake?' So, are you awake? Or is this some weird kind of sleepwalking thing?" Gillian teased, the girl and boy she was with laughed a little at the joke. They looked almost as reckless as she did, but something about Gillian screamed that she had everything together. They were all wearing dark clothes and heavy eyeliner, all things Sasha was well accustomed to. The girl had long hair but half her head shaved. The boy had stretched ears and two rings in his nose. She thought back to her own jewelry she'd taken out before coming here and almost took a step back from the railing, but at the sight of Gillian's wide smile, didn't.

"I'm awake."

"Oh, good! We're going to a concert at some hole in the wall, wanna come?" Gillian asked, everything about her being begging Sasha to say yes. It wasn't something that went unnoticed.

"I don't know…" Sasha replied, looking back out to see the ocean in the distant background, all lit up from the moon. She didn't know that she felt like going out.

"You going to hang out with old rich people the whole summer? C'mon, don't be lame, you seem better than that," Gillian said, almost a little too loudly. Sasha took one step back.

"You don't even know me, okay?"

"I know! That's the point! So get down here!"

Something about the way her voice sounded or perhaps how desperate her eyes looked all lined in black and lit up by the moon caused Sasha to feel that same stirring in her chest when the heroine in the play had made her difficult decision. It was the same kind of feeling she felt when she held Melrose's hand or pushed her parents out of the house for at least one walk a day. She'd felt it when she watched the sunset and meteor showers with Calliste on his roof or sipped wine at Davey's and listened to everyone getting loud and then louder, their stories always competing. She'd felt it when all her friends were around the bonfire by the old *Chateau*, when Hailey was still with them.

Hailey. It always came back to her.

She'd tell Sasha to go.

"I'm coming, okay. One sec," she replied, disappearing into her room to change out of her dress into black jeans, boots, and a ripped-up tank top. She'd snuck the clothes in later, after her mom had left the room. She felt she'd need them. Now she knew why. The house was so massive it was easy for her to tip toe down a few vacant halls and make it out a small door in the back. She was immediately cast into the darkness of the night and could only hear a few whispers and small laughs before her eyes adjusted and Gillian and her crew approached her.

"Don't you look nice. C'mon, we don't want to be late," Gillian said, tapping Sasha gently on the shoulder, sending a heat wave through her. Quietly, she followed Gillian through the garden and out the back gate to the road, the other two kissing every now and again and giggling incessantly. Gillian looked back at Sasha for a moment as they walked.

"You alright? This will be fun, I promise," she said, slowing her own stride so Sasha could keep up with her. She walked in a fast, meaningful way. Sasha, on the other hand, had a slower pace and could never make it in a straight line.

"What kind of band is it?" Sasha asked, her arms crossed as she kept pace with the only friend her age in the little seaside town. Gillian flashed her a giant grin, her teeth so white they seemed to shine even in the darkness of the night.

"A rock concert. It'll be the bee's knees," she said, silliness in her voice, putting her arm through Sasha's crossed arms and dragging her along. The four of them talked a little on their way to the venue, laughing and joking, and taking shots from a flask the other girl had brought along with her. Gillian seemed impressed with each new move Sasha made, and that gave her a new kind of empowerment she hadn't felt in a very long time. She wasn't pressured. Rather, Sasha felt she could do or be anything she wanted to be. And that was very freeing.

"Come on, I know the guy who works the back," Gillian said as they approached the venue, young people everywhere in various styles of dark clothing and heavy makeup. She pulled Sasha off to the side down the alley, losing the two friends she had come with as they met up with others in the front of the building. The place seemed old, and the outside of the building was far from extraordinary. Sasha followed her new friend down the side alley and around the back where there was a large patio and bar area. Gillian pulled her over to the shed and offered a boost.

"I thought you said you knew a guy?" Sasha whispered, not sure how she felt about having to scale the fence by means of the old shed roof.

"Yeah, I knew the guy who built this shed. C'mon, the fun's just starting, you know?" Gillian said, and with a roll of her eyes, Sasha stepped into her hands and grabbed onto the top of the roof, grabbing Gillian's hand and pulling her up, then together they belly crawled to the other side.

"When the bartender isn't looking, just jump, okay?" Gillian said, pointing to the two guys they were trying to avoid. Most everyone on the patio seemed drunk enough, and the lighting was dim, coming from nothing more than strung-up lights over the whole expanse. Sasha felt a pounding in her chest, and for once, she was thrilled by it.

"Go!" Gillian shouted in a whisper, and without hesitation, Sasha threw herself over the edge of the shed, dodging the fence, and landing on her feet, more or less. Gillian was right beside her, standing upright, looking down at her, flashing her that same giant grin. She threw her long brown hair, filled with large waves, over her shoulder before offering Sasha a hand to stand up.

"That went well. A drink, and then we should dance," Gillian announced, grabbing Sasha's hand this time and heading over to the bar where she promptly ordered two 7 and 7's. Since they were already in and didn't have a black X drawn on the top of their hands, getting refills was as simple as asking.

"Perks of not using the front door," Gillian said as she handed Sasha her drink. She followed her into the concert hall, music playing loudly. They each drank their whiskey before Gillian pulled Sasha out onto the dance floor, where together they danced, drank, and laughed at how much fun it all was.

The over-head lights were dim, but the flashing lights from the stage lit up everything just enough for Sasha to watch Gillian as she danced, roughing up her hair now and again. Sasha danced just as well. The space between them was electric, and it didn't matter how many other people were around. Sasha enjoyed the lack of control; she was thrilled that Gillian made all the calls, all the choices. And now, together, they danced and sang, not even knowing the words. Their faces were lit up with different shades of the rainbow as the stage lights rolled over the crowd, and Sasha almost didn't notice how Gillian moved closer to her, touching her shoulder every now and again, or grabbing her hand for long moments.

"Isn't this fun?" Gillian laughed, her lips touching the soft part of Sasha's ear as she shouted her words. Sasha nodded her head, looking up at the tall girl before her, long hair still wavy, rolling down her back, her clothes black and gold, her bright eyes lined brilliantly.

"This is fun," Sasha replied, spinning in a circle, happy.

13 – SWEETNESS

"What *is* that?" Davey asked, watching as Jimmy cut thick leaves off a potted plant on the back porch of the lake house. Jimmy chuckled, cutting the leaves in half to reveal the slimy insides, a bright and happy green.

"It's called an aloe plant, and it'll help with your sunburn. Who knew someone could turn so red?" Jimmy asked, more to himself, as he walked up to Davey's bare chest and back and carefully laid some of the leaves on the worst parts. Davey inhaled sharply but settled down the moment his skin started to feel cool for the first time in days. His face visibly calmed, and it was something else Jimmy found funny enough to laugh at.

"I can't believe you didn't say anything sooner, dude. You're a little uptight, you know? You gotta calm down a bit. You're gonna die of a heart attack like my old man," Jimmy said, sitting on top of the thick railing that ran along the sides of the small wooden porch. Davey looked up, confused for a moment.

"Isn't Nick…?" he started to ask. Jimmy shook his head.

"Nah, you'd think. He's a good guy, though. I like him," Jimmy said, squinting his eyes from the sun as he looked out at the lake where the other kids were mulling around on the beach, Nick and Sidney trying to work on the old pontoon boat to get at least a couple rides out of it that summer. It was quiet for a moment,

Davey not sure he wanted to know more. Jimmy didn't say anything more about it.

They watched for a long moment as Sidney and Nick cheered each other on after each attempt to start up the old rig failed, the engine giving out a tiresome groan each time, desperately waiting for them to quit trying. They didn't, though they did take small breaks to splash each other in the face with lake water. The corners of Jimmy's mouth edged up ever so slightly.

"Are you guys going to sit on this porch all day?" Karen asked, coming up from the beach slowly until she met them at the house. She had an interesting gait.

"Just trying to get this aloe to soak in for a bit," Davey replied, looking at the leaves on his shoulders and chest, moving them around a little so that the transparent gel touched every part of his red skin. Karen chuckled.

"I thought Italians didn't burn?" she said, looking from her brother to her cousin. Jimmy shrugged, still not wearing a shirt; his skin perfectly browned, even though he continued to look slightly overworked.

"I've never burned before and don't plan on it again," Davey insisted, noticing that she was just as tan as her brother, though with two streaks of white where the top straps of her shirt always rested. She nodded with a bit of mockery, as if he had a choice in the matter. He rolled his eyes at her.

"It'll be fine," Davey insisted once more.

"Dude, that's going to peel," Jimmy said, leaning over from his perch, looking over at him.

"It's going to be just fine," Davey said, once more. Jimmy shrugged, letting it go, just as Sidney began to jump up and down in the water excitedly, waving her arms in the air. Nick's roaring laugh made its way to the back porch and both Karen and Jimmy jumped down excitedly. The engine of the pontoon boat was loud and rough but powerful and consistent. Nick was twirling Sidney around in the knee-deep water, drops of the lake spinning out away from her as her feet grazed the surface. Jimmy started to run out there, catching up to his sister. He stopped for a moment long enough for Karen to jump onto his back, then together they ran down the grassy lawn to the dock, throwing themselves over the deep edge. Sidney and Nick laughed at them as they all climbed up into the pontoon boat, waving to the other cousins to come climb aboard their newly sea-worthy vessel. Davey just shook his head, smiling a little, and walked over slowly.

He wondered what it would be like to have a sibling. With his parents, there had been only the briefest thought of another child. It had been a hard time believing that Davey could even exist. He was their miracle child. Marie had several miscarriages before she got pregnant with Davey, and the constant trying was hard. When she made it past the first trimester, she was over the moon, and so was Vince. The next two trimesters were tough. It was an almost impossible pregnancy, and Davey was born two months premature. Even keeping him inside of her that long had been a horrific challenge. But he lived, and he grew up to be just as strong and tall as all of his Romano cousins. They had miscarriages after Davey. And then it all just stopped. They had to be happy with one. And they were very happy with the one they had.

Davey wondered what it felt like to have a sibling. And what it felt like to share some of the responsibility he shouldered. It was always just him.

"'Bout time you made it out here, jeez. You obviously don't know the story of this old lady," Sidney said, grabbing Davey's hand to help pull him aboard from the dock since the boat was already drifting out. She tapped the side of the old pontoon with affection as she sat down on a patched up seat, looking over at the captain.

"This gal only works a few weeks every summer. You have to appreciate her while she lasts," Sidney explained, looking over at Davey, who was otherwise silent. He sat next to her, looking out at the water, the other cousins sitting at the very front of the boat, pretending to push one another in.

"Something up?" Sidney asked, touching his shoulder slightly.

He shuddered.

"No, nothing," he replied quickly, lost in thought again. Sidney held a small smile at the corners of her lips as she tied her blonde hair back loosely, reaching for the sunglasses that rested on the carpeted floor of the boat.

"Your parents used to love this boat, you know that?" she asked, leaning back in her seat and looking over at her cousin's son. He wasn't anything like she'd imagine he'd be. He wasn't like Marie, and he wasn't even like Vince. At least, how Sidney remembered Vince. Davey looked back at her, his skin red and peeling, his brown hair pushed back in simple waves, a little stiff from lake water and direct sunlight. Around his neck, she noticed, was a golden crucifix. Real gold, no doubt. The chain was beautiful, two gold strands tied together, meeting at the bottom where Jesus was strung, bleeding, looking right at her.

"Did they?"

"Oh, yeah. We used to have parties on it late at night. We'd have some friends over, and all of us would go out on the lake in the middle of the night and anchor it down. We'd drink and go night swimming and sing and dance. You know, all the things young people like to do," she teased, hitting his arm gently for emphasis. He smiled at the thought of his parents doing something like that.

"I didn't know my dad ever came out here, to this side of the state," Davey replied as Sidney snorted, taking a sip of her water that she wished wasn't just water. She looked out at the waves, watched as they hit the sides of the boat with little force. Nick was pushing the boat to go fast, but she didn't care. She liked the wind and liked the way the sunlight reflected off the water's surface. She'd never let go of the past; never forgot about it.

"He did, quite a bit in the early days. He lied to his mother about it, though, you know. She didn't like us at first. The *only* thing that kept her from losing it, I think, was that *at least* we were Italian," Sidney continued, forgetting for a moment that this woman was also Davey's grandmother. Davey didn't mind, in the moment. He was becoming curious about how his family looked from the other side.

"Why didn't she like you guys?" Davey asked, leaning back to get his torso out of the sun and to catch every word Sidney said. She was certainly chatty.

"Ah, well. You know. We lived in the woods; we didn't go to church every Sunday. Only Marie ever did go to college. And the wine! That damn wine. We gave Vince a bottle of our Bianchi wine, and Marie came back with crazy stories about how she threw the whole bottle out. Poured it all down the sink. Can you believe that?" Sidney asked, getting a little fired up about it. Davey could, actually, believe that. But something about the way Sidney told the story made him feel upset about the loss of the wine. Mostly, he was upset his mother had known.

"Yeah, she doesn't like sweet wine," Davey laughed, a little awkwardly.

"Well, the woman needs to sweeten up," Sidney replied, crossing her legs and rolling her head back for a moment to stretch out. Davey didn't know what to say.

"Anyways, we always had fun, Nick and I, when your parents would come out. Vince is a really funny guy, your father. He's so wild. He was always taking dares. Real sweetheart, though. I'm happy Marie has him," Sidney replied, her voice getting a little quieter at the end, looking over at Nick. He was grinning ear to ear, half sitting at the seat behind the wheel. His hair flew out around the edges of his hat, and from somewhere, he'd managed to find a cigar and light it. The sun had already damaged his skin. It seemed a permanent dark hue, rough and coarse, burned forever. He looked wild and so happy. He was much older than Sidney.

"So where did this come from?" Sidney asked, breaking their silence. Davey looked down to where she was pointing – the crucifix that rested on his otherwise bare chest. He touched it for a moment with his fingers, always comforted by it.

"It was my dad's; he got it when he was in Rome. My grandparents took him to the Vatican when he was around seven or something. He made his First Communion there," Davey replied, always entranced by the story. Sidney nodded, chuckling a little.

"Ah, well. It's beautiful. Quite the story," she replied, happy to see that next to it, there was also a golden charm of a bull's horn, the *cornicello*.

"And that's for good luck?"

"Yeah, something like that," he replied. They didn't talk for awhile after that, both of them looking out at the water lapping the boat as they made their way around the lake, the sun still shining brightly overhead, the air heating up as afternoon set in. Davey had different thoughts about the water's depth than anyone on that boat. A bit of it splashed up, hitting his face sweetly, mocking him. He wiped the drops away as if they were bitter tears.

"Davey! Come here, man," Jimmy called out from the front, and carefully Davey made his way up to sit with him and Karen, who each had their legs draped over the sides. He watched as the water turned violently right below his feet, churning, then going under the boat, disappearing entirely.

"Isn't this kind of dangerous? The propeller is right back there..." Davey started, looking at Jimmy with a bit of anxiety. Karen laughed, and Jimmy clapped him on the back, his skin instantly stinging viciously.

"I guess. Just don't fall in," he replied, as if it was really that easy. Maybe it was, but he certainly didn't think so, not with Henry, Celia, Hannah, Alex, Jimmy, and Karen still messing around, pretending to throw one another off. He looked back for a moment to see Nick standing behind Sidney, who was working the wheel. She looked like a young girl, learning to drive the boat and pretending to mess up now and again to hear Nick give her grief. It was a joke; they were always joking around.

"My mom give you the third degree back there?" Karen asked, breaking Davey from his thoughts. He shook his head.

"Ah, no. Just telling me about some things her and my mom used to do," Davey said, not sure why Karen would think otherwise. Her mom didn't seem the type.

"Well at least she wasn't reading you the Riot Act, never let her do that," Jimmy complained, leaning back a little and balancing his weight on the palms of his hands.

"The Riot Act? What's that?" Davey asked, Karen just laughed.

"Don't you worry about it, church boy," Jimmy replied, grinning through his teeth. It was quiet for a while, only the sound of the motor working hard filling the air. They drove around the entire lake before heading back to the house, where parking it was a hassle. Nick wasn't very good at drawing the boat in, and it took every hand on deck to help tie it up to the dock and make sure it didn't crash into the old wood and collapse. Karen did the best job of driving it up close enough to the dock to jump off and tie it, and she gave her father plenty of grief for it as everyone unloaded. They all spent some time in the sun splashing around in the water. Davey kept his whole body submerged, trying to keep his skin from frying any more. Once it all healed, he would be using generous amounts of sunscreen.

"Hey, do you guys want to pop by the Garfields' place tonight? I'm sure they're having the usual festivities," Sidney asked, her feet dipped in the water as she sat on the dock, working again on a tan. Everyone agreed in earnest.

"Who are the Garfields?" Davey asked.

"Neighbors across the lake. We spend the evenings with them when the boat is fixed, and we can get over there easily. It's a fun time. They're really cool people," Karen replied, swimming circles around Davey as he treaded water. He believed her.

After an hour, they went back inside, eating all the leftovers and cold meats and cheeses for lunch. Sidney made a tomato salad with spinach and onion, and Nick tossed out extra slices of calzone and grilled chicken and meatballs. Davey was getting used to eating cold lunches and then not having any dishes to wash right after. More often than not, they were using paper towel as plates. Everything was quick and easy; nobody made a big deal out of anything.

That afternoon, everyone took a nap. Davey found himself

getting tired in the middle of the day, and sometimes he couldn't fight to keep his eyes open anymore. No one else even tried to fight. They just found an open couch or bed and lay down, taking an hour or two out of their day just to dream and sit in comfortable warmth, letting a breeze from the window keep everything simple. The twins slept curled up together, Karen claimed the overstuffed first floor couch, Sidney fell asleep in an outside chair, and Nick passed out on the boat. Jimmy and Davey made their way to their own beds and slept only for an hour, waking up before anyone else did. They spent some of the time in silence but some of it talking. Jimmy was never serious, but there was strangely something very serious about him. It didn't come out often, verbally at least, but that afternoon the two boys lay in their separate beds and talked about their families, their friends back home, how badly a sunburn hurt, and how hard it was to watch someone walk with bowed legs.

"You feel bad for her?" Davey asked, not sure he really understood.

"No, I don't feel bad for her. She's fine," Jimmy was quick to say, then sighed a little, trying to find the right words to say what he meant.

"I just feel bad that other people give her shit for it, that's all. I don't know. She's her own person. She's good, she just gets blamed for too much," Jimmy replied, picking at the skin around his fingers instead of looking over at Davey. Both were lying on their backs, looking up at the old cracked ceiling instead of each other.

"She's kind of devious," Davey said, trying to draw him out of whatever he was trying to say. He knew he wasn't saying it correctly, and it frustrated him. Jimmy felt trapped in a swirling dark hole, and was glad Davey threw him a lifeline.

"That she is, and it's always her fault when there's no ice cream left," he replied.

"I already figured she was the thief," Davey replied, chuckling. They talked absently a little while longer, only getting up when they heard footsteps downstairs on the old creaky wood that made up the floorboards. The sun was already making its descent in the sky, shining almost too brightly through the open sliding doors.

"Sweetheart, you going to be ready in a few?" Sidney asked, getting together a cooler of things to bring over. Jimmy nodded from the couch, where all the cousins had gathered after their nap. They had all set strange objects on a sleeping Karen, wondering how many things they could stack on top of her before she'd wake up. The grand total had been three shoeboxes, two sandals, a bag of marbles, one bible, a television remote, an old CD by The Cure, and a jar of cat food. She'd thrown the cat food right at Jimmy when she woke up, almost breaking the television that only worked if there was a DVD in it.

Davey watched as Sidney packed snacks and meat for grilling, a case of beer, and two bottles of white homemade wine. He missed the bitter red he was used to having every night at dinner. It always helped with the after-eating conversations and production line the dishes created.

"Load 'em up! Let's hope my old lady will start up again for us. Twice in one day, I know, asking for a lot, but it would be great," Nick said to whomever would listen as the family headed out the back and towards the dock, the sun bright as ever right above the tree line of the woods that covered everything the water didn't. It was such a sharp contrast. Dark shadows or bright orange light. It was less harsh, too, and Davey's red skin felt the best it had in weeks, especially when the boat picked up speed and the wind ran through his greasy hair. He hadn't showered in a day or two.

Docking the boat at the neighbor's house was an easier task. There were quite a few skilled boaters; all of which cracked jokes and drank the rest of their beer while helping Nick and Karen tie up their boat to a free spot at the dock. Davey followed his cousins down the dock, setting the food and wine they had brought near the grill on the back patio and then all choosing a spot to sit on the benches around the fire pit. The atmosphere was calm, but it was decorated with a lot of loud laughter and crude jokes.

"Hey Karen, hey Jimmy," a girl greeted, walking over with a plate of burgers recently cooked, handing them out. She sat cross-legged on the thick grass in front of the bench where Karen had already laid out, stretching her legs as far as they would go. The other cousins were splashing around in the water with other neighborhood kids. Davey couldn't get over how easy the conversations were, how simple the greetings. He didn't say much, just looked around, noticing it all, taking it in.

"Kate, how was your year?" Jimmy asked, holding his burger up for a moment in thanks then took a huge bite of it, ketchup and mustard spilling out of his mouth and making a mess on the ground in front of him. Karen rolled her eyes, and he smiled at her, mouth full of food. The girl, Kate, laughed a little before folding up her legs tighter and replying.

"It was alright, the same old thing. You guys? Who's this?" she asked, eyeing Davey quietly. It made his stomach tingle; turning it into a home for butterflies all swirling around trying to find the way out.

"My cousin on my mom's side. Who knew?" Jimmy replied, finally swallowing his bite, elbowing Davey in the side. He shrugged, trying to laugh it off.

"Well, nice to meet you…" she trailed off, leaving it open.

"Ah, Davey," he replied, awkwardly sticking his hand out to shake hers, and then almost pulling it back, but she latched onto it and gave him a firm hand shake, as if it was just what people did. He liked that. She tucked a piece of her short brown hair behind her ear, looking off at the lake, her eyes getting lost in the sunset for a moment. She was a quiet girl; sweet. They chatted for a while longer, about their past school years, what the rest of the summer was going to look like, if maybe they'd have to sneak a bottle of wine or Sidney would get too drunk to keep count of how many half glasses she was pouring.

As the sun finally disappeared, Jimmy helped some of the others start a fire, but it wasn't until Karen came in and built a tepee of wood in the pit that anything truly caught on fire and continued to burn. Kate came and sat next to Davey, and at first, she didn't say anything. Together, they paid attention to all the adults, drinking and laughing, talking about the past three seasons and how much better everything seemed at the lake. Jimmy and another girl started to dance around the fire after a few glasses of the family wine. Karen had given him some to taste.

"A sip won't kill you. And besides, you drink Romano wine all the time, you said," Karen reminded, pushy. He took her cup, smelling it for a moment. It seemed so light and fresh.

"Yeah, red wine, the good stuff," he teased, but appeased her and took a sip. The liquid almost fizzed on his tongue, an instant shot of warmth traveling down his throat and into his chest. It was too sweet, and his lips puckered a little at how sugary he thought it tasted. Karen laughed but rolled her eyes and wandered off for more.

"You don't like white wine?" Kate asked, her own cup between her knees.

"I just didn't grow up on it, I guess. We only drink red. Really dry stuff, but it's good," Davey replied quickly, feeling the need to defend his family's creation, even though Kate wasn't challenging him about it.

"I like the red. But I also like the white. It's kind of happier, you know? Everyone can drink it," she said, taking another sip, letting some of it sit on her lips for a moment, letting them glisten in the light from the fire. Her whole face seemed to spark.

"Are you having a good summer up here so far?" she asked. Davey shrugged, but then saw her waiting for more. He wasn't sure what to say.

"I mean, yeah. It's great up here. Beautiful, really. It's just…really different from home," he replied, trying to put into words what he was feeling. He figured he was just homesick, but deep down he thought it was something else. Any of his friends would have told him it was something else.

"Yeah, but I think that's what makes lake summers so great," Kate replied, taking another heavy sip of the wine Jimmy had poured her. Together they watched as people danced to the music playing over the speakers, some laughing and telling what only appeared to be wild stories, and others drinking quietly and soaking it all in.

"You have to give it a chance at least, right?" Kate asked.

"Yeah, definitely," Davey agreed, almost instantly.

"No, you really have to give it a chance. A real chance. You have to try and have the kind of fun they're having," Kate pushed, pointing at Jimmy and a neighbor girl, Becca, dancing in circles around the fire, doing a drunken version of the waltz.

"You're saying you want to dance like that? I only had one sip," Davey replied, leaning back a little on the bench, away from the fire. He laughed, thinking about dancing in front of all these strangers. Kate smiled, but it was kept small.

"A kiss would work, too."

Davey hesitated. It took him a moment to process her words. Then another moment to figure out if he wanted to. He realized he did, but didn't know why. He didn't know anything about her. Her name was Kate, she was pretty, had short brown hair, and a gold earring in her tragus. He had all these voices in his head, from people back home, asking him questions about her. He knew none of the answers. He couldn't answer any of the questions they would ask, that they were asking right now, in his mind. He thought they were important; was raised to think they were important. Besides, she was drunk on wine. White wine, it always got people drunk too fast. It was too sweet, too easy going down. You could drink white but had to sip red. He realized that he was taking too long. He looked back at her, into her eyes, and everything in his head quieted. Her lips were still glimmering, firelight casted on the dampness of the wine. The answers to all his questions were the same. She was Kate.

They kissed.

14 – FLOWERS

He found himself sitting on the roof of his house, trying to see the sky in the same way his friends' did, as something more than just the sky. He didn't get it. He took another swig of beer, his body instantly calming as the warmth radiated down his torso. It was the only thing that made him feel good.

Melrose slid his hand into the pocket of his jeans, pulling out the tattered piece of paper that had been living at the bottom for a week. He took another sip of beer. He'd been at the convenience store, eyeing the liquor shelves and wondering when the lady at the checkout counter would go on her break, so that the old man who asked for a twenty when the bottle was fifteen would be able to check him out. Marie Romano had surprised him.

"Melrose, I thought that was you," she'd said, pushing her cart over to him. He looked at her, stunned to hear his name in her voice. She looked at him, her eyes soft, but it was something much more real than pity. Melrose's throat had gone dry.

"Oh, hey," he'd managed to choke out. He eyed her cart of groceries. She looked over at the large liquor display the store had to offer for a long moment.

"I bet it's been hard, being the only one," she said. It had sounded like a question, but the more Melrose thought back to that moment, he no longer thought it was. He had just nodded, not sure what else to do. He had suddenly felt self-conscious, not even sure the last time he had showered, or combed his hair, or rubbed the sleep out of his eyes.

"Yeah, it's been fine," he'd mumbled, after she had waited for an answer.

"Yeah, fine. Well, I don't know if you have this, but I have a number for the landline at the cottage Davey's at.... there is no cell service out there. Here, why don't I just..." she had mumbled, going through her purse for her phone, then searching for a piece of paper and pen. Quickly, she had scribbled the numbers onto the paper, and then handed it to him carefully. He took it after a second passed.

"It's a little bit quicker than mail," she said, touching his shoulder as she started to walk by, pushing her cart forward.

"It was good to see you, Melrose," she said, her voice calm. Melrose had watched her walk down the aisle and then disappear off to the produce section or the meat counter. Melrose had felt paralyzed for a long time.

Now, fingering the piece of paper, he thought about calling. His inhibitions were low, especially as he took another sip of beer. It was almost empty, but he had many more to drink.

He dialed the numbers and hit send.

"Hello?"

Melrose almost laughed. It was Davey who answered the phone. Of course it was. Not even his house, yet if something had to be done, he couldn't resist doing it.

"Hey, man," Melrose greeted.

"Mel? Is that you?"

"The one and only," he replied, laughing a little. He hadn't realized how drunk he was until he started talking to Davey.

"Man, how are you?" Davey asked. It was a loaded question. Melrose shrugged, scratching his head.

"You know, I'm alright. Listen, I just, uh. Well, I ran into your mom at the store and she gave me this number and I'm really just doing her a solid by calling. She said you might like to hear my voice, or some shit like that," he teased. Davey chuckled.

"Oh, really, my mom said that?"

"I swear on the Holy Bible," he replied.

"You're ridiculous."

"How's the lake?" Melrose asked, thinking about the water. He was curious if he liked it. He tried to envision what it must look like there, but the shuffleboard houses and looming power lines surrounding him hindered his imagination.

"It's pretty good. It's so different though. I mean, really beautiful. I think you would like it here. There's a lot of stuff to do, but we kind of all sit around most of the time," Davey said, looking out the window at the deck where everyone was sitting, playing a game of euchre.

"I don't know if that's really my kind of place," Melrose said a little gruffly, finishing his beer and opening another one. He threw his empty can into the neighbor's yard. The old man never went back there unless it was to take a piss off the porch when his wife wasn't looking.

"C'mon, I know you would," Davey said. Melrose didn't say anything for a moment. He didn't say it to mock him, though Davey was sure Melrose was taking it that way. Davey knew there were pieces of Melrose that were missing, and he wanted to help his friend find them again, put himself back together. He was there; sure, he still said the same asinine things, yes. But he was hiding, steering clear of all things living. Davey knew he wasn't much better most of the time, but it felt different when it came to Melrose Bartlett. It was something they both knew.

"I'd drink too much for your liking. Hell, I'm drinking right now," Melrose said, turning harsh. Davey sighed.

"I know that."

"Oh, do you now?"

"That's why you're calling, isn't it? How many shots have you taken?" Davey asked. Melrose nearly growled, but kept it back.

"It's my fifth *beer*, actually."

"Oh, my mistake," Davey replied, then sighed. He didn't care that Melrose drank a lot. There had even been a few occasions where he'd gotten drunk with Melrose in his basement, or out in the woods once even with Sasha there too. It just made Davey mad that alcohol could get him talking, yet he couldn't.

"You should have come out with me for the summer," Davey said, his words seeming to fall too quickly out of his mouth.

"Hell, don't start with that soft shit now. I was just calling to see how things were. You don't write as much as you said you would. Lying is a sin, you know that, don't you?" Melrose muttered, trying to be funny again, but not being able to pull it off. Deeply, he wanted to be there with Davey. He wanted Davey with him on the roof. He wanted to talk, but couldn't make it past the many barriers he had built stone by stone, all on his own. He'd realized far to late that barriers like that kept you in, not others out.

"I mean it," Davey said.

"I know you do," Melrose said.

"Has the plant been shitty?" Davey asked, already knowing.

"No, it's been fine. There's a lot of overtime. The money's good. I like the guys I work with, they seem alright. It's really been fine," Melrose said. He was usually good with his lies because he never over did it. Davey was a hard sell, though.

"Well, if that's all it takes these days," Davey said, and although his words seemed harsh, his tone was soft, and Melrose let all the tension slide.

"Summer's not too much longer," Davey said.

"Ah, don't kid yourself, I know how a calendar works," Melrose laughed.

"Have you talked to Calliste or Sasha?" Davey asked, curious. Melrose shook his head, even though Davey wasn't around to see.

"I get their letters, but I didn't run into their moms at the grocery store to give me landline numbers," Melrose pointed out. Davey nodded.

"I'm glad you called, honestly. You're going to be okay, alright?" Davey said.

"Yeah, man, I know. Light off a firecracker for me, or whatever the hell you're doing up there," Melrose replied, thinking about what it would be like to be by all that water and all that sky for three months. The thought kind of terrified him.

"I'll be sure to. Drink a beer in my name?" Davey asked, and Melrose laughed, holding the current beer in his hand up to the orange-lit sky.

"Already am," he replied.

"Good. Call again sometime, okay? I'll keep writing, though," Davey promised. Melrose nodded, though he knew he wasn't going to call again.

"Yeah, no problem," he said.

"Okay. Alright, man."

"Alright. Bye," Melrose said, hanging up only after he heard the landline click. He sat on the roof awhile longer, drinking. He suddenly felt very alone, and the longer he drank, the more he felt abandoned rather than cared for. He slid off the roof, landing roughly in the front yard. He started to walk. He was glad he had the next day off, for no other reason then he hated going in.

One thing that was nice about working, and not going to school, was nobody asked about the bruises. Black eyes, swollen eyes, red eyes, it didn't matter. Could you work? Still screw on the axel? Still spin on the tires nice, straight, balanced? Okay.

Melrose had entered the summer with intentions of sobering up, to stop drinking altogether. It wasn't good for him anymore. It didn't do the things it used to. That thought was now far away. He was drinking almost every night. He had to be; otherwise no one would fight him.

In the summer, in his stretch of the neighborhood, there was always a party going on. Melrose would often just walk up the steps around midnight, never really knowing anyone there. He'd walk around, get some more drinks, smoke a little, kiss a few girls, and then find some guy who would be easy enough to piss off so he'd take it outside and throw a few punches. Melrose loved that.

"Man, I think I made out with your girl just now," Melrose

would start, pushing some guy in the shoulder, laughing a little as he took out a cigarette and placed it between pursed lips. Lips that had apparently been all over his girlfriend.

"What did you just say to me?" the boy would say, standing up straight, no longer leaning against the porch while he smoked. Melrose would turn around slowly, his eyebrows arched, his eyes already a little wild and bloodshot.

"Yeah, that brown-haired girl. I don't know, she let me do all kinds of things," he'd usually continue, but that guy couldn't stand even the smallest bit of teasing. It took only a moment, one shove, for Melrose's blood to boil over, his hands to turn into fists. He used them well – not just anyone would fight him. The two wrestled in the backyard of whatever shitty house the party of the night was at. The grass was overgrown, dead in most areas, littered with garbage. The light from the porch only illuminated half of each boy, making the blows they dealt to one another dangerous. People cheered, egged them on, dumped beer over their bodies. Melrose loved every single moment of it. The pain radiating through his face with each hit was a release of the tension that grew within him, eating away at his insides. Each punch he dealt gave him the same relief, but he almost liked taking hits more.

Deep down, Melrose wanted his dad to hit him. He urged him to all the time, but Bernard never carried through, always beat around the bush, and that made the tension Melrose felt inside his soul tighten; suffocating him. If they could just fight, he thought he'd feel much better. It would never happen, though. This fight was just practice for that, because if anything, he was still hopeful.

Depressingly hopeful.

"Chris! What the hell! Chris, what are you doing? What are you doing?" a girl yelled, running out of the house and down the wooden steps of the pouch, coming upon their fighting circle. Melrose was getting a little dizzy and swayed away from his opponent for a moment as he went to the girl, fists in the air, angry.

"You made out with this piece of shit? Huh?" Chris asked, getting in the girl's face. She looked confused in the best way.

Chris calmed down, seeing it was genuine.

"I've never even seen that guy before. I was with Rachael and Casey, ask them," she said, waving her hand back to her friends. There was a bit of a crowd on the porch now, looking down at Melrose, mostly. He was struggling to stand up.

"Hey, I kissed your girl," Melrose mumbled, drunk, beaten. His head pounded, his body wanted to rest. But with everyone staring at him, the tension was rising again. He just wanted the fight to last a few more moments. He wasn't ready for it to end.

"Man, you're sick. Get away from me," Chris said, pushing Melrose back with such force he tripped over his own legs, falling onto his back. He just laid there.

"Crazy ass piece of shit," Chris mumbled, his arm draped around the girl who gave Melrose a dirty look before focusing forward and walking away. Everyone else seemed to go back into the house, and without the movement, the porch light clicked off.

Lying on his back, blood pouring from his nose, he looked up at the sky, able to see quite a few of the stars with all the noise and lights far away. The grass made him feel safe, taller than his knocked-down form. His eye felt like it would be swollen in the morning. He pulled at small pieces of the grass, trying to focus on one star at a time but it was an impossible task. He thought he might cry. Then, a piece of glass hidden in the grass sliced his finger, and he yelled out angrily, sucking the blood, feeling the metallic taste of what flowed within him, making him live. He thought about life a lot, what a body needed to survive. He felt like too many things depended on each other. Everything would be easier if things were more separated. Melrose was just one piece of a much greater scheme, and he was tired of paying for the sins and choices everyone else around him was making.

He knew it wasn't his fault. He knew that. But his entire life seemed to reflect otherwise. Sasha was always telling him that, with Davey looking down at the ground awkwardly, or Calliste trying to add a few points. He couldn't stand it when they did that to him. He just wanted the noise to stop.

He fell asleep for a few hours in that backyard, amongst old tires and pieces of metal and glass. A car was rotting away back there, tied up in the thick grass and small, un-pruned trees that grew wickedly along the back fence. He didn't roll much, so the glass stayed out of his skin, for the time. He woke up when the sun was just starting to peek over the horizon, a dull orange light covering the world around him. He felt wet, covered in dew. Slowly, he stood up, feeling a general soreness radiate through his body, first his hips, then his torso, his shoulder, and finally his face.

"Ugh, damn," he mumbled, touching his face slowly. He'd been in worse situations. He brushed off some dried blood on his face and walked very slowly inside the house, surrounded by a slew of sleeping teenagers. Carefully, he walked around them, grabbed a bottle of water from the counter, a bagel from above the microwave, and then headed out the front door. He walked a few blocks down to his house, thankful for the day off, thankful it was so early in the morning.

He ambled home, smoking the second-to-last cigarette in his pack and finishing the rest of the bagel. He wished he'd looked through the fridge for some cream cheese before taking off, but wasn't feeling the wrath of Chris that morning. He remembered his girlfriend; she was hard to forget. They'd been sort of friends back in middle school, but that was a long time ago.

As he walked home, he passed an empty and abandoned lot, almost reclaimed by the woods behind it. A doe was grazing near the edge, but when the deer saw movement, it whipped its head up to stare at Melrose; it's wide eyes gazing into him. He was transfixed for a moment by the creature, then felt uncomfortable under such a heavy stare. He threw the rest of his bagel at it, and the deer quickly bounced back into the woods, disappearing.

His father's truck wasn't in the driveway when he walked up, because he had probably taken an early shift that morning. Whenever there was overtime, Bernard took it. Melrose probably would, too, but so far, he hadn't. As he looped around to the back, he tried to sneak in the back door and let his mother sleep, but to his surprise, she was awake.

"Hi, honey. Do you want some breakfast?" she asked, standing by the stove, frying up some potatoes and eggs. He felt like he should say no and just disappear to his room, get some real sleep, but he didn't actually want to do that. Just felt like he should.

"Yeah, uh…sure. I'll take some," he replied, carefully walking over to take the farthest seat at the table. She quickly went and got him a plate after pouring him a glass of orange juice. He sipped at it as he watched her stir the food in the pan, noticing things about her that he always tried to forget. She was pretty and small, and she looked a lot like someone else he used to know. Daisy was too kind, and it showed in her face. She cried if a spider or moth died, so she certainly cried over sad movies and arguments. Her long brown hair and eyes were much lighter than Melrose's, who had black hair and what looked like dark, shifty eyes. Well, maybe it was more than a look, maybe he really did.

"Did you have a good night?" she asked, looking over at him. Daisy was so kind; people often thought she was stupid or weak. They took her kind words as her overlooking the obvious. She couldn't possibly be so kind if she knew the actual truth about people and what they had done. If Bernard were home, he'd see Melrose's bruised face, his dirty clothes, his bloodshot eyes and know immediately what he'd been up to last night and yell. But something no one thought about was Daisy saw all the same things, she knew all the same things, and still thought Melrose needed a warm breakfast. She wasn't stupid or weak. She was very kind. Others saw trouble. She saw troubled.

"Yeah, it was alright," he replied, unable to stop his mouth from salivating a bit as she pushed the eggs and potatoes into his plate, giving him a huge helping before giving herself just a small plate. He wondered how she knew he'd be home this early.

"I think your eye needs a little ice," she continued, looking over at her son, taking in everything that was rough about him and thinking about all the reasons why. Some of it was the place he grew up, the smallness of their house, the way Bernard turned every emotion into anger. But some of it was the responsibility and what happens when you are forced to feel responsible for everything.

"I'll get some in a bit," he said, taking a bite of the food, feeling it almost melt in his mouth. It was so good. He hadn't really eaten her food in such a long time. Breakfast was always the best meal she made.

"So, how are you? How's summer been? You know, you work so much I never get to see you," she said, pulling her legs up on the chair and into her chest. She was just wearing a loose tank top and shorts. The air conditioning didn't work very well in their little house, and Daisy was always feeling the heat.

"It's been good. The money's nice," he replied, eating in between his words. He thought it was nice that she blamed work for the reason she hadn't seen much of him this summer. He knew she was kind.

"Miss your friends?" she asked. He stopped chewing for a moment.

"Uh, sorta. Nice and quiet without them," he tried to joke. She didn't pretend to smile. He felt terrible because he knew that she missed his friends. She had thrived on hosting bonfires and barbeques, yet somehow, Melrose had forgotten that. She loved each of them but hadn't seen them very much in the past few years. Some of that was just life, but a lot of it was Melrose's purposeful doing.

"How are they doing?" she asked, looking right at him. She only did that when she wanted a real answer, more than just the sugarcoated reply. Sometimes she was tired of having to interpret everything.

"Well, Davey is having a great time at his mother's cousins' place. Just running around getting a tan by a lake," he said and she nodded, probably picturing it perfectly.

"You think he's using sunscreen?" she asked.

"Obviously. This is Davey we're talking about. The guy

wouldn't know how to make a bad choice even if he wanted to," Melrose laughed, and his mother shot him a small smile.

"Yeah, and uh, Calliste is alright. I don't think boot camp is quite his thing, but he's smart. He's getting through it, making his old man happy," he continued, scooping a huge amount of food into his mouth this time. Daisy watched him chew. She waited for him to swallow.

"I hope he really is alright. I worry about him at a place like that. I just don't see it…being good for him. Not sure what Adam is thinking, but then again, no one seems to," she commented, thinking about the last time she had seen either of Calliste's parents. After his mom got sick, his father seemed to retreat from everything. It was Alice who opened the world for him, and it was her condition that slammed the door shut.

"And Sasha?"

"She's fine," he replied. His mother gave him the same look again.

"What is she doing?"

"Living the rich life up at the point with her grandparents. You know that," he replied, trying desperately to just keep eating and not talk anymore.

"Melrose…" she started, but as soon as he heard the tone, he started talking.

"She's fine, she's doing good. She's making new friends. Hanging out by the beach. Maybe doing some surfing or watching the sunsets. All the same things she's always done, okay?" he said, finishing it. She gave him a different look this time, one that excused him. She was fragile, too, in different, more obvious ways.

"I doubt those new friends of hers are as good as you guys," she said, taking the empty plates to the sink. Melrose nodded, zoning out a little and thinking about that. She'd told him about Gillian in a letter, about the concert she'd snuck out to go see. He felt something about Gillian, but couldn't place his finger on what, exactly. She wasn't explicit in her letters for both of their sakes.

"And you're good, Mel? You're good?" Daisy asked, breaking

him from his thoughts, her hands in the soapy water of the sink. He nodded. He was good, always was good. Never mind the drinking, the smoking, or the fights. The thing no one realized about Melrose was he was kind, just like his mother.

When asked, what did he say?

"I'm fine, Ma, just fine."

15 – Exposed

Almost two months had gone by.

It felt like ages. He missed the quietness of his house. He missed the birch trees in his backyard. He missed his own bed, his own shower. He never knew that what he'd miss most about his home was the solitude. He'd always thought that was what he wanted to get away from, but now, that was all he could ever hope for. A quiet moment in the showers before hearing low whistles and vicious laughs. A quiet moment out in the fields before the booming of guns, or the pounding of running feet. A quiet moment while he ate instead of the jokes flying over his head or the clanging plates as food was taken from his tray. A quiet moment. A safe moment.

"Martin, you doing alright?" Sergeant Adams asked, during his free day. Once a week, on Sundays, they were given a few hours to wander around, take some time for themselves. Calliste relished in the opportunity. He often retreated to the back woods, climbing a tree and laying down on a low branch, writing letters, doing little sketches, or just thinking while looking out over the fields. He rarely ever took the time to realize despite everything, this camp was situated in a very beautiful place.

"I'm doing fine, sir, thank you," he replied, using all the correct words, all the correct inflections on his words. Sergeant Adams just nodded; looking up at the boy perched in the tree. He had thought, for even a little moment, that Lukas and he would be friends, would get along, could help one another out in a place like this. Adams was rough, hard, often callous, but he did have a mother and two sisters, and his life hadn't been complete abrasion.

"Sounds convincing," Adams replied, catching Calliste off guard for a moment. It was a comment that sounded almost too personal; faintly sarcastic.

"Sir?"

"Carry on, Martin," Adams replied, waving to him half-heartedly as he walked back down to the mess hall. Calliste watched him go, studying him for a moment. He walked with a faint limp but otherwise was both tall and solid, a perfect picture of hardness and perseverance. He started to sketch him, from a side angle, his face mostly hidden. He used his pencils to shade him in, carefully shaping all of his curves and corners and angles. He spent his free hours working on it, satisfied when it was done. Calliste felt that was the best way to capture him – with his face mostly hidden.

Late that night, after everyone was in their bunks, and the big room was more or less filled with snores and heavy breathing, Calliste found himself still rolling around in bed trying to sleep, but his mind was racing through too many places. He thought about his mother, whom he hadn't talked to as much as he had promised he would. He just couldn't do it. She'd know something was wrong the moment she heard his voice, and he didn't want her to worry anymore than she already did. Perhaps she would think he was having such a good time that it was hard to get to the phone. Perhaps.

Alice was a thoughtful person. It was the best way to describe her. Always, her mind was working, thinking, chiming away at something beautiful or something ugly. It didn't matter what the subject was. Alice always had an opinion, a way of thinking, and a way of making her thoughts into feelings. Maybe that was why she was sick now, forced to battle her own brain. Calliste knew that was what his father blamed it on.

Adam had never been one for feeling. He was set in his ways, his education. He felt that life, truly, was all a matter of careful, logical choices. If you made the right choice, the honest one, then you could live any life you wanted. And he was right, mostly. He brushed his teeth and never got any cavities. He did his school work and went to a good college on a scholarship. He chose to study math, and it never hid from him or lied. He was set to make big money and be in bed every night by nine. There was only one time the world did not act in the way he expected, and that was because of a computer glitch. A computer glitch that landed him in a poetry class as an elective, not his chosen class on the study of Nazi Germany. Adam hadn't been happy when he discovered the mistake and chose to sit in the back, mumbling about how feelings were subjective, by the way, and not important enough to study.

Alice had never thought ahead a day in her life. She sat next to Adam because she was running late, and no one else had wanted to sit next to a cross, stuck-up grad student. Alice didn't mind. She loved poetry. And when the man sitting next to her said it was stupid, she thought about it. She thought about reasons why he would hate poetry, why he thought feelings were a waste of time. She tried to convince him he was wrong, and in many ways, she succeeded. They got married only a year later. Adam was a man of decisions, and after a month of sitting by Alice, feeling things, he knew she was the one; she was worth it. And for Alice, there was probably many of *the one* out there, waiting for her to grab onto them. But she felt something around Adam, too, a kind of stability that let her thoughts grow into even bigger un-pruned gardens. So they got married, and they lived a very happy life in the beginning. Calliste was born four years later, after they had graduated and traveled a little bit. He was perfectly planned, of course, but Alice had chosen his name at the last minute. Her parents were French; had immigrated to the States when Alice was just three years old. So, she wanted a name that honored that tradition. She liked the sea, and she liked soft men. So she named her son Calliste.

Because she felt it was strong and kind, reminiscent of the sea, which does many different things. And Adam liked it because Alice did.

They never saw Adam's family much. There was a reason he was so hard, so controlled. They spent all the holidays with Alice's family, enjoying the French foods that her mother would cook and the amazing adventure stories that her father would tell with a big booming voice that felt comforting and all encompassing. Everyone was happy.

When Alice had her stroke, Adam seemed to forget everyone was happy. Alice was still happy. She accepted her limitations and didn't focus on them, but Adam became obsessed. He loved her and wanted her back. Alice never left, but in a way, he seemed to help in her disappearance. Alice's parents died within a year of each other when Calliste was twelve years old. With the finality of their deaths, the effects of Alice's stroke seemingly permanent, and her husband keeping all the doors locked, she retreated into her thoughts, often with her eyes closed. That was when Adam became cold. He stopped talking to Calliste unless it was informative. He stopped going out unless it was to the office. He wanted desperately for Alice to come back to him, but he couldn't feel anything, and he didn't know how to without her.

Calliste became a little ghost, something only Alice thought she could see every now and again. Someone who was small and quiet but came back to tell her stories of what the outside looked like and what all the little faeries were doing. One of them was dark and strong, another considerate and a little anxious, and the last one was good with animals and liked to watch sunsets. She made up her own stories about them, little faerie characters in the wild world that only existed in her mind, something Adam couldn't see.

Adam didn't feel anything, but eventually, he started to feel something, a deep hurt that grew in his chest and started to spread throughout his whole body. He worked hard to get rid of it. He tried to kill the little ghost and instead turn him into a man, one who was calculated and would go to a good college and not fall in love with a girl in a poetry class because those kinds of people are always damned. It was as if they knew some secrets about the universe and when they shared them, they started to die and take everything with them, like a star that turns into itself and becomes a black hole. Adam never belonged in a poetry class, and he thought all the pain in his chest was because of poetry, but really, it was the lack of it. Calliste didn't know how to tell him that. Alice couldn't anymore.

Calliste knew their story, part of it he had even been around to see. But he liked the beginning the most. He animated the pictures he had seen of his mother in his head, playing out the way she must have acted when she had long, thick, wavy hair and dangly gold earrings. He thought about how his father couldn't possibly be the man he thought he was if he had fallen in love with his mother. If he could let Alice in, he could let Calliste back in, too. He was so tired of feeling so isolated.

Calliste felt very much alone, and because he was his mother's son, he cried silently about it, but because he was his father's son, he cried silently about it and didn't tell a soul.

On Monday, a field practice was scheduled. Because he had little sleep, it took Calliste a lot of energy to keep up with the other marching boys as they followed their leaders through the wooded trails and into the great big meadow. On the way, Calliste spotted a few deer out in the midst of the woods; frozen as they watched with big eyes the predators walk by. Something about their look hurt Calliste; he hated to be grouped with men that would make those deer's hearts race. They took off with their tails up.

He started to feel panicked. He knew he was feeling too much, taking things too personally. He wanted to get away from the tension of the group; all the power and anger that seemed to roll off the backs of the boys in front of him and hit him square in the face. He stood in the back of the group patiently as rules were explained, directives were given, teams were split up – all while he stood tapping his foot, eyeing another tree to climb up into, take cover, do anything for a while as he waited for the game to be over. He knew that his little plan wasn't a secret anymore, but he figured he could hide for a long enough time to calm down, get a few shots in, have the game end sooner rather than later. Maybe he'd even get to finish half of his dinner that evening without someone stealing the rest of it. Not that he cared. He wasn't very hungry anymore.

"Alright, head out!" Sergeant Adams called with two other men beside him, watching the game as if it was a match of soccer, and they were the referees. Calliste almost rolled his eyes at the thought. He headed into the woods almost immediately, slithering through the brush until he came to the tree he wanted. A few leaves bit into his skin, but he brushed them back without a second thought. He made it up into the tree about midway until he realized that he could hardly see anyone and not because he wasn't high enough.

The field seemed dead. The woods oddly quiet. His eyes perked up, looking around, searching desperately for any kind of motion. A few of his teammates were out there, taking shots at others, but it wasn't right. Too many of the boys were missing. He grew small against the trunk of the tree, perched on its branch ready to jump somewhere, but not sure where that somewhere would be.

He heard a whistle behind him, and without thinking, immediately turned to face it, to see where the noise he was searching for so intently was finally coming from. His heart was pounding.

"Gotcha," Jack Turner said, shooting up at Calliste. He wasn't the only one. He had seven others with him, and they all took a shot at Calliste from extremely close range. They didn't stop at one. The pain fired through him, spaced out from different points but all reaching his core at the same time. He yelled out even though he didn't want to, trying to hold onto the wood of the tree, shielding himself behind the trunk. They were too close; he was sitting out in the open. He wanted to reach up and climb higher, but the little plastic bullets kept pelting him, and after one attempt to move somewhere better, he took a misstep and fell out of the tree, the wind whooshing underneath him before the hard thud of the grassy ground caught him with unforgiving force. The shots didn't stop, and even though he wanted to at least crawl away, all he could do was curl up and cover his face.

"He's dead already! Stop he's dead! He's out! What the hell! What the hell are any of you doing? Jesus, I don't want to fill out paperwork. Stop it!" Adams yelled out, running over, the boys scattering, as if they had nothing to do with the pathetic small child curled up in the grass, covered in little red blisters.

The other two men stayed behind and yelled at the boys, talking about honor and loyalty and the rules of the game and discipline. Adams stayed quiet beside Calliste, who stood up slowly on his own and started to walk away. His whole body ached, but at least the spinning was starting to stop. He hadn't hit his head that hard. He probably just needed some water.

"You just need some water. C'mon, Martin, just drink some water; brush it off," Adams mumbled under his breath over and over again. Calliste couldn't tell if Adams was concerned about him or the potential paperwork. He couldn't take it anymore.

"Sir, I am *fine*," he said, his words so curt that Adams instantly stopped talking. He sat under one of the trees at the opposite end of the field, drinking some water, looking out over his meadow, feeling everything about it was ruined.

Almost, anyway.

He felt dead.

16 – Signs

Get me out of here.

Sasha was all about giving her more distant family a chance, but the conversation had gotten entirely too uncomfortable. She'd never felt so attacked by malice. Weeks had gone by, weeks of her telling her mother everything was fine, weeks of learning about her grandparents and spending time making small talk with Ann, weeks of living in it and seeing what a little money and some class could get you in the world. It had all been good. She'd enjoyed it, even.

"You know, it's challenging because they just don't work as hard as they used to. I just don't get it, you know, Richard? Here I am, just trying to turn a profit for the company, and nobody wants to work hard at what they do?" a man said, glass of champagne in hand as he made what he considered small talk with Richard Raskova. Sasha listened quietly as she tried to stomach the glass that her grandmother had given to her with a wink. Sasha had smiled, thinking it some kind of joke.

"Oh, I know it, John. I know it. This year, I had to make cuts somewhere, so I started layoffs. But the real thing is, you know; just hire a few more people in later, part time. It can really do the trick. They'll work the senseless hours, the late hours. It works out all the same. For them, I mean. That way, we're still in the profit," Richard replied, standing a little too close to John, laughing at their cunningness. Sasha watched with wide eyes. They were hosting a dinner party with a massive attendance. Her grandmother had already introduced her to several partners in the companies, employees at different branches, the mayor, some lawyers, a few doctors, and even some folks who limited their employment to the word *financing*. Sasha took another sip of her drink. It was too bubbly. She wished for something more bitter.

"I just need them to work harder. I'm working hard. It isn't easy making these kinds of choices. And the EPA is all over my back about this and that, and then there was that issue I had in PR not too long ago. It's like nobody thinks about these things but me. It's outrageous," John replied, tapping his glass with his finger and almost instantly getting a refill from a voyaging waitress.

"I did hear about that, yes. But you recovered fantastically; I have to really give it to you. It's like you still have an unblemished record over there," Richard said; clapping John on the shoulder in a way meant to egg him on, comfort him. Sasha nearly choked. It hardly looked like John was suffering.

"Thank you. I had to make some really tough calls out there; people are coming around, calling me cold and crass. Well, someone had to make those decisions, you know? Someone had to make those hard calls," he replied.

"Its just business. People always take things personally, but it's really – "

"Just business," John finished, clicking their glasses together as they both finished what was in them. Tossing them aside, they followed one another in stride to find something a little stronger to drink. It made the fiery opinions come out with a little more emphasis. Suddenly, Sasha's glass of champagne tasted dull.

"Sasha! Come over, I want you to meet someone," Ann called excitedly, waving her granddaughter over. She was wearing a light pink dress with pearls and jewels sewed around the collar. She looked elegant, if not a little dated. Carefully, minding the drunken people, Sasha made her way over to her grandmother and two smiling older women with gloved hands. They shook Sasha's hand daintily as she was introduced.

"This is Eleanor, Mr. Hawkins is her husband over there. Remember, from finance? And this is Sylvia, her husband is over there talking to your grandfather right now," Ann said, pointing to the bar where Richard and John were still talking, now laughing loudly with one another. The women looked a little tight and smiled with a bit of regret.

"We've heard a lot about you, Sasha. Your grandmother says you do very well in school and that you're very smart. You're going into your senior year?" Eleanor asked, looking over Sasha instead of looking at her. It felt a little uncomfortable.

"Ah, yeah. I do all right. And yes, I'll be a senior in the fall. Not too far away," Sasha replied, thinking for a moment about the waning summer. She felt almost in the belly of the beast, having wandered a long time down a cave she thought would be safe only to find that the end was full of skeletons.

"Do you know where you'd like to go to school? What you'd like to do?" Sylvia asked, sipping her drink, waving her hand in dismissal when a waiter came by and offered her hors d'oeuvres. Sasha took one readily, however, hungry and almost unable to wait for dinner.

"I haven't really figured that out…the last few years have been kind of…hectic," Sasha replied, trying to accurately sum up how she felt. She didn't know how to talk about any of her time in high school. It had been much more chaotic and terrible than she could have imagined.

"Well, whatever you choose, I know my husband would have no problem getting you an internship of some kind or a job eventually," Sylvia replied, smiling a little as she looked over at her man, wearing a suit that must have cost at least a grand.

"That would be nice and all, but I kind of care about the environment, so…" Sasha mumbled, joking awkwardly, but immediately sucked in air in disbelief. There was a moment of silence that fell over the group; the cloak of kindness brutally ripped off.

"Excuse me?"

"Oh, nothing. Sorry, bad humor. I just read about the thing...somewhere. And the protesters. Sorry, bad taste. I'm sure that was very annoying and very hard to deal," Sasha mumbled, hating every word she said, giving up her values more and more as she spoke. She didn't know what was happening to her, but she felt so small in that room. Everything she cared about, talked about to her family and friends, was wiped away with one icy glare from a woman who had to be at least sixty but didn't look like she was aging at all.

"No, it's still a sore subject. John is rather sensitive about it," she replied, just as John's booming laughter could be heard across the room, where he was more animated than ever with Richard, both red in the face from each other's jokes. The tensions among the four women only heightened.

"Excuse me," Sasha said quietly, wiping her mouth with a cloth napkin she held in her hand, setting her glass down on one of the many small tables. She walked quickly but with control out into the hallway. She searched for a place with some air and finally settled on the balcony. It did have a beautiful view of the water.

Able to breathe, Sasha shuddered. She couldn't help but think about all the words and phrases she'd heard thrown around that evening. She missed her friends. She missed bantering with them, saying exactly how she felt, exactly how she saw the world. Mostly, they agreed with her. As the breeze cooled her warm forehead, brushing the fringes of her hair back away from her face, she thought about how maybe she'd turn out like the women in the room if everyone she knew were the same. But no one around her was quite like the other. She thought of Davey's crooked smile, and the amount of effort he put into everything he did. She thought about how smart Melrose was, and how good he was with his hands, because he could fix almost anything and make it seem brand new. And Calliste, her poetic little friend, he was so forgiving and kind and patient. She appreciated it the most. They were all the best in their own right. She twiddled her fingers together on the metal railing, focusing on her breathing. God, she missed them.

"Did it get too tight in there?" a girl's voice broke into Sasha's thoughts. She turned, surprised to see Gillian there. Her outfit suggested that she was serving drinks. Sasha laughed quietly to herself for a minute. To think Gillian wouldn't be there was ridiculous. She was everywhere. She bit her lip a little before walking over to lean against the railing with Sasha, their arms almost touching one another.

"Wonder how you could tell," Sasha responded, dragging her eyes away from her new friend back out to the ocean across the road. It was dark out, but the light from the day was still evident in small spaces around the horizon.

"It always does. You lasted awhile though," she complimented with a bit of happiness in her voice. Sasha took it as mockery. Gillian touched her elbow to Sasha's for a moment. She felt the tingle of the touch race all the way up her arm, then flow steadily, slowly, down the rest of her body. She liked it. The two girls stood silently for a few minutes, warming up, watching the sea glisten under such a full, bright moon.

"Are you going back in?" Gillian asked, after a few minutes. Sasha sighed, rubbing the sides of her head with her fingers. She didn't want to, but knew she had to. Distantly, she thought about calling her mom and telling her that she was right all along. People were sharks, even if they pretended to be really colorful fish for a while.

"Yeah, yeah. In a minute. I think I need another minute," she said finally, a tightness clenching in her chest. Without thinking, her body moved closer to Gillian's, her side resting against hers, her head falling onto her shoulder, begging for some kind of companionship. Gillian didn't move, but her body didn't go cold, either. Her body language was welcoming; she didn't want to scare anyone away.

"Well, I've got to get back. Will I see you later?" Gillian asked, raising a brow as Sasha picked her head up and looked over Gillian, at her, not over her.

"If you'd like to," she whispered.

"I know I would," Gillian said, disappearing through the side door, covered in the darkness from places the moonlight didn't hit. Her absence left Sasha with a shiver and a new sense of loneliness she hadn't felt in a long time.

She headed back inside to the party, grabbing another glass of champagne from a waiter. If you did things with purpose, no one questioned you. She mingled with the crowd, talking to people, making connections, giving her grandmother a wide smile as they passed one another in their rotations. A switch had flipped in Sasha, and she was eager to win the game. Finally, she had noticed, that was all this was. Some people had been playing the game so long; they'd forgotten they were in the arena, not out in the world where the people were. While she talked with attendees, she spotted Gillian a few times, looking more elegant in her white button-down and apron than a lot of the guests at the party. Her long hair fell in waterfall curls, her strong jawline jutting out from it, showing her confidence. Sasha watched her flirt with some of the guys, getting extra tips tucked into her apron pocket. She watched the way she smiled at some of the ladies she served, her eyes sparkling. She was something else. There was a loneliness Sasha felt inside of her, but Gillian wasn't looking to fill it. She was something else.

After having several drunken people offer her internships, acquiring several offers for scholarships, invites to theatre outings, and enduring a last toast at the end of the evening, she wandered upstairs, forgetting about everyone, and falling asleep almost as soon as she hit the bed.

She slept fitfully.

It was close to three in the morning – witching hour. She couldn't sleep, thinking now that it must be a sign, not the alcohol. Sasha often convinced herself of signs from the other side. She needed there to be one. With that feeling strongly rooted inside of her, she got up and slid on a sweater, laced up her sandals, and quietly left the house. The walk down the street to the one road she had to cross felt claustrophobic between all the houses and trees, but finally, after crossing the street, she reached the beach. She took in a deep breath. At this hour, she felt so small in a space so vast.

The sky, the deepest of blues, stretched out for miles, to places Sasha could never fully see. It was decorated with stars, alone and in clusters, vast pinpoints in the drape over her reality. The sea it touched was just as dark, with no light, the moon refusing to show itself anymore that night. She walked over the cool sand to be closer to the lapping waves at the shore; it always seemed to want her to.

Where was Hailey? Was she up there in the sky? Did she ever leave the deep water? Sasha, for a moment, could feel water filling her own lungs, her body sinking – feeling the panic that raced through her nerves at the idea of not being able to tell which way was up from which way was down. She shook her head quickly, clearing her mind. Sitting on the beach, the water lapped at her feet, reaching for her but unable to. She looked up. She cried. She missed Hailey. Her best friend. Her best person. The keeper of her secrets. Sasha had never been called quiet until Hailey had left.

The grief consumed her, eating every part of her body and soul. It had been two years; it came and went often. She could never fully shake it. She cried louder. Her insides were torn. Forever was much too long.

"Hailey!" Sasha yelled, trying to break into the void.

"I need you back," she whispered, crying.

17 — BLOODLINE

Blood flowed quicker than he thought.

For a moment he watched it seep out from between his fingers as he pressed down on the cut firmly. He started to laugh. Just a few chuckles at first, but then a few more, louder laughs. Jimmy looked up at him, a little puzzled, but laughed with his cousin. He was pleasantly surprised, having thought Davey as someone to cry rather than laugh about so much spilled blood. Slowly, they were ceasing to seem so foreign to one another.

"Are you in shock there, Cuz?" Jimmy asked, peering over at the blood that was covering Davey's arm, dripping onto his legs a little.

"Nah, not shock. This is just ridiculous, you know?" Davey replied, his voice only slightly shaky. Jimmy took off his tee shirt easily; surprised he even had one on. He wasn't worried, but there was a lot of blood. He noticed that Davey's skin was almost as dark as his was now, all the red having vanished and turned into a stunning bronze.

"Let's go back to the house. I think we can finish this up later," Jimmy said, glancing over at the fort that they were attempting to make. They'd told Nick and Sidney that it was going to be a deer blind for hunting season in the fall, but truly, they just wanted to make a fort out in the woods.

"Yeah, not the worst idea you've ever had," Davey replied, wrapping Jimmy's shirt around his hand tightly. It was starting to clot; he was sure of it. They left the hatchet behind, the blade having already done its job. They trampled through the woods with a bit of a rush in their step, finally breaking out into the opening where the old house was. Sidney was lying out on the back porch, reading a novel that looked like it had made its way around. She noticed the boys coming up quickly, and set her book aside, covering her eyes with her hand a little to see them better.

"Please tell me you still have all your fingers attached," Sidney said, staying still in her chair as they came up the steps a little haphazardly. She noticed the bloody tee shirt. Davey nodded quickly, while Jimmy shrugged off her question.

"I mean, we still have all ten with us…" he began, teasing her a little. Sidney rolled her eyes, standing up quickly and ushering the boys to follow her inside. She wasn't worried anymore. Her bare feet beat against the ground of the kitchen as she directed Davey to the sink while she looked through the cabinet for any kind of first aid kit. She finally found one, something that belonged in a museum, but she held it up victoriously. Jimmy was sitting up on the counter, looking down into the sink full of blood and dirty dishes.

"That's disgusting," Jimmy scoffed, looking up at his mom. Sidney shrugged as she turned the water on, making the messy sink slightly worse.

"Maybe you should do the dishes, then," Davey replied, looking up at Jimmy, rather than watch as Sidney unwrapped the tee shirt from his hand. She held it up over the sink for Jimmy to take.

"Nah, that's not mine anymore. It's got another man's blood on it. All yours, Davey boy," Jimmy replied, holding his hands up. Sidney simply tossed it into the other half of the sink, holding Davey's hand underneath the water. It was a long cut down the top of his hand, and it was deep, but after further inspection, Sidney decided no one was at risk of bleeding out.

"Do you want stiches?" she asked, still looking at it, moving his skin a little.

"Ah, no?" Davey replied. Sidney nodded.

"Cool. I didn't want to drive into town anyways," she replied. After pouring some peroxide on it and drying it off, she taped it up, bandaged it, and put gauze around it just to be safe. It looked like he'd really done a number on himself.

"And the man will live!" Jimmy declared, roughing up Davey's already long and messy hair, hopping down from the counter and grabbing an apple from the basket on the island counter. Some of the fruit looked like it had seen better days, but after rubbing the skin on the hem of his shorts, it seemed edible enough.

"Of course he'll live. You didn't seem too worried," Sidney replied, leaning back on the counter, looking over her son. He was a ragged mess, a consequence of running around wildly in the woods all summer. He seemed happy, and she liked that he was an outdoorsman, even if it often meant he was barefoot and bare-chested.

"You two look like a mess," Karen commented, coming down the steps and entering the kitchen. She looked Davey up and down; then glanced into the sink.

"Um, that cannot sit like that," she said, looking back up from the sink. Both boys had their hands up in the air, not ready to address the mess.

"I can't get my hand wet," Davey said, already starting to walk away.

"Mom's the one who cleaned it in the sink," Jimmy replied, throwing himself onto the couch, putting his feet up on the armrest.

"I literally have no part in this," Karen said, looking around at everyone like they were crazy. Sidney laughed and headed over to the sink.

"I will take one for the team, but only this time! Besides, I think there's some law about how many kids you can keep in a house at one time, and this sink is definitely a health hazard," Sidney said, starting the water and pulling dishes out of the mess.

"Mom, that's a rule for dogs. You can only have so many *dogs* in a house," Karen replied, sitting on the armrest of the couch, pushing away Jimmy's feet.

"Oh, is it?" she asked, laughing a little. Karen rolled her eyes.

"What were you guys doing out there?" Karen asked, looking from one boy to another. She'd been feeling tired the past few days, too much sun and not enough water. She had resorted to asking them about their adventures instead of trying to keep up.

"Building a deer blind for the fall. What were you doing?" Jimmy asked, a little annoyed. Karen huffed, sliding down the armrest onto the couch, pushing his feet even more out of her way, but he was fighting her every moment.

"You don't even hunt," she replied.

"Well, maybe this is the year I do," he commented, not looking at her. She rolled her eyes and crossed her legs awkwardly, swinging one foot in the air as she turned her attention to anything other than her brother. She mumbled something about how Jimmy could never kill a deer, but the rest was mostly unintelligible. She looked at Davey's hand for a long moment but didn't say anything about it. Sidney moaned the entire time she cleaned the sink, talking about health hazards and the mental burden it was to do chores in the summertime.

"Let's go back out," Jimmy said suddenly, finally throwing his legs away from Karen and onto the floor, standing up abruptly. Davey followed suit, and he barely got a chance to wave goodbye to anyone before running out the door after Jimmy. It was only a little past noon; they still had the whole day stretching out before them.

"I can like, taste the end, you know?" Jimmy asked after they'd trampled down the trail for a few minutes, putting some distance between them and the others and the house. Davey could still hear the waves from the lake, but no matter how far he looked out, he couldn't see where the water was. Most of the time, it felt like it was all over. Jimmy grabbed a stick and whipped it around as he walked, knocking down tall grass and small trees that had barely any time to grow. Davey wasn't sure what he was thinking.

"The end?"

"Yeah, the end of the summer. The end of all of this," Jimmy replied, exasperated, waving his arm around as if Davey would be able to see his words.

"We still have like, another month. It's not quite doomsday yet," Davey said, feeling very much in the middle of something rather than staring the end in the face. He cradled his hand to his chest, pain starting to seep out from under the bandage. The adrenaline had almost worn off.

"You don't know how this works. You've never done it before," Jimmy said, quieter this time, thinking more as he whacked at the weeds before him, heading back to the fort that sat only half built. They'd had to go back, anyway. Nick would have been furious if the hatchet was left out all night, and he wasn't wandering through the woods to get it himself, that was for sure.

"Dude, I think you need to relax. We still have some time. Summer isn't over yet. I'm having a great time, even with this," Davey replied holding up his throbbing, bandaged hand. He probably did need stiches. Jimmy turned around to look at him for a moment, cracking a small half smile, one that made him look like he knew something no one else did.

"Yeah, you're having a great time finally, aren't you?" Jimmy asked, and Davey shrugged, agreeing. His skin was tough and tanned; his hair had grown shaggy and wild, only being pushed back with a few handfuls of water from the sink in the late mornings. He hadn't done laundry in two weeks and had started to eat lunch out of the fridge without washing his hands.

"Listen, we'll finish building this monstrosity, then we'll pack up some of the Birolodo and fava beans, grab a bottle of wine and drink it by the fire. And you'll see summer is far from over, alright?" Davey asked. Jimmy almost couldn't believe his words. He knew Davey was wrong. He had too much sun in his head; he couldn't see the days were getting shorter now. Jimmy nodded anyway.

"You're going to drink some wine?"

"Yeah, I'm looking forward to it," Davey replied with what he hoped sounded like utter confidence. Jimmy laughed, shaking his head a little. He'd tasted the Romano wine. It was too bitter for him, and it warmed him up too quickly, much too deeply. He didn't even know how Davey could harbor bad feelings towards Bianchi wine.

"Davey Romano is looking forward to getting drunk on white wine. Am I dreaming?" Jimmy asked, looking up to the sky for effect.

"Hey, I said I'd have a glass, not get drunk off it," Davey reminded.

"Who only drinks one glass?"

"It's a social thing, you know."

"No, I have no idea what you're talking about," Jimmy replied. Davey rolled his eyes and used his one good hand to throw some of the larger branches they'd already cut over to Jimmy. They joked a little more about the reasons for drinking wine as they worked, weaving the wood between stakes they'd pushed into the ground. Every so often, they'd push down on the small walls they were forming, making them tighter and more solid, allowing less space and empty gaps. When the sun started to wane in the sky, their stomachs both begging for food, they looked back at their creation. It was almost done, a little taller than they stood, and so sturdy they were sure it would last the winter and still stand tall next summer. The fort on the island was still left unfinished, but Davey and Jimmy had both felt it inside of them to build something new, together.

"This one came out better than anything we could have done on the island," Jimmy said once they were done and stood back, admiring their work.

"Yeah, and if we were out there, then I might have bled out by the time we got back to the house," Davey replied, bumping his shoulder into Jimmy lightly. He chuckled a little, picking up the hatchet as they headed down the trail back to the house. When they reached the little clearing, everyone was already loading the boat up with dinner treats and blankets to sit on around the fire. They were going back to the Garfields', the unofficial dinner host a few nights every week. They liked the company, had the best house, and everyone knew what to bring and how to be helpful.

"Were you going to leave without us?" Jimmy asked Nick as he limped up the dock, carrying a box filled with side dishes and a couple sodas.

"Maybe. Heard you did a number on your hand there, Davey. Is your mother going to come after us? Are you going to lose some fingers?" Nick called out, not exactly smiling. Davey quickly shook his head, keeping it down.

"Ah, no. She'll be fine with it. It'll be all healed by the time she comes back up here, anyways," Davey assured. Nick didn't look convinced but waved the two boys up onto the boat anyway. Sidney sat back on the bench in the boat, looking at Nick and then at the two boys and smiled widely.

"Nicky, since when are you a hard ass?" Sidney asked as everyone boarded the boat. He shook his head, turning his hat backwards and trying his best to maneuver the boat out of the dock without incident. He was getting a lot better at it, even though Karen offered several times to give some advice if he found himself in a pinch.

"Accidents have consequences, Sidney Clare," he replied so quietly that almost no one heard him, yet everyone did. No one said anything the rest of the ride to the Garfields', but Davey nervously snuck glances at everyone. Sidney focused on her husband's face, even though he wasn't looking at her. Karen stared out at the water lapping the sides of the boat; Jimmy studied the floor intently. Davey kept sneaking glances over at Nick, studying his leg. It didn't look messed up, but it obviously was. Davey wondered about that accident. He had thought everyone had made peace with whatever it was; that was just how things seemed to be done up north. Yet, despite all the jokes, there was still some small part of Nick that wasn't okay with it. Davey wanted to ask someone about it but resolved to keep his curiosities just curiosities. He didn't need to know everything, always.

When they docked, the silence was over. Karen helped her father with excellent talent, then jumped off the boat herself, faltering a little in her step, but in a way Davey almost didn't notice.

"You going to make out with your girlfriend again?" Jimmy teased, his face lighting up. Davey shrugged, then looked up and smiled as he grabbed a box to help carry up into the yard.

"Don't forget you said you'd drink some wine this time," Jimmy reminded, eager to get his cousin to share in the pleasure. Davey was growing on him; he liked the companionship his cousin gave. It was solid, yet full of places to lean into.

"Dude, go get a glass right now. My god, I didn't forget," Davey said.

"Is this real?" Karen interrupted, listening in.

"You heard it here first. Our cousin is breaking out of his uptight shell," Jimmy announced, clapping Davey on the back and nudging his sister a little.

"About damn time," she laughed. Davey mingled for a while, learning names and faces, not tired of hearing the same crazy stories over and over again. He spotted Kate easily; she was only pretending to hide from him, teasing him. They'd seen each other a few times since that first kiss, and there had been many more kisses since. She was fun, Kate. She had a good mind and a nice view of the world. And it was summer. Who could say anything about that?

"Took you guys long enough to get here," she said, coming up behind him as he flipped some burgers on the grill, given the task when the regular burger flipper was too drunk to continue and kept leaving his post and burning the food.

"Ah, we got a little held up. I'm here now, though," he replied. She smiled, but it faded away when she caught sight of his wrapped-up hand. The bandage made it look worse than it was. Sidney was hardly talented in the field of first aid. She stared at it for a moment and then looked up curiously.

"I hate to be the one to tell you this, but Big Foot is real, and he lives here in these very woods," Davey replied, so seriously that it took a moment for the joke to settle in and for Kate to laugh, shaking her head.

"It was a tough battle, but you should see the other guy. I really did come out on top," he continued. She touched his shoulder lightly as she laughed, sending tingles down his whole body. He really did like her.

"Does that mean I don't have to worry about running into him out there myself?" she asked, her eyes sparkling a little as she looked up at him. She always seemed to have glassy eyes, bright eyes. He shrugged.

"Probably not, but just to be safe, I'll accompany you into the woods anytime," he offered, and she laughed louder this time, flashing him a grin and an upward look with her eyebrows raised.

"Don't burn those," she said, glancing down at the burgers Davey was neglecting. He quickly started flipping them over, removing the ones that were already done and settling them on a plate next to the grill. When he looked back up, Kate was gone, chattering away with someone else and drinking more wine, but the two kept giving one other little glances, which caused shy smiles.

"Took you long enough to make these," Jimmy commented as Davey came by to sit next to him and Karen, with three plates in his hands filled with food. They both nodded their thanks.

"It's an art, grilling meat," Davey replied.

"Oh, not you, too," Karen groaned, rolling her eyes all the way to the back of her head. Jimmy nudged her with his elbow, and she came back to the present, still annoyed with the comment. She was sitting cross-legged on the grass beside the chair Jimmy had found himself. Her legs were bowed too far apart, and she couldn't use her lap for a table.

"I'm mostly teasing, Karen. Calm down," Davey said and she looked at him incredulously.

"Don't tell me to calm down. Grilling meat isn't an art or a talent. It's almost ridiculous what passes as a skill for you guys these days," Karen rambled. The boys looked at her, but didn't seem to really see her. She wanted to give up, she almost couldn't take it sometimes. She didn't know why she tried to hard. They did nothing, yet it was all praise. She didn't need admiration for all the things she knew how to do, and how to do well, just wanted some kind of acknowledgment. A simple nod would have made her content.

"Don't be upset they asked the new kid to grill over you," Jimmy teased, and Karen stood up abruptly, grabbing her plate and wandering off to go sit next to Sidney. Jimmy curiously watched her walk off.

"I don't know why that made her so mad," Jimmy mumbled a little under his breath. She'd been acting a little different the past week or so, and he couldn't tell what was bothering her or what she was feeling. They were a lot more open with one another at home. Here at the lake, everything was better when things were fine.

"I'm sure she's okay," Davey replied absently, taking a bite of his burger as his eyes kept focus on Kate, who was eating with her family across the yard.

"You don't even care. You can't take your eyes off the neighbor girl," Jimmy replied. Davey dragged his eyes over to his cousin, who didn't look mad at him, more impressed with his transformation thus far. There was really only one more thing he wanted from him.

"You need a glass of wine," Jimmy said, pointing at him as he stood up and walked quickly to the table with all the bottles on it, messing up Karen's hair as he glided past her. He didn't hesitate to pull the cork out of the Bianchi bottle of homemade vino, pouring two very full cups for both himself and his cousin. He walked back a little slower, trying very hard not to spill the precious liquid in his hands. As Davey watched him walk over, he gazed out at the lake, the setting sun. He looked over to where Nick was laughing loudly, Sidney telling a story in earnest, and the neighbors chuckling and holding their beer bottles or plastic cups close. He felt very content where he was, very calm for the first time in what seemed like forever.

"Here you are, Romano," Jimmy said, handing him a glass.

"This is not a glass. This is like half the bottle," Davey said, looking at the crazy amount of it. If it was red, he knew how he'd feel after so much. But he looked up at Jimmy anyway, and he was smiling.

"It's the good stuff, kid, drink up," he said, holding his glass out to Davey. He paused for a moment, then looked back up and tapped his own cup against his cousin's, a few drops running down the sides of the cup. Jimmy took a big gulp, but Davey started off with a sip. It was sweet but didn't taste so much like candy or sugar as it had before. This time, it tasted more like the way the world smelled out on the lake in the morning of a warm day. He held his glass up one more time, Jimmy matching him, and then both of them took a large drink.

Davey drank the entire glass of white wine, and the sweetness settled in him, and he felt very light, very warm, and very happy.

18 – WATER

The grime was making him hard.

He couldn't stand it anymore; it was everywhere, all the time. He already felt dirty. He didn't need to actually see it all the time, have it stain his skin for the rest of the world to see it, too. It was constant, working near all the oil and grease. He had gotten quite good at his job, always turning out product, and never late. He was even starting to take overtime whenever he could get some. He hated it, but he hated sitting on the roof of a collapsing house alone even more.

Doug could see how angry Melrose got every time the bell would ring for break, lunch, or the end of the day. He would just take a moment to look down at his arms, stained with oil and grease. He was beginning to act a little compulsive about it, scrubbing extra hard at the sinks to get it off every inch of him, even under his fingernails. Especially under his fingernails. Doug thought it was amusing. He often did; he saw humor in everything. Nothing really bothered him.

"Kid, now, c'mon. Are you enterin' a beauty pageant at the end of the day or what? Nobody got to be that clean to go home and eat," he would say, watching Melrose constantly use the rags he kept in his overall pockets to wipe off new spots on his skin. He almost considered using gloves but was allergic to latex.

"It's not about that, Doug," Melrose would mumble, annoyance soaking every word he used, but of course, Doug didn't hear it. He kept talking.

"What's it about then, huh? What you need to be so clean for, huh? You got some lady to impress every night of your damn life?" he'd ask, and the questions would go on and on and on. Tom always stayed quiet during these discussions. He'd work on his own parts on the other side of the axel, pretending to be so in tune with his work that the words spoken were flying past him. Occasionally, he'd look up. He'd see Melrose's face, know what he was feeling. He could see the craziness that rested there. Tom knew exactly how Melrose felt. He knew how the thoughts just crept in, and how people would notice the odd behaviors, and how you'd feel like it must be obvious that you needed help. You were drowning. But Tom also knew that wasn't how it worked. People let you drown.

"Dougie, why don't you leave the kid alone for a few minutes?" Tom interrupted one day, his voice quiet and even, but with a very clear tone of firmness. Melrose felt uneasy for a moment, but Doug just seemed confused.

"What? I ain't bothering him. I'm just talkin'. Why you always get so upset when people talkin'?" Doug asked, more to himself than to Tom. Although the two were good work friends and even went out together with their wives for dinner once in awhile, there was a hierarchy in place. Tom had constructed it, and Doug felt it.

"I know, Doug. But sometimes people like to work in quiet for a little while," Tom replied, his voice even lower than before. Doug mumbled something under his breath, but they were all innocent, soft words, and then they were all finally able to work in quiet.

It was nice, exactly what Melrose had wanted, but Tom demanding it made him feel uneasy, uncertain. Melrose snuck looks over at Tom, who seemed to not have a single care in the world other than screwing on every car part he was required to do. He noticed how Tom seemed to stay clean, his hair always combed over and cut neatly, his overalls pressed and washed, even his boots stayed perfectly laced. His hands were dark, but not as dark as Melrose felt his whole upper body was. How did he stay away from the grime?

The silence continued until the bell rang for lunch, and Doug mumbled a few more things before wandering up the stairwell to the top and disappearing for lunch. Melrose almost felt bad for needing the quiet but knew after thirty minutes of eating, Doug would come back talking up a storm again, his hurt feelings completely repaired.

"Join me for lunch, Bartlett," Tom said, rubbing his hands with a rag before setting it down on the bench behind him. Melrose froze for a moment but nodded, waiting for Tom to go up the stairs before him. While Tom got his lunch, Melrose repeated his ritual of furiously scrubbing at his hands and arms, trying to get rid of everything just to eat a sandwich and watch his skin get dirty all over again.

"That's clean enough, kid," Tom said, coming up to him at the sink. Melrose didn't want to be done washing, but something about Tom's voice forced him to stop, and after quickly grabbing his lunch out of his own locker, he followed Tom to a corner table in the break room and sat across from him.

"Now, you've graduated, right?" Tom asked, taking a slow bite from his own sandwich and looking right at Melrose, causing him to squirm a little. Tom was very even, very calm, but Melrose could feel something deeper in him, always stirring in the dark. He simply nodded, then remembered Tom's issue with silence when asked a question.

"Yeah, I did a few months ago," he replied. Tom nodded. Something checked off a list in his mind.

"And what was your plan in all of this?" he continued, eating his sandwich evenly, looking into Melrose, not at him. Although the focus was still uncomfortable, the question bothered Melrose. Every adult in his life asked him that question, or used to, rather. He never had the answers they wanted. He hadn't expected something so mundane, or easy to answer, from Tom.

"Here I am, this is the plan. C'mon, man," Melrose said, sitting back in his chair a bit, already acting dismissive. Tom stayed even, but his eyes held a darker spark.

"Oh really?"

"Yes, really," he replied.

"How were your grades?" Tom pushed, and this time Melrose could barely stop from rolling his eyes. Tom shook his head slightly. It made his skin prickle. Melrose was used to the plain anger on someone's face or in their fists. He never respected that; he was able to fight it. But Tom's silent statement was chilling.

"They weren't all that great," Melrose replied, leaning in a little now, fiddling with his bag of pretzels. Tom nodded, but sighed a little, as if he understood, but was still disappointed. Melrose felt that wave of disappointment, and it almost cut him deeper than anything his father had ever thrown at him.

"You can't get stuck here. People get stuck here, you know," Tom said softly, almost done with one half of his large sandwich, pieces of lettuce sticking out the sides.

"It's their job," Melrose said.

"It's a job," Tom replied.

There was a moment of quiet between them.

"Listen. I'm going to be real honest with you for a moment. You're going to die if you get stuck here. Do you hear me? This isn't a place that treats people hiding from something, or running from something very kindly. Do you understand that? You have to get out into the world. It's not about the money," Tom said, saying more in one breath than Melrose had ever heard from him before.

"But money is what pays the bills and feeds the kids," Melrose replied, merely because he was getting nervous. Their conversation was steadily pushing him towards an edge. Suddenly, Tom's eyes turned all the way dark, and he set down his food, pulling the air between him and Melrose so tightly together it was nearly suffocating.

"I have a wife, I have kids. I feed them, I house them. But you want to know something? I threw away my life, and I hate myself. I love them, but I'm not happy. I feel stuck now because I had them too early. Before I got my life together. I was going to go to Harvard. Did you know that? Smart enough to go to the Ivy Leagues, and yet I'm stuck here trying to stay clean. You don't think I see how crazy you're getting about all the grime this place has to offer? It's all it has to offer! It pays the bills, sure. But you have to pay something to work here. *Your* goddamn sanity. This place is good for a lot of people, but it isn't good for you," Tom said, his voice low but his tone a solid blow. Melrose just looked at him, seeming to finally notice what Tom looked like, what kind of person he was, what he stood for.

"Why didn't you go to Harvard? Why did you stay?"

"Because I got in trouble. I did something stupid, something because I was bored. And I paid for it, believe me. And then it felt like it was too late to go. So I did what all my friends were doing. I got a job at the factory, and I found a wife, and we had kids, and I thought that was supposed to make me okay. And I love them, but you know what? I feel like I can't stay clean," Tom replied, his hands on the top of his thighs, kneading his fists into his own skin, trying to stay calm. His whole life was now dedicated to staying calm, keeping the buzzing in his head low, smiling when he came home. It was a miserable existence; it required so much work.

"Listen, maybe you think it's too late. Maybe you didn't get the best grades. Maybe you did something stupid, too, and you feel like you're paying for it. I understand how your father is. My father was like that, too. But consider this a message from the you in the future. You have to get out; you have to go after more than this. I can see that you want to, that you need to. Don't lose sight of that," Tom said, looking right at Melrose this time, into his eyes, trying to search for anything that resonated with what he was saying. Tom rarely pushed out of the walls he had built for himself, and he wanted it to mean something for the dark kid sitting in front of him that he hoped he wouldn't see past the summer months.

The worst part of the speech, to Melrose, was that he felt

doomed. He knew that what Tom was saying was right; he did need to get out. But the bad things were too great already, and here was his last warning to bail, and he couldn't. He felt trapped.

"I know what you're saying," Melrose said quietly, looking down at his half-eaten lunch. He felt too nauseous to continue. The room had felt so silent during Tom's talk, but now it was buzzing again, and Tom was chewing the rest of his sandwich, and his eyes weren't dark anymore. Everything was the same, but Melrose wasn't.

For the rest of the workday, Doug talked on and on about nothing, and Tom and Melrose worked quietly, nodding when appropriate. When the bell rang signaling shift change, Melrose passed by the sink and walked right out the door, past the parking lot, past the neighboring field, and into the woods. He didn't wait for Bernard, and he didn't tell him he didn't need a ride that afternoon. He just needed to walk, to be quiet, to go back to the damn wall. It gave him solace, somehow.

It took him almost two hours to make it through the woods to familiar territory, and then to follow the right deer paths to the old crumbling wall. He leaned against it, welcoming an old friend for a moment. Running his hand over the stones, his fingers felt the little slips of paper he had placed there over the past couple years. He thought about all the letters he'd received from his friends. He read a lot of them out by the wall, and if there were no new ones in the mail, he would reread the old ones.

Sasha was living the rich life, making connections and going to fancy plays. Her letters were sarcastic, but he felt she was just teasing him. She wrote him the most, and that made him mad, too. Calliste's letters were short and bland. He was curious as to what was happening to him, why he wasn't talking about something like flowers or feelings. Davey's letters were the most infrequent and the wildest. Melrose laughed at the thought of his church boy loosening up and running through the woods half naked. Still, Melrose never wrote any of them a letter back. He didn't have time. He was in their world for only a moment, then thrust back into machinery and the goddamn grime. He was becoming mechanical, his only human moments reduced to the few mornings he'd look at the sunset from on top of the roof.

Why didn't anybody see that? He was drowning.

He didn't head back until it was dusk. He wandered home slowly, kicking the ground a little as he walked, his work boots heavy on his feet. He'd taken off the top part of his work suit, tying the sleeves around his waist to keep them up. Even his white undershirt had oil on it somehow. Carefully, he untied his boots and kicked them off in the backyard, then wandered up the path from the garage.

He paused for a moment before opening the back screen door. He could hear his father yelling inside but wasn't sure what it could be about. Bernard almost never yelled at Daisy. Carefully, Melrose crept into the back hall where the laundry room was, the voices louder now and coming from the kitchen. He walked in to water all over the floor, Bernard on the ground with some tools, and Daisy hugging herself in the doorway to the front living room. Bernard saw Daisy's eyes flutter up to greet her son. He turned around quickly, taking in the dark Melrose. He started to curse.

The pipes were leaking again.

Melrose couldn't contain himself anymore. In his father's presence, he was always moody, always quietly sarcastic, pushing the boundaries with one finger instead of two hands. But in that moment, staring at the rising water, the ruined floorboards, Bernard was about to go too far. He was going to push his son in too deep. It had been boiling for a long time.

"Where have you been? Where the hell did you go? You're an inconsiderate piece of shit, you know that? Where did you go?" Bernard yelled, his face red, his body seeming to grow taller and wider from all the rage. Melrose watched him grow.

"Nowhere, really," he replied quietly, almost a whisper.

"Nowhere? Are you kidding me? Always nothing! Always! If you could just do something. I mean, my God, you never do anything good!" he yelled at his son, meaning more than just laziness, more than his lack of consideration, his lack of decent grades back at school, his lack of acceptable crowds. Hell, his lack of being able to tighten the pipes under the kitchen sink. Melrose could sense that his father was hinting towards the *big thing*, finally. His fists shook, the expression of every emotion he felt.

"You're so stuck in your own head, your own world. Why not try paying attention to the people in front of you?" he continued. Melrose breathed in deeply. He was trying so hard to just absorb the angry words and not lash out. Sasha would be proud.

"Leave him alone, Bernie. He does enough," his mother whispered, trying to keep her own tears in. She knew what he was talking about, and she cried daily for the cause, the water staining her cheeks.

"Does enough, Daisy? He doesn't do anything. Is that enough for you? Huh? Nothing? It's not enough for me," Bernard growled, inching towards Melrose. His father had never hit him before, not with a full fist, but Melrose recognized a shaking similar to his own in his father's fists.

"Why don't you just say what you mean, Dad? Say it. I know what you're always thinking about," Melrose said, finally egging him on, adrenaline pumping, giving his father the excuse he was looking for to hit him. It was boiling over. The weight was all too much, and he was finally tossing it off, letting his head get light and his vision cloudy. He didn't do anything? It was so much work carrying the blame.

"Hey, you know. I'm sorry I'm so lazy. I can't drive your truck, I can't fix the dishwasher, I can't even stay sober for more than a day and hell, you know, I never did like the water much," Melrose spat, shedding light on some of the beast. Bernard lunged for him; Daisy crumpled to the floor. He pushed his son back into the kitchen wall with such force that for a minute all Melrose could do was sink down onto the wet kitchen floor, knowing for sure they had broken the drywall. Seconds later, Melrose dove for Bernard's legs, causing him to stumble back. It was his one attempt at offense. He stood up, trying to gauge his next move, looking at his father, but his father wasn't seeing him. Melrose was a fighter, he was quick and fast, but against his father and the anger Bernard had let grow, he was no match.

The fight lasted no more than one minute. It ended with two swift hits to Melrose's face, the first one knocking him back, the second one causing him to see stars. Melrose almost laughed as he stared up at the ceiling, lying on the wet floorboards of his kitchen, tasting blood in his mouth, hearing his mother sob in the corner, looking up at the fractals of light on the ceiling. He blinked a couple of times to make them go away, but they stayed for a few more moments. He never went to watch the meteor showers with Sasha and Calliste, but he wondered for a moment if this was what it was like.

19 – VINO

It had been the best time.

Davey thought about it, stretched out on the dock by himself one early morning. Everyone else was asleep. It was the one thing he hadn't completely let go of. He liked sleeping in, found the idleness appealing, but there was also something about being the first awake, surrounded only by the singing birds as the first light hit the world that he really liked to be a part of. It had been the best time.

There were only a few weeks left of the summer, and like Jimmy, he was starting to feel the time closing in on him, like sand whistling out from between his fingers. He didn't want it to end. He was realizing how much he liked not working for his aunts and uncles, how tall grass was beautiful, how sweet white wine was. Sitting on the dock, brushing the bottoms of his bare feet on the top of the lake water, feeling the warm sun welcome him – he loved it, all of it. Now, more than ever, he could see the appeal. He was thankful for that gift, if not a little saddened by it. He was past being shocked about how easy it was to transition. He loved the anxiety-free life. He'd never known a world where worry wasn't woven into it, where even a sliced hand and a lot of blood was just a small blink, a few jokes. It barely even hurt anymore, and he wasn't sure if it ever had.

"What are you doing out here so early?" Karen asked, wandering over to him. She startled him for a moment, but he quickly recovered and beckoned her to join him at the end of the dock to sit and enjoy the sunrise.

"I could ask you the same question," Davey asked, bumping her shoulder a little. She smiled and nodded. She was still wearing her pajamas, small silky shorts and a tank top with lace trim. Her white blonde hair was a mess, even though she'd tried to pull it back into a ponytail of some kind. Her hair was an odd length, not really short, but certainly not long.

"I haven't been sleeping a lot in the mornings anymore. Besides, I like being up early," She said, setting her own feet into the water below, smiling a little as small minnows came up and tickled the bottoms of her toes, eating away at the dead skin.

"Why can't you sleep?" Davey asked. She paused for a long moment, and then looked over at her cousin.

"Why can't you?" she asked slyly.

"I used to wake up early all the time. Eight used to be sleeping in for me," he replied. He'd have to go back to it soon – he had no delusions about that –he felt dread thinking about it.

"Why? What did you do?" she asked.

"Just starting the day off. I live on a street with a lot of family, there's, like, group breakfasts all the time, everyone's getting ready for work or school. We all help out with one another. I know it sounds weird, but it's like an Italian thing, all living close to each other," Davey went on. Karen had her palms on the ends of the dock boards, her shoulders up close to her head as she peered over at her feet. She was listening.

"You don't have to justify it to me. I'm Italian, too, you know, cousin," she said, and he kind of laughed at her reminder. But she was smiling. She was a lot like her mom, it seemed, but a lot like someone else he knew. He couldn't quite place it, though, not at the moment.

"That's true, you are, cousin," he said back.

"Are you excited to go back home?" Karen asked.

"Actually, I was just out here thinking about that. I don't know. I mean, I miss people back home but all of this..." he said, gesturing to the house and the woods and the lake, "I don't know, I like this a lot." Karen nodded, understanding exactly what he meant. This was her seventh summer spent up north at the lake. She loved it too.

"I know exactly what you mean," she said quietly, moving her feet in the water a bit, scaring the fish away for a few minutes. They came back soon enough. Davey looked at her, trying to take in her mood. The sun had fully risen, but it still felt like dawn, not morning. There was a difference.

"How have you been lately? You've kind of disappeared from our usual antics," Davey said, his voice soft but with sincerity. She froze for a second, then let out a sigh, looking everywhere else but at him.

"Did Jimmy ask you to ask me that?"

"No, not at all."

"Well, I'm fine. Just a little tired lately. It happens," she said, looking out at the far reaches of the lake, the houses on the other side barely visible through the rising fog the morning sun brought out. Davey thought about her answer for a moment, and didn't say anything, but suddenly she continued.

"I don't know, I just get sad sometimes. I'm in a funk, but how many problems can one person have?" she asked, rubbing her hands down both off her bowed legs, following the irregular shape of them with her fingers. Davey watched her, looking at her legs genuinely for the first time. He'd always glanced at them, noticed them for a second, but he took the time that morning to actually focus on them. She didn't mind. She wanted him to. She hated when people didn't.

"I have a friend like that," Davey replied.

"Yeah? What are they like?"

"He's got more problems than one," Davey said.

"Don't we all," she commented. Davey thought about his

friends for a minute, about each of them individually. He felt a pang of anxiety. He hadn't heard from any of them in awhile. He felt lost without them, without knowing. His eyes were focused on Karen's legs the whole time. They were more twisted than he had thought.

"I think you see a lot, and feel a lot, but you don't involve yourself enough. The rules seem to hold you back too often. They aren't always the things that help people, you know?" she asked him, her sudden honesty taking him by surprise. He did know. Looking out at the water, seeing the stillness in some parts, but the small breaks in others, he knew exactly how the rules don't always save people, how they didn't always allow you to be there the way you desperately needed to. There was a sense of guilt that had sprouted from Davey's hardwired anxiety.

"I know," he said simply. She sighed.

"I'm glad you came out here this summer. It's been fun," she said. He nodded, smiling a little at her. They stopped talking and leaned back on the dock, watching the water for a while before going inside and making a big breakfast. The rest of the family slowly wandered downstairs as the smell of cooked eggs and fried bacon wafted up the steps to all of the bedrooms.

"I kind of missed the responsible Davey," Jimmy mumbled sleepily, smiling a little as he ran his hands through his hair, trying to push it back and push it down. It wouldn't cooperate, and after the teasing look Karen shot him, trying to cover her laughs, he walked over to the kitchen sink, turned the water on, and stuck his entire head under the tap, dousing it pretty well. Karen laughed from her perch at the island in the middle of the kitchen, sitting up on one of the barstools.

"That's not where people take a shower, Jimmy," Karen said, looking at him as he dried his hair with some paper towel and then smoothed it, finally calming it down.

"It seemed to work out alright for me," Jimmy said with a silly smile, looking at his reflection in the surface of the microwave. Davey rolled his eyes and laughed to himself as he flipped over the eggs he was frying and put them on the plate he had ready.

"What do you want to do today?" Davey asked.

"Well, I know you got stuck helping my mom fix the stairs yesterday, but as a reward for letting us get out of helping her, I spent the time with my dad fixing the old four wheelers in the pole barn. We can take them out for a spin if you'd like," Jimmy said, the excitement on his face obvious. He could drive the boats, but he preferred driving on land. He felt more in control there, able to take more risks and have them turn out all right in the end. Davey nodded; he was up for anything.

"Karen, you want to come?"

"I don't know," she said, looking out the window.

"Just sit behind one of us as we ride around. If you want to look out a window all day, the next best thing is looking out from the back of an ATV," Davey reminded, teasing her a bit. She looked up at the ceiling, contemplating it, but finally nodded. Jimmy looked surprised, but Davey was pleased as he stirred up the potatoes.

"Now someone is really trying to earn their keep around here," Nick said, coming down the steps, his voice booming over the otherwise quiet kitchen. He looked around at all the food Davey had out, the fried ham, bacon, eggs, and potatoes.

"I can make pancakes, too, if you'd like," Davey said sweetly. Nick shook his head, laughing as he helped himself to a huge plate.

"This is more than enough," Nick replied, sitting next to Karen and eating.

"We were going to take the ATVs out today...if that's okay," Jimmy said, leaning against the counter, his hands behind him yet flat on the countertop, his arms at awkward angles. Davey noticed he usually was in a twisted shape when he asked Nick something, but he didn't know why. Jimmy couldn't stand straight around him, but Nick never had anything bad to say.

"Sure, that's what we fixed them up for, wasn't it? Just be careful out there. No more injuries allowed. The ones that happen at the end of summer are never the good ones," Nick mumbled, between bites of eggs and toast.

"Good morning," Sidney yawned as she walked down the steps into the big room, looking pleasantly surprised at all the food on the counter.

"Well, don't mind if I do," she murmured to herself as she made a plate, taking the third and final barstool on the other side of Karen and started to eat. Jimmy nodded to Nick that he knew to be careful. Karen gave him a look with her eyebrows raised, something only the two of them shared. He waved her look away. They ate their breakfast, talking about something ridiculous that had happened the other day while they were fixing the stairs, and then everyone set their dishes in the sink and walked away from them, even Davey. Sidney and Nick decided to go into town and see a movie and relax before the big bonfire that night. It was the only one that had been formally planned because the end of summer was approaching, and people wanted to have fun while they felt they still could.

Davey, Jimmy, and Karen wandered off to the pole barn in the far back of the property, opening it up and finding the two ATVs ready and waiting. Davey looked up at the hatchet that hung on the wall, smiling at it a little.

"Ready? You can drive one of these, right?" Jimmy asked, throwing Davey the keys to the yellow one, while he sat up on the blue one. Davey nodded. He certainly did.

"Take Karen. You have the bigger one," Jimmy said, putting his ATV in neutral and pushing it out of the barn with a little bit of effort. Davey and Karen did the same for the yellow one and soon enough, they were all perched on their vehicles, turning the keys in the ignition and hitting the gas. Davey shifted up a few gears and sped off, following Jimmy's lead, trying to not only catch up to him, but also keep up with him.

Jimmy knew the woods well, and he had a spot in mind that he wanted to visit. They followed the trails around the lake a bit, having to watch their speed because of all the twists and turns and uneven ground. Finally, they made it out into a clearing, a huge field with small hills and mostly cut grass. When Jimmy entered the field, he took off, hitting the gas hard and shifting all the way up to fifth gear. Karen pointed to a different path to take around the field.

"You can cut him off if you go this way. Catch up," she said, quickly wrapping her arms around Davey's torso as he took off down the path she told him to. She was light, and the ATV was big, and it went just as fast as Jimmy's could, even though Jimmy didn't think so. They spent a long time riding around the field, trying to keep up with one another, trying to go faster than the other. It was all about enjoying the speed and wind, the wide-open skies and bare fields.

Something wild happened. Jimmy was off in the trails down in the woods around the field, scaring the birds out of the trees, but he found something else. As Davey and Karen drove around the outside of the woods, trying to gauge where he'd come out, a herd of deer jumped from the brush, at least seven or eight. They ran across the field, trying to steer clear of Jimmy's antics, but they couldn't avoid Davey and Karen's presence. Davey hit the gas, driving in the middle of the herd, keeping up; not chasing them. Karen laughed wildly as she watched them run right by her on either side. Their bodies were swift and strong, running with a purpose, in unison, their white tails up high in the air. Davey slowed down as they reached the edge of the property, letting the deer sail away into the woods once again, gone from their sight.

"That was awesome! It was so incredibly awesome!" Karen yelled, jumping up to stand on the footrest of the ATV, completely taken by her excitement, breathing heavily as if she had just ran the whole time. Davey laughed at her excitement, feeling it in his shoulders from the tight grip of her hands. He was breathing heavy from his own well of excitement. He'd loved driving beside them, looking into their eyes as they ran. Maybe they were scared of him. He didn't know. They hadn't seemed like they were. They were just running, moving, living.

"That was awesome. Damn," Davey said, thinking about it.

Karen sat back down, holding onto Davey as he drove off up and down the hills, getting a little air each time, going to find Jimmy. He wanted to tell him about it, but didn't get a chance to say much through Karen's excited chatter.

"It was so crazy! There was like ten of them, all running beside us the whole time. And we were going fast, too. It was just so cool, you can't even imagine," she rambled as they pulled up beside Jimmy, both engines still running. Her story made him happy.

"So, I guess you guys were lucky I'm a little faster on this thing and scared them out of the woods your way," Jimmy teased. Karen waved his words off, still thinking about the deer running beside her.

"I'm just joking. That sounds really cool; I'm kind of sorry I missed it," Jimmy shouted over the noise of the engines. He looked over at Davey.

"A few more laps?"

"Hell yeah," Davey replied, taking off before Jimmy got the chance, finally getting a leg up in the unofficial race. His confidence had grown, and he took the hills a little faster, getting a little more air each time he sailed over, feeling Karen grip his sides tighter so she wouldn't fly off. He was really learning to love the quickness, appreciate the wind for once. They were things he hadn't thought about often enough when he was at home, on the street where every Romano seemed to live.

They headed back to the house around three, eating a late lunch and snoozing on the deck in the sun until it started to set. They woke up to the sound of Nick starting up the old boat, which had apparently lasted a lot longer than ever before. Nick made sure everyone thanked the old girl as they boarded. Everyone sat in front this time, feeling the wind in their hair as Nick pushed the boat to go as fast as she could through the turning water as they headed to the Garfields' for the biggest bonfire of the whole summer.

"We brought this. It's from 1968. It's the good stuff, it was a good year for grapes," Jimmy said as they unloaded the food from the boat to bring up into the backyard. Jimmy touched the glass of the wine bottle in the box, showing Davey. There were only a few bottles left of the aged wine, and they were only brought out during celebrations or endings. Davey looked at the bottle the entire time he carried the box to the wooden balcony at the top of the backyard. It looked weathered and old, the wine a dull color, aged as much as the stained label.

"Hey there, stranger," Kate said, exiting the house through the large glass door as Davey set his box down by all the coolers of drinks. She was wearing jean shorts and a white tank top that was loose and a little too short to cover the waistband of her shorts. She looked warm and sunny, happy. She was always happy; it seemed so easy for her. Davey admired that. He grabbed her hand, pulled her over, and kissed her. She was taken back by the surprise and suddenness of it but smiled only seconds later, while his lips were still on hers.

"Going to miss me in a few weeks?" she asked.

"Something like that," he teased, smiling back at her as he let her go and she wandered a few feet from him. She smiled and waved to him as she walked down the back steps, going to greet Karen probably. She'd be back. He'd find her.

Jimmy and Davey were on burger duty, while a lot of the other men drank their beer and their wine and talked around the fire while not helping anyone do much of anything. Sidney never helped, either. She served herself, gave out orders every now and again, and essentially accepted that self-service always worked out. They ate a big meal that night, extra neighbors coming to join in the biggest bonfire of the summer, bringing all kinds of side dishes and desserts. After the grill was finally turned off and everyone had their fill on hamburgers and pasta salad, someone found a box of firecrackers.

"They're going to light themselves on fire," Kate said, coming up beside Davey and Jimmy with Karen not far behind her. They watched as a few of the kids held burning matches under the wicks of their sparklers and fireworks, which shot up in the sky and dazzled everyone with their green and blue glimmering lights.

"No way," Davey said.

"You know what my father says. The accidents that happen at the end of the summer are never the good ones," Jimmy replied a little quietly, just throwing a thought out into the open, watching it fly up with the fireworks and fizzle out. As each one exploded in the sky, there was an uproar from the crowd, enjoying the light show, excited by the noise, and moving on from their day drinking.

"Let's have that bottle of wine," Davey said, looking over at Jimmy. His eyes lit up at his cousin offering to drink his own wine with him. He hadn't made that bottle of 1968, but he had made many bottles like it. Sometimes, it was hard to pass out the white.

"I'll get the bottle," Jimmy said, walking off. Karen rolled her eyes.

"He's been waiting all summer for you to say that," she commented, watching him almost run back with the bottle. The four of them found a spot by the fire and sitting on the cool grass, poured themselves a glass and swallowed the wine easily. They continued to pour themselves glasses, and soon enough, Jimmy wandered off to find another bottle of wine. Karen and Kate stopped after they were a bottle in, choosing to sip at their wine instead of drink it. But Davey and Jimmy couldn't stop; everything was getting better. Davey didn't stop pouring.

He found himself singing, his arm wrapped around his cousin's shoulder, Jimmy doing the same to him. They were around the fire, standing up, dancing and singing campfire songs while the rest of the crowd was egging them on, laughing with them. Davey could hardly believe how loose he was. He was mad drunk, and he hadn't realized it until he stood up and started to sing. He was so happy. Kate and Karen sat back, watching them with their eyes lit up by firelight, moving their hands in the air as if they were conducting an orchestra. There was more laughing than actual singing, and each boy looked at one another and tried to convince themselves to take it seriously, to really sing a song all the way through.

It was beautiful. The night sky was bright, more stars in the sky than Davey could ever have imagined there were. The fire was massive, wood crackling loudly as it broke apart and sent sparks up into the air that danced all the way into the sky until it looked like they became stars themselves. Davey couldn't stop singing. A sugary taste was in his mouth, resting on his lips, making his face a bright pink as he sang and danced with Jimmy, who looked just as happy with his bright, reflective eyes. They did the song and dance bit for quite some time; before all the energy left them, and all they wanted to do was sit down for a while and smell the wood burning. Kate followed Davey to the front of the house where the fire was not, and they kissed for a very long time.

"C'mon, man, we gotta go," Jimmy called out as he stumbled around the house, meeting Davey in the middle, holding the hand of a smiling Kate. Jimmy smiled at her.

"The 'rents want to go, party's over," Jimmy said, a far away sound in his voice as he looked out at the dwindling crowd and the fading fire. It had looked so powerful before, like it couldn't possibly burn out.

"I'm coming," Davey said, kissing Kate on the cheek before she wandered up the balcony into the house and then he held onto Jimmy as they walked over to the dock where the boat was tied. Karen just shook her head, hands on her hips as she watched them struggle to walk in a straight line.

"You two are going to fall in and drown," she teased, helping them into the boat. Davey stiffened at her candid words, thinking about something bitter. But the sweetness of the wine came rushing back, warming him up; making him feel safe. Sidney and Nick said nothing as the two boys fell down on the front seats as the engine started. They just looked at the kids, then at each other, then at the sky. They were happy, too.

Sidney and Karen helped the two boys up the steps and into their room, both of them falling into bed easily. Davey looked out the window for a moment, letting his heart settle, watching as the curtains drifted in the wind from the open window. He didn't think he had closed that window once the whole time he was there.

"Tell me about your dad," Davey whispered, hidden under his bed sheets, his whole body radiating with warmth from the wine, the fire, Kate's kisses, and all of the people. Jimmy was feeling the same kinds of things in his bed, looking up at the ceiling. He was surprised Davey asked, only because he had been thinking of the old man in that moment already. He had a picture of him, hidden in a suitcase in the closet. He never really looked at it, but it was nice to have.

"My mom and Nick have been together since she was in high school. They broke up for two months when she was twenty-four or something like that. Anyways, I guess she had a fling with this guy, and she found out she was pregnant the day her and Nick got back together," Jimmy said, his voice higher than a whisper, but the tones low and mellow. He'd removed himself from the story a long time ago.

"Did you ever meet him?" Davey asked, feeling a tightness in his chest that came naturally with controversy. He figured it had all worked out, in the end. Something about the sweet taste of the wine was still on his lips. He was starting to understand the need for sweet wine – why it was okay. Why sweet wine was more than okay.

"Well, yeah. A few times. He didn't want a lot to do with me, but he didn't know that at first. He tried for a little while. I think it made things harder for Nick, y'know, to think of me as his. It was weird for a few years, especially when Karen was born and she was going through her medical things," Jimmy said, his voice tapering off. He loved his sister. He didn't want anyone to think she made things harder for him. If anything, he knew he made things much harder for her. He regretted it, but she was often the one who had to look out for him, protect him, make sure he felt the world wasn't really such a harsh place as the city streets and broken concrete in their driveway back home made it seem. And that was hard for her.

"So things are good now?"

"Things are great now."

Great was a strong word, but Jimmy still felt sweet inside, too, and just hours ago, singing by the fire, listening to Nick play the harmonica, his mother and sister pretending to play drums and the neighbors joining in the chorus, things did seem great; a little white wine amongst a sea of red bottles, a few stars in an otherwise dark sky. It was all the same. Davey thought about it.

It had been the best time.

20 – Northern

She was getting used to the water. First, she'd dip her toes in; then let her ankles get covered. Soon enough, the water was at the middle of her calves, then her upper thighs, later her hips, her chest, and finally, she was submerged.

Sasha wasn't particularly fond of swimming in the ocean, but she thought it was important she got used to it, understand that the sea was not the enemy. Things were still beautiful, even when bad things happened there. The past few weeks she'd taken to swimming in the early mornings before her grandparents even thought about hosting a brunch. She was trying to get back into the nature scene; trying to appreciate all the things she loved most about home. Feeling the sand clump between her toes felt better than any of the luxuries she'd been given the past few months. She wasn't alone.

Gillian surfed. She came out in the mornings, too; catching whatever waves she could for a few hours before work. They'd started coming together, getting closer. Sasha floated in the water a bit as she watched Gillian catch a medium-sized wave, letting it carry her forward quite a few feet before dissipating, and she sank low on her board to avoid falling in. She'd offered to teach Sasha, but she hadn't been interested. Just being in the water in the early mornings was good enough for her.

After her swim, she laid out on her beach towel, welcoming the heavy rays from the morning sun, warming up her body before going home to shower in some kind of cherry blossom soap. Her phone rang in her bag, and she almost ignored it, but figured it could only be one person.

"Hey, Mom," she greeted not even checking the ID.

"So, you are alive!" Vivienne replied, pacing around in her office, looking from her computer to out the window at all the chickens running around in her backyard. She was working hard on a story, but none of it was coming out the way she had hoped. As far as she was concerned, the whole summer had been a bust, and Frank was too occupied with his art installments to notice. She needed her daughter back.

"I am, and I see you are, too. How crazy is that?" Sasha replied smoothly as Gillian walked up from the shore, casting her board aside and laying out her own towel. Sasha watched from under her sunglasses as Gillian began to peel off her wet suit while trying to listen to whatever her mother was saying. Gillian was taking her time, throwing her hair off to the side to avoid complications with the zipper.

"Believe me, it's pretty crazy," Vivienne replied, biting her fingernails, still pacing the floor of her office.

"Why? What's going on? Have you and Dad not seen signs of life for over a week again?" Sasha asked, mostly teasing, still lying down on her back and looking up at the sky when she wasn't looking at Gillian. She didn't miss Gillian's face contort a little as she overheard Sasha's commentary.

"What does that mean?" she whispered, lying down next to Sasha on her stomach, propping herself up on her elbows, her long hair thrown back to dry in the sun. She was getting sand everywhere. Sasha waved her hand to shoo away her question.

"No, we've been out. I just miss you. When are you coming home again?" Vivienne asked, this time standing still in front of the large windows that covered the back wall of her office. She loved them and hated them all at once.

"Not for like, two and a half weeks. You could have come out here to visit me and your parents, you know," Sasha said, not looking at Gillian anymore, but fully aware of how intently Gillian was looking at her, studying her.

"Oh, hush. You're rude sometimes," Vivienne replied.

"Are you alright? What's going on over there, honestly, Mom," Sasha said, sitting up halfway, holding her upper torso up with her elbows planted in the sand beside her. Gillian rolled over and put little sand piles on Sasha's leg absentmindedly.

"I think there's something wrong with your chicken. She has bubbles pouring out of her nose. It's so bizarre, and I don't know what it means, and I don't know how to fix it," Vivienne said, angry with herself for being so helpless outside of her office walls. The windows were beautiful, but they reminded her of all the things she wasn't good at. If it weren't for her daughter, the backyard would have been useless.

"Bubbles?"

"Yeah, clear bubbles. She's sneezing and breathing funny. What does that mean?" her mother asked. Sasha just shook her head, looking out at the waves hitting the beach. She couldn't look at Gillian; the piles of sand were moving up her leg.

"Mom, that's not even an issue. Is this Freckles? She probably just has a virus or something. Our chickens have had it before. There's a yellow powder in the back shed, just follow the instructions on the back of the box and mix it with water. Let her drink it for a few days, and it should clear up. I'm sure the Internet would have given you a similar answer," Sasha said. The sand was up very high now, and it tingled as she felt each little piece of it fall onto her leg in a small pile. She glanced down for just a second and thought there had to be at least thirty little piles laid upon the top of her leg. She felt like she couldn't move at all, so she lay back down to look at the sky and nothing else.

The piles started on her other leg.

"I'm sure. Are you having a good time? Where are you now? I hear something," Vivienne asked, trying to get the attention away from her minor meltdown about chickens. She didn't want to fail her daughter. She thought she already might have.

"I'm at the beach right now. Just laying out, I have a friend here," Sasha replied, the sand piles inching up her other leg slowly but surely.

"Ah, a friend?" Gillian mumbled, laughing a little. She was bored not being able to talk to Sasha, but at the same time, she was interested in her phone conversation.

"Oh, that's nice. The beach there is a really great place," Vivienne replied, thinking back to it and all the times she went night swimming. It had been her favorite part, the water.

"Can I talk to Dad? Can you go find him?" Sasha asked, forcing her mom out of the office she knew she was living in. Vivienne let out a hesitant sigh.

"Well, he's really busy…" she started to say.

"I'm sure he will put down the paint to talk to his finest creation," Sasha replied forcefully. Gillian looked up at her, sensing the command in her voice. She was interested, more than ever before. She was running out of skin to build little sandcastles.

"Obviously," Vivienne murmured, walking through the house and glancing around in empty rooms looking for her husband. She knew he was in the art studio downstairs but wished he was somewhere else. She wished she were, too.

"Honey, it's our daughter," Vivienne said, coming down the steps and into the big room. It was a walk-out basement, windows covering the whole back wall to look out onto all the property they owned. It was a mess, but in a huge clearing in the middle stood Frank and a giant canvas half-filled with his work. He looked up at his wife, taken out of his thought process for a moment. He thought she looked beautiful. As he smiled at her, he went over and put some paint on her forehead before kissing her, then taking the phone from her hand.

"Sweet pea!" he said, and Sasha giggled at the childish

nickname he had always reserved for her.

"Hey, Dad. How are you? How is everything over there?" Sasha asked.

"Same old, same old. Miss you terribly, though. The chickens have come to hate us. I think they are starting to realize we are incompetent. It's about to be *Animal Farm* over here," he replied, smiling as he talked to her. He took personal failings a little less personally. He was happy, generally. Vivienne just wanted Sasha to be happy.

"That's funny, Dad. I think you guys can hold out another few weeks. How's Mom? Are you guys going out at all? I think you guys need to go out today," Sasha said, holding her hand to her forehead and pressing down on the skin. She was getting too hot. She flipped over onto her stomach, letting all the sand piles fall away from her. It wasn't long before she felt them come back, this time, on the back of her legs. She shivered at the sensation. Gillian was bored.

"We're fine, honestly. But maybe we could go out for dinner or something," he suggested, raising his eyes to look at his wife who was sitting on the stairs. She smiled at the thought of that and how much thought her daughter put into them.

"Good, please do. You guys are getting restless over there. Want to go on a hike or something when I get home?" she asked, the sand piles slowing down as they reached the back of her upper thigh. She knew it was a matter of seconds before Gillian started on the next leg, and she was right.

"Yeah, of course. That sounds awesome. We really do miss you, Sasha, but I hope you really are having a good time out there. Getting whatever you were looking for," Frank said, his daughter understanding exactly what he meant. A lot of thought had gone into creating her, after all.

"I am, Dad. I am. Tell Mom goodbye for me. I love you both. I'll be home before you know it!" she said. Frank told her that he loved her before hanging up and going to sit next to his wife on the steps, putting his arm around her and just sitting there with her as they looked out the back wall at the chickens mulling around and the acres of land that stretched back out of their line of sight.

"Was that your parents?" Gillian asked. Sasha hadn't moved, and neither had Gillian, who was sitting up beside her, still making little sand piles on the backs of her legs. The sand started spilling onto her back moments later.

"Yeah. They worry a lot," Sasha replied, thinking about home, feeling the sand move up her spine. She wasn't sure about anything, except she liked it. She liked it.

"I have to go to work in a minute, but we should hang out later? Tonight? If you want to," Gillian offered, brushing her hands together to get all the sand off her skin before standing up and grabbing her bag and board, tossing her towel over her shoulder. She looked so strong in the way she moved. Sasha peered up at her, covering her eyes from the harsh sun. Gillian smiled down at her, wanting her to say yes.

"We could go night swimming," Sasha offered, thinking about her mother.

"I'd love to," Gillian replied with a smirk, then started to run to the top of the beach, turning around only for a moment to give a short wave before hopping over the small guard rail and heading off into the parking lot. Sasha decided to leave soon after.

When she returned to her grandparents' house, she ate a quick brunch with them and talked the usual social politics, something she had gained quite a bit of insight into. Her grandfather was almost impressed with her, and although he didn't say much to her, he regarded her highly as he peered out at her over the brim of his newspaper. She was beautiful and talked about things like his daughter had, but Sasha had a tone of honesty and character that Vivienne hadn't discovered yet at her age.

When the table was cleared, Sasha walked barefoot up the marble steps to her bathroom on the second floor where her room was. It was a huge space, all marble, with a large Jacuzzi facing out over the gardens. She left the windows open, the thin filmy curtains moving quietly during her time in the tub. She took a long bath with all the soaps and bubbles she could find. She washed her hair and conditioned it, scrubbed her entire body, and shaved her legs. When she dried off, she lathered on lotion, wanting to be smooth, clean, and pretty. She knew that she smelled like roses when she walked carefully to her room in her robe. It took her a minute to pick out an outfit, sifting through all the new clothes she'd gotten that summer, but she finally settled on her standard uniform from back home. She pulled on loose cotton pants that were cuffed at the ankles and a tight, cropped tee shirt. After combing her long hair out for a while, she carefully braided the sides, then the middle, and then interwove all the braids into an up-do that framed her face. She felt like she hadn't looked like herself in awhile and wanted to see what it would look like to be the real Sasha and walk around such a grand house and such a beautiful garden.

She spent the rest of the day until dinner in the garden, resting on the hammock, drawing the flowers all around her in her sketchbook, then the faces of her friends and family. She first drew her parents, just a quick freehanded sketch. Then she drew a picture of the boys, the three of them with different expressions on their faces. They were all so different. The next face she focused on was Hailey's. She hadn't seen it in awhile. Since she had passed, she'd hidden all the pictures of them together in a drawer in her closet. She wished she hadn't done that, resolving to rehang them when she got back home. As her hand moved over each feature, she realized she hadn't forgotten what her best friend looked like after all. Mostly, Hailey had been a force in life, until she wasn't.

"You'd like it here," Sasha mumbled to herself, finishing up the drawing. She looked young, and Sasha realized that she was and always would be. It gave her a strange feeling, but she let it roll over her shoulders. She missed Hailey so much; it engulfed her. But running away hadn't helped; facing it did.

She ate again with her grandparents for dinner, and it lasted longer than she thought it would because they had guests over, so the meal was upgraded to five courses and a lot of long conversations about things Sasha now knew plenty about but still didn't care for. She thought about interjecting but stayed silent. Although some of the things seemed terrible, Sasha wanted to keep the happiness on her grandmother's face alive. It was so fragile, she had learned, and relied on so many different things that were always out of her control. Sasha had learned that Ann was a good person; she had just never learned how to stand up for herself. She thought for at least the last few weeks she was there; she could keep the waves from rocking the boat too much. Her mother had almost sunk the boat.

After dessert, when her grandparents and their guests retired to one of the dens, Sasha felt free to go. She went back up to her room and watched the sun set on her balcony, legs held tightly to her chest. She'd found a note on her bed, a simple word scrawled in cursive, from Gillian, no doubt.

eleven

Sasha had purposely stayed away from the rooms she was working in the house that day. She'd wanted some time to herself. It only seemed right. Besides, she would see her that night. She was starting to feel the tension.

Ten minutes until, she slipped on her bathing suit under her clothes and carefully snuck out the back door. She'd already said goodnight to her grandparents an hour before, claiming too much sun had done her in.

The walk down the dark sidewalk to the beach was nice. She liked how the trees loomed over her and how with each step the smell of salt water surrounded her more and more; so much so that she felt it was pulling her to the beach, as if it would carry her if she wanted it to, all the way to the place where the waves hit the sand. Sasha got down to the beach a few minutes past eleven, walking over to the place where she and Gillian usually spent their time, away from the tourist spots and the crowds and families. She found Gillian's towel and bag left out on the dark sand and strained her eyes to see if she was already out in the water. She was.

After she stripped off her clothes and left them on her own towel, she ran down to the shore and kept running until the water was waist high. Everything around her was different shades of black, from the night sky, to the banks of the beach, to the waves in the deep water, but the moon highlighted everything just enough that she didn't feel lost. The water was a little cold, but she could hear Gillian laughing and telling her to jump in. Sasha took a deep breath and dove under, swimming for a few seconds until she surfaced again, closer to Gillian, who met her halfway. She was shivering a little from the cold water but also from excitement. She loved night swimming and couldn't believe Sasha had suggested it.

"Have you done this before? Swam so late?" Gillian asked, looking up at the starry sky before looking back at Sasha, who was treading water and trying to float on her back but not doing very well even with the small waves.

"My mom used to do this all the time," Sasha replied, still trying to float but not keeping her back straight enough. Gillian snorted a little, pushing her wet hair out of her face and swam closer to Sasha.

"Girl, keep your back straight or this will never work," Gillian said, her voice full of command that was unique to Sasha. She placed her hands underneath Sasha on her back, not really touching her, but pushing her back up if she started to go under again. Sasha kept her back as straight as she could, and each time she did, Gillian's hands raised to force her to keep it even straighter.

"See, you're doing it right now," Gillian said, happy that Sasha was getting it. She let go, and Sasha saw that she could float on her own. She almost started to cry. The water was holding her up, she could swim, she would float. She could do it. She looked over at Gillian, who was smiling at her, face lit up by the moonlight. She could do it.

They swam a little longer, messing around and splashing each other, but after half an hour, the air was much warmer than the water, and together they ran out of the sea and up to their towels where they fell down and breathed in deeply. They were quiet for a moment, just breathing and looking at the night sky. It was so much brighter over the sea, where there was no light to pollute the sky, to cover such a masterpiece.

"I'm leaving soon," Sasha said. She didn't know why it was on her mind.

"Yeah, I know. End of the month? Summer's almost over," Gillian replied, her arms hanging off her knees, looking out at the waves and sky too.

"Yeah. It went by really fast," Sasha said. She felt almost ready to go back.

"Summers around here usually do. It feels like forever in the middle, but at the end, you can't believe it was any longer than a week," Gillian said. She was playing with the sand in between her fingers again, this time putting the little piles of it on her own feet, covering them up slowly.

"I think that's just how summer goes, in general," Sasha said, laughing a little. She picked up a little bit of sand, moved a little closer to Gillian, and started a pile of sand on her other foot. She put a pile on her each of her toes, and after a few moments, Gillian stopped putting sand on her own foot and watched as Sasha did it for her.

"Hey," Gillian whispered. Sasha turned her head and looked up at her, but Gillian's face was already there, so close. Sasha felt lips on hers. It was slow for a second, not unsure, just hesitant. But when Sasha didn't recoil, when she even kissed back a little, Gillian moved closer, kissing her more deeply, her face very much against hers. There were no thoughts in Sasha's head. Her mind was off, but her body wasn't. She kissed Gillian back, just as deeply, again and again.

Gillian turned her body, balancing on her knees, facing Sasha, still kissing her. Gillian's steady hands held Sasha's face for a moment, then one hand traveled down her neck a little and off to her shoulder. Sasha kept kissing. Gillian moved her hand from her shoulder down her back, her fingers softly trailing down the skin covering her spine, causing her to shiver and feel warm all at the same time. Gillian's lips were forceful and soft, all at once. Sasha kept kissing her, following her lead because her mind wasn't on, and her body was open. The hand on her back moved down lower, past her mid-back, down to the top of her bathing suit shorts. Her finger ran along the hemline a little, then with a full hand, Gillian pushed down at the bottom of Sasha's spine, pulling her closer into her embrace.

With that move, Sasha found herself underneath Gillian, who was kissing her face and her neck, slowly and with intention. It was all happening very slowly; time was hardly going by. It made her feel every little touch, every single moment. Sasha's hands moved from Gillian's shoulders down her arms, down the center of her chest and across her stomach, lined with muscle, moving over Sasha with grace. She left one hand on Gillian's hip, her other hand traveling up to cradle her face, pushing her wild dark hair out of her face. Time slowed even more, and it seemed to go on forever.

"Do you like girls?" Gillian asked, after the kissing. Sasha shook her head.

"I just like people, I think," she answered honestly, confused. Gillian didn't say anything after that, but she seemed satisfied. The two laid next to each other, Sasha contained within Gillian's strong arms, deliberate in everything that they did. They didn't talk for a while, but it was okay. The moment didn't need conversation. They were both happy, both accepting of their realties. The tension was finally gone.

"Look at that, we're about to get a show," Gillian said after a while, and Sasha looked up to where she was pointing in the sky. Faintly, off in the distance, the sky seemed to slowly get lighter in color, first a pale pink, then a stronger orange, and then suddenly it grew bigger, engulfing more and more of the sky. Sasha sat up, her heart pounding as she watched, Gillian letting her arms fall off to her own sides, equally entranced by the show.

The dark sky made room for the colors that were beginning to move over across the vast expanse covering the ocean. The hue turned from orange to a more muted green, then a vibrant one. The lights moved across the sky, changing colors, changing depths, sizes, and shapes. It was awe striking. Sasha had never seen such a brilliant display of color in the sky; she'd never been somewhere so dark and vacant that it could make room for so much motion and light. At first, she felt strangely small under such a sky, her eyes transfixed on all the light. But her heart was pounding, and her palms felt sweaty, and she felt a bad feeling begin to creep over her shoulders and cover her chest, and she didn't know what that could be.

"It's the Northern Lights, whoa. I've never seen them so intense," Gillian said in a hushed tone. Both of them were laying on their backs, looking up at the sky that held so much green light at such a dark hour, it was unbelievable. It looked magical.

Sasha couldn't shake the feeling. It was only growing. Her mind started to race, putting together weird images she couldn't get out of her head. Mostly, she thought about how Calliste would love to see this. Calliste. His name wouldn't leave her mind, and as she heard his name over and over again in her mind, the feeling grew, covering her skin and making it tingle and giving her the feeling that at any moment, she'd fall.

Gillian held her hand as they watched the sky together, the lights so stunning it was like everything around them was under a spell. Gillian was thinking about their kiss, but Sasha was thinking about something else. In that very moment, under all the darkness and green light, Sasha knew that Calliste wasn't okay. The realization made her heart sputter and fall.

She kept looking at the sky and gripped Gillian's hand tighter.

21 – LIGHTS

A shift had taken place.

He thought it was for the better. After all, being invisible was better than being tormented, wasn't it? No one really looked at Calliste anymore. They didn't talk to him, acknowledge him, or really even see him. And Calliste didn't care. He welcomed the invisibility. After weeks of being on everyone's shit list, it was nice to take a breath and know that no one was going to knock it out of him.

That was what he thought, anyway.

Besides the sergeants, only Lukas talked to him every now and again. Sometimes he'd eat a meal with him out in the yard, where no one could see. Sometimes he'd share a joke when in line for drills or activities, mostly under his breath, so no one could hear. They even spent some of their free time together; taking walks through the woods, out to the meadow, when he thought no one was paying attention. Calliste knew he didn't have a friend in Lukas, but it was nice to have someone to talk to, a person to face and have some company now and again. He was counting down the days until they sent him home. He couldn't wait. If anything, he knew he could handle whatever his father threw at him. He was ready for that.

"Do you want to go to the meadow tonight?" Lukas asked, a little abruptly, as he tossed his food tray onto the ground next to Calliste, plopping down with some confidence. It was dinnertime, and Calliste was once again sitting with his back to a big oak out at the farthest stretch of the yard instead of in the mess hall. Calliste thought about the question for a moment.

"Sure, but why? What's there to do at night?" he asked.

"I heard there was suppose to be some show in the sky. A meteor shower or something like that," Lukas said, eating his food quickly, as if he hadn't had a bite all day. Calliste noticed the change in him; he was a lot more confident, a lot more virile. He thought about how this was probably how Adam had hoped he'd turn out, staying at a place like that all summer.

"Yeah, I'll go. I actually love stuff like that," Calliste replied, taking a tentative bite of his spaghetti. He was starting to get used to eating and not thinking about it. At first the food had made him sick, then he had felt too sick to eat the food, and now, he was resigning himself to simply having a workable relationship with the food at camp, nothing more. It was certainly nothing to write home about.

"Do you? I would have never guessed," Lukas teased, taking a few bites of food off of Calliste's tray. In turn, Calliste stole his apple, pushing the rest of the spaghetti over to his sort-of friend. Calliste almost smiled.

"Yeah, this outdoors thing is something I like," he said, looking out into the woods a bit, wondering if there were any deer watching him.

"So, meet me out in the yard at like, ten? It's supposed to start around eleven, I heard. Well, read. I read about it in the newspaper," Lukas said, his mouth full of pasta.

"You? Read a newspaper? I'm shocked," Calliste said half-heartedly. Lukas didn't seem to notice much as he ate the rest of the spaghetti and the extra roll Calliste had given him. He was actually working hard at drills; he probably did need the extra calories to keep him going.

"Oh, I read just fine, Mr. Intellectual. I gotta go, but I'll see you tonight," Lukas said, standing up without waiting for a response from Calliste and leaving both trays by the side of the tree. Calliste just shook his head as he watched Lukas run off down the hill. Probably couldn't be away for too long, lest the other boys suspect he had been fraternizing with the enemy.

Calliste spent some more time out there in the yard, working on a few of his drawings. He had learned everything from Sasha's father. Frank was happy to give him a few lessons, and unlike Sasha, he really liked it. Mostly now, Sasha did quick sketches that she kept hidden away and considered them nothing but impressions. Calliste, on the other hand, drew until his heart was content; he worked hard at his drawings, trying to make them all full, beautiful pictures. Most of his drawings were hung up in his mother's room. She liked to look at them and see the places her son went.

When the light started to fade, Calliste went back to his bunk, set his notebook on the side table, and grabbed his things for a shower. He took a long one, using most of the hot water. No one else showered so early, and he liked the time to himself, without hearing all the loud voices on the other side of the curtain.

He went back to his bunk and read for a while, then contemplated writing a letter to one of his friends. He tried to draft one to Melrose but didn't really have the heart to send it. Besides, he'd be back in a few weeks time, anyway. Then he thought maybe he could send one to Davey. He'd heard from him the least that summer. But Davey was too happy where he was, wandering around the woods, swimming through the lake. Calliste didn't even know what to say to him about that. Sasha was out of the question. She'd read into his words too much, think something was wrong. In his mind, nothing was wrong, there just wasn't anything more to say. His summer had been awful; he hated camp, the food sucked. There was nothing more to say.

Ten o'clock couldn't come soon enough. Calliste really wanted to see the meteor shower. He had been building up his excitement for the past few hours even though he hadn't meant to. Lukas probably didn't even know what he was talking about; the most they would see would be a few shooting stars. Still, Calliste wanted to see that. He wanted to see anything. He hated camp so much.

"You made it," Lukas greeted as Calliste ran across the lawn to the flagpole where Lukas was already standing, hands in pockets. Calliste nodded.

"Of course, man," he replied.

"We should go, Lord knows I probably read that paper wrong and mixed up my times or something. Shit, if I get this wrong, too," Lukas said, as he turned away and started to walk out towards the woods. Calliste followed but then had to lead once they got on the trail, Lukas already forgetting where the meadow was and unable to navigate the trails in the dark. He had a small flashlight with him, and it helped a little. Their feet made crunching noises as they walked, breaking small pieces of wood and slipping on wet leaves throughout the trails. Calliste welcomed the noise. The walk took about twenty minutes, a bit longer than usual because it was so dark in the woods at night. Eventually, they emerged into the meadow to the spot where they stood the first time they had discovered the place right by the grassy banks of the creek. The water gurgled a little as it rolled by the stones and dead wood in the shallow stream.

"We made it," Lukas whispered, taking in the meadow that looked quite different at night, when he was alone with Calliste and in the dark. The sky above them held a spectacular amount of stars, and the moon was shining down brightly, allowing them to turn off the flashlight and still be able to see where they were going quite clearly. Without really talking about it, Calliste headed to a big rock dug into the bank of the creek and climbed up on top of it to sit. Lukas did the same; it was big enough for at least four people.

"This place looks really different at night," Lukas commented, slightly dumbfounded. He was thinking about weird things like how pretty the place looked, how it seemed almost a little magical. He tried to shake his head from those thoughts; they made him uncomfortable. Calliste seemed content to him, steady as ever.

"I kind of like it. It's calm," Calliste mentioned, looking around. The grass was long and dark, flowing in different directions all over the field, looking more like something out of *Charlie and the Chocolate Factory* than a real place.

"It's certainly quiet," Lukas murmured, choosing to stop looking around him at the field and instead focus up on the sky. He was impatient for the shower to start.

"Are you excited to be going home soon?" Calliste asked, brushing some of his blond hair from his face. They had to keep it short while they were there, but Calliste had stopped buzzing it, and Adams hadn't said a word about it. Lukas shrugged.

"Yeah, I am. A lot, actually. But this place turned out not to be so bad for me," Lukas said, his voice growing quiet at the end. He knew the same thing had not happened for Calliste, the first person to be kind to him at the beginning of the summer. He felt badly about that but didn't know how to fix it. Calliste didn't seem to mind; he just kind of nodded his head at the answer, like he understood.

"Yeah," Calliste replied.

"You got a lot going on, back where you're from?" Lukas asked.

"I have some friends and family, I guess. Yeah, I like it back home. I didn't really feel like I had to leave or anything," Calliste replied, trying not to think about it.

"That's nice," Lukas said, picking at the skin around his thumb a little, then lightly hitting his fist into the section of rock beside him. He was impatient. They sat out there quietly for a little bit longer, both looking up at the sky, admiring it, appreciating the view that the meadow provided them with. The sky really was spectacular. It seemed so dark, yet there were so many stars and then wide swoops of milky light. Some of the stars seemed to blink out there, and as they waited, Calliste took the time to point out all the constellations he knew, which turned out to be quite a few more than he thought. Lukas only knew the Big Dipper, and was fascinated by how many Calliste could point out and how he made them all feel alive. Soon, the quiet was gone, and they were talking and laughing about all the constellations and their stories, trying to make up some of their own.

"Well, what's going on out here?" a voice asked from the darkness of the field. Lukas's heart dropped instantly, and he turned around abruptly. Calliste's breathing quickened a little, but he calmly turned his head to look back and see Jack Turner and a few other boys from the camp standing in the grass, close to the rock. Lukas jumped down from the rock suddenly, seeming to want to put immediate distant between him and his sort-of friend. Calliste stayed sitting cross-legged on the rock.

"What're you guys doing out here, all alone and in the dark?" Turner asked, his voice turning to a laugh, filled with menace and vindictive hate.

"Nothing. We're not doing anything," Lukas quietly rebutted, his voice a little shaky, his eyes focused downward at his shoes. Without meaning to, Calliste thought about how if Melrose were here, he'd yell at Lukas to look up and keep his voice solid. Calliste tried to embody the kind of confidence his friend had, but all he could do was sit quietly and not say anything.

"So, you're saying, that you and Blondie over there walked all the way out here to do nothing? Is that what you're saying?" Turner asked, a couple of his friends laughing a little, moving closer, like a pack. Calliste stayed up on the rock. He wasn't the focus, not yet. Lukas took a step back, his second mistake. Melrose had taught all of them never take a step back; it was only permission to keep pushing.

"C'mon, we wanna know. Just tell us what're you doing out here. Stargazing together?" Jack asked, barely finishing the word stargazing before someone erupted into laughter, pushing his friend a little bit as if it was the funniest thing he'd ever heard. It made Calliste sick. It made Lukas sick, too, because what more was watching a meteor shower than stargazing? He had no response.

"That's what I thought. Are you two boyfriends or something? Slippin' back here for some alone time?" Turner said, looking over at Calliste for the first time since they had gotten out there. A couple of the boys whistled, and Calliste felt his face turn red. His heart was steady, but his breathing was sporadic at best. Nothing compared to how badly Lukas was sweating. He was so embarrassed.

"Who's on top?" Turner asked, his voice hushed, his lips pursed as he said the last word. This created howls from the other boys, and they moved a little closer to Lukas. Calliste wanted to move or at least stand by him. He was being pathetic, but Calliste felt the same fear he did, just not the same humiliation.

"What-t-t? N-no one. I'm not-t gay," Lukas mumbled, almost inaudibly.

"I'm sorry, what was that? I couldn't really hear you," Turner pushed, holding a cupped hand to his ear, sticking his face so close to Lukas it was like they were kissing.

"I'm not gay," he said again, just a bit louder. The other boys kept howling, louder than Lukas could ever be. Turner wasn't satisfied. He waited.

"I'm not gay. I'm not goddamn gay," Lukas said, a bit more forcefully, anger in his voice this time. It was beginning to collect in the pit of his stomach.

"One more time for the people in the back," Turner urged, his face so entertained by the fear and harsh declaration he was forcing Lukas to make.

"That's disgusting. I'm not, I'm not gay," Lukas said. Calliste closed his eyes for a minute. He saw what was happening; knew what was probably going to happen.

"Ah, thought I heard you say something," Jack said, slapping Lukas hard on his back, pushing him out of the way so he tumbled into the dark grass, into the darkness, seemingly disappearing forever. The boys kept howling, kept whistling.

"So, that leaves you," Turner said, pointing at Calliste up on the rock. He walked a little closer, but Calliste didn't move, didn't think he could. He felt paralyzed. He didn't want to say the things Lukas had said, didn't want to sound like him. He didn't know a way out of this, either, but certainly didn't want to go down the way his sort-of friend had.

"What are you doing out here, you little meadow fairy?" Jack asked, walking around the rock a little, hitting his hand into the side of it, just begging for Calliste to come down there and face him. Still, he didn't move and didn't say anything. The boys began to demand some kind of response. The quiet was getting them agitated; they had come riled up; they weren't looking to calm down just yet.

"I'm talking to you," Turner growled, jumping up and grabbing one of Calliste's feet, pulling him down off the rock with hard force. The surface of the rock scraped at his back and arms, but he managed to catch himself so that he didn't completely crumble when he hit the ground. Jack stared down at him, so much bigger than he was. It was almost ridiculous. Calliste breathed in deeply, trying to stay even. He stood up tall. He didn't take a step back. He thought about those things.

"You gay, little fairy boy?"

"No," Calliste said, not in a whisper, but not loudly either. It was just the truth.

"No, what?" Turner pushed, stepping closer to Calliste.

"I'm not," he said simply.

"Not what, fairy boy?" Turner growled, his anger mounting, his disgust evident. It wasn't even so much that Jack Turner thought Calliste was gay. It was more about how small he was, how smart he seemed, how quickly he evaded him and his rules. It was annoying, agitating. Mostly, he hated losing in drills and races when he had to deal with the pretty boy. His world was much more limited. Calliste didn't reply.

"You have a little crush on our commanding officer?" Jack asked, reaching into his pocket, pulling out a folded-up piece of paper. Calliste looked down at it curiously for a moment, unsure of what it was. Realization hit him soon enough. It was the drawing of Sergeant Adams he had done a few weeks back. He remembered sitting in the tree sketching it, focusing on making it as realistic as possible. More than anything, he wished he'd put his sketchbook away.

"No, I don't," Calliste murmured, but this time, Turner wasn't so easily persuaded. He pushed Calliste hard back into the rock, his head and shoulders taking most of the hit. He swayed a little, pain coursing through the back of his neck, shooting up and down. He wanted to rub his shoulder but decided it better to still not move.

"Oh, you can't lie to me now. We came all the way out here just to talk about it," Turner said, looking back at his entourage, enjoying the ridiculous noises that rose from the pits of their stomachs.

"I doubt that," Calliste said with his last bit of confidence.

"Well, if you say so," Turner growled, hitting Calliste across the face, causing him to stagger backwards. Before he even got his footing back, another blow came from the other side, this one with more of a closed fist than an open hand. Falling back into the rock, he tried to hold onto it for support, to take a moment, see where all of the anger and motion was coming from. They didn't let him. Turner pushed him back again, no longer teasing, no longer waiting for some sly words to come out of the pretty boy's mouth.

"Hey! Blondie is cryin'!" a boy shouted from the back. Turner stopped for a moment, looking down at Calliste, who was still holding onto the rock, trying to find his footing, his face turned away from all of them. Where was Lukas? Someone was probably holding onto him. Not that he was going anywhere. Turner knew that boy would stay silent. He looked at Calliste's face, the wetness under his eyes lit up by the moonlight; the small hushed gasps bubbling up from his throat. He got off on it.

"Why are you crying?" he asked.

"Why aren't you?"

That was the last thing he let Calliste Martin say. With a

completely closed fist, he punched him solidly in the face, feeling blood dot his knuckles as it poured out of his nose. Calliste fell down, off to the side, away from the rock. He tried to crawl out of the way, but Turner was faster. He walked up and kicked him in the side, then picked him up to get him to stand once more. One of the other boys came forward, pushing him hard into another boy, who did the same. Another boy kicked him in the back, causing him to fall forward again, and then, Calliste lost track of how it happened or who did it.

There was pain everywhere. There were blows dealt on his face, his torso, his ribs, his back. He felt the sharp pain of a heavy boot slam into him time and time again. He couldn't see, the darkness surrounding him, his eyes swelling shut to try to save something, anything. There wasn't any thinking. He kept trying to crawl away, but there seemed no path to escape the howling, the dancing, or the intensity.

He started to choke, a rising panic within him as he realized he couldn't breathe, that he was face down in something thick and didn't have the energy to turn over. He was gasping. Right when the darkness seemed to enter him, his body was flipped over onto his back, his mouth open wide, reaching for the air that he felt around him, but couldn't get in. Each breath was sharp and painful. Trembling, his hands tried to run over his body and see where the pain was, how to stop it, anything. But they couldn't. They barely worked. As he tried to move once more, his arms trembled at the motion, and he fell back down, gasping loudly. His eyesight was blurry, it was too dark outside, and everything seemed to be spinning. The howling hadn't stopped, but it had changed. The tone was crueler, meaner, and had taken a few steps back.

"No one's crying but you, pretty boy."

There was one final kick to his side, and with it, a horrible cracking sound and an awful shot of pain that seemed to explode within his chest. Breathing felt almost impossible, but his body kept forcing him to do it. He was crying, sobbing. Over his whole body was a radiating sense of agony, filling every single nerve ten times over. His foot was numb, his side was filled with shards of pain, he couldn't move his neck, and there was blood dripping down his face and into his mouth, the metallic taste stinging the last bit of sanity he had.

The howling stopped. They were gone. Calliste's ears were filled with silence for a moment, his labored breathing, and then the gurgling of the creek beside him. Water. They had left him on the dark grassy banks of the creek. Things were starting to go cold. For a few moments, he tried to open his eyes and managed to keep the left one open for a little while, focusing on one point in the sky to try and still the spinning. It wasn't dark anymore. There was a light in the sky, and it was growing. He started to laugh, but it hurt so badly it immediately turned to cries. He was losing it. Painfully, he looked up at the sky, watching it grow in light, watching the colors change. It helped. It made the darkness creep away, made him feel less alone out there in the meadow, surrounded by animals and trees that could not help him.

He lay, gasping, each cracked rib making it harder to draw in air, each forced breath accompanied by a deep groan that ran through his frozen body, unmoving; beaten. Why was he so cold? He watched the sky. Lukas had been wrong. It wasn't a meteor shower at all.

It was the Northern Lights.

22 – Crumbling

The sun was piercing.

At just the right angle, it blinded him for a heavy moment, forcing him to stumble back and sacrifice an arm to raise and cover his eyes, shielding them from the sheer brightness. Cody Hertz took heavy advantage of tossing Melrose into the sun, watching him burn for a moment, disoriented, before lashing out at him again. Things were slow for that moment, in the sun, both boys breathing heavily, a deep silence. The only thing they could hear was a sharp ringing. Then, just as quickly, the world caught up, and the sound of fist hitting flesh broke the barrier, and everyone else yelled and roared along with the struggle.

"C'mon, I know you've wanted to do this for awhile," Cody coaxed, knees bending up and down, ready to move left or right at a second's notice. Melrose took a moment to get his bearings after the last punch, his anger only growing from being attacked first. Fighting with Melrose wasn't an easy task, and it wasn't for just anyone. After the rumor had run rampant through the neighborhood that Melrose was someone who got knocked around by his old man, his reputation had grown massively. Besides, he had the bruises to hold up the story.

"You piece of shit," he muttered through the pain, lunging at Cody with frightening speed. Cody attempted to dash off to the left, but Melrose clipped his right shoulder, pulling him back toward him. With a swinging fist, Cody tossed another punch on his way down, hitting Melrose's chin this time but with little force. In an instant, Melrose jumped on top of him, dragging his face towards his own, just to hit it left, then right, then left again. Cody was far from done, however, and managed to kick his back with a free leg, causing him to stir just enough for him to throw Melrose to his side, and then dragged him back, kicking him hard in the side again and again. With a cry of pain, Melrose crumpled for a moment, then managed to get ahold of the fighting foot, ripping it back, landing Hertz on the rocky ground, hard.

They fought some more.

Sasha looked on, first entranced, later in horror at how far the fight was going. Before, Melrose had always thrown a few punches, both boys calling it quits after a little blood and a few bruises. It was just the way he was; how he handled the pain and the expectation. That had changed this summer. Sasha couldn't understand this fight. Cody Hertz had always been a rival, someone constantly in a dark corner laughing and taunting. This fight was something out of a dark dirty basement, a thing of malice, not an effort to overcome.

Her heart pounded as she watched. She didn't think Melrose had even seen her yet. He didn't even know she was home. Somehow, she wanted to intercede, to tell them to stop killing each other. They were killing each other. No one else seemed to notice. A few others gathered around, cheering them on, seeming oblivious to the utter pain they endured. Instead of horror, the crowd fed off the bloodshed, off the mockery, off of the lack of pain management that had brought Cody Hertz and Melrose Bartlett to that dusty ground, ready to bring each other to ruins. It was how their neighborhood worked.

"Your girlfriend is out there," Cody laughed, making a kissing face through the blood pouring down his face; his teeth crimson in the light of the sun.

"Surprised she took you back, you know, after that whole thing with your sister," he spat. It took one second for Melrose to see nothing but red. He lunged. In one swoop, he grabbed up Cody's throat; slammed him to the ground, and punched him directly in the jaw, letting loose the most sickening cracking sound. The crowd hushed immediately, the noise yanking them forward into the sun, into reality.

Blood flowed from Cody's mouth, drenching his shirt – the color making his eyes flash with anger, then pain, as he fell back. Melrose was wild, thrusting out another fist, connecting it with Cody's shoulder as he went down. He met the ground harshly, gasping. His jaw lay at a crooked angle – broken.

"You're gonna kill him!" Sasha yelled. An eager crowd had hidden her before, but now it was disappearing, and quickly. Melrose didn't even hear her as he jumped onto Cody's body – only hearing the taunts Cody could no longer speak. Pushing her way through, she ran at Melrose and tried to drag him away. Cody lay where he was, moving slightly, moaning horribly, trying to touch his jaw but unable to from the sheer pain radiating from it. It was absolutely broken, smashed in half, and torn apart. Melrose tried to push her away, seeing only red, but Sasha grabbed his hair and held as tightly as she could, slapping his cheeks to make him see her. As he whipped around, he faced her, grabbing at her arms forcefully.

"Stop! Hailey would want you to stop!" Sasha shouted, staring the beast right in the eyes, watching it leave Melrose as he realized who she was and that she was really there, standing in front of him. Her eyes did not drift from Melrose's eyes, and together they stood in absolute stillness as Melrose's racing heart calmed, taking in the reality around him. He loosened the grip around Sasha's arms, and in a moment she ripped herself away from him, running over to Cody on the ground. He was panting heavily, blood flowing freely down his throat, over his face, across his body. The sun captured the essence of his eyes for Sasha to see, the utter fear ripping through her own body as she tried to help him breathe.

"Get the hell out of here!" she yelled at Melrose, who stood motionless, sucking in air, not sure if he was going to cry or collapse. She heard sirens. For a moment, she watched as Melrose leapt away, disappearing into the woods, then looked back at the broken boy in her arms.

"Cody," Sasha said calmly, cradling his head, preventing the blood from choking him. She was gentle; she was soft, but he wasn't innocent.

"You don't know who did this, okay?" she whispered, looking him right in the eyes. She meant it. Inside of her was a storm, pushing at all corners, trying to break free, but for now, she stayed still, stayed calm.

"Okay?" she asked.

He didn't move.

"Okay?" she asked again, touching his cracked jaw with just a little pressure from her thumb. His hand gripped her forearm, and he quickly nodded as best he could, closing his eyes. She took her fingers away from his jaw, holding his face gently and offering her company as the sirens grew closer, and she knew someone, somewhere, had called an ambulance for him. He probably wouldn't have told, anyway. That wasn't how things like that worked. Not there, anyway.

When the medics got there, Sasha was alone with a terrified Cody, stating that she didn't know who had done it or what had happened; just that there had been a fight that got out of hand, and once the jaw broke, everyone booked it. As soon as they loaded him onto the stretcher, Sasha disappeared, giving Cody's hand a tight squeeze before departing. The flashing lights were the last things she saw before she was fully hidden by the woods. She found a stream to wash her hands off, not realizing how much she was shaking until she attempted to rub off all the blood on her arms. In the moment, she started to sob. She cursed Melrose, and she cursed Cody Hertz.

She wept for Hailey.

An hour went by before she fully calmed down, allowing her mind to file through the wreckage. She was angry, sad, hurt, confused, and burdened. However, casting all of it aside, she knew that Melrose was sitting somewhere contemplating something much worse. All she wanted was for Davey to have to go find him, or Calliste, even. They couldn't. She had to.

There was an old crumbling stone wall that Sasha knew about. She had found it by accident one time, walking through the woods. Wandering along it, memorizing its every crack and crevice, she had immediately recognized that Melrose too knew of it, when he once mentioned finding a special kind of rock barrier dug into a bank. It was the wall. She began to frequent it, and although she never saw him there herself, she saw evidence of him. Little pieces of crumbled paper stuck into the rocks.

Messages to someone who could never unfold the paper.

She thought about how pitiful it was to have to communicate that way as she walked through the woods, hearing the birds flutter around, oblivious to the shallowness in her own heart as she walked. She had missed her own woods and felt a little warmth inside of her as everything around her fell into place. She felt at home.

"Thought I might find you here," she said, seeing the back of his head just over the top of the wall he was leaning against. He hardly moved.

"Are you dead?" she whispered, climbing over to face him. He looked more like a ghost than a boy. Blood covered, darkened eyes, beaten skin, and tattered clothes, he was as good as a corpse sitting out by his own tombstone. She sat carefully in front of him, keeping her breathing to a soft sound. He was shaking. Her malice towards him evaporated. He was so hurt, and she had always known that.

"I want to be," he stuttered, voice as uneven and shaky as the rest of his body. Completely tormented, this was the real Melrose, the one that lived inside of him, heartbroken and shamed his entire life by every little thing and moment.

"You think that'd help?" Sasha asked, her own voice straight and direct.

"It would fucking stop this," he replied, bringing his shaky hands to the sides of his head, trying to hold it all together but unable to exert enough force. They dropped down to his sides. Tears streamed down his face, mixing with the blood. His whole frame was colorless and frail.

"You can't lock it all up in your head, you have to let it out. And not…not with your fists," Sasha tried to explain, trying to coax him to just talk to her. Their relationship was built on subtleties. That couldn't be the case here; that kind of communication was failing to save a teetering Melrose.

"It's not your job to fix this," he spat, gesturing to himself.

"Your job was over when Hailey died," he said, gasping at his own words, crying out a little louder than before, trying to bury his face in his own chest.

"We didn't love you and let you in because you were Hailey's older brother. We love you because you're Melrose. It's always been that way," Sasha assured, but her words hardly penetrated the wall Melrose had built so well, unlike the crumbling one behind him. She wasn't sure how to reach in and grab him.

"I hate you for saying that. I hate all of you. You're dead weight. You were all here because of her, and then you all left. I know it's been two years, but you all left me and didn't look back once. How was your summer, huh? I bet it was fucking wonderful," he mocked, his voice thick, his eyes shifting back and forth. He was so angry, but it was fading. His anger was trying to root onto something so that it could stay, but nothing was strong enough to hold onto those lies and keep them alive.

"We're all here for you," she said, pushing for him to understand. He rolled his eyes, but nodded, wiping tears and snot from his face, looking off to the right, anywhere but her face. He wanted to stay angry, but he couldn't. The anger could never hide the pain all the way; it never had.

"I know it's not your fault," she whispered, echoing a lie she knew he lived with, had heard small pieces of in conversation. Sasha didn't pretend to understand how hard it was to lose a child or pretend to know what that grief looked like, but she did hold a small piece of contempt for Bernard Bartlett for allowing his son to think it was his fault. Melrose had never told her that.

"I know," he mumbled.

"There was nothing you could have done," she whispered. He nodded, barely listening to her, trying to focus on anything else. His heart was pounding in his chest, his breathing thick and heavy, and his hands were shaking and fidgety. He wanted it to stop.

"This will pass. And it will still not be your fault," she said.

"Sasha, I know," he choked out, wiping his eyes, but his sight was still blurry.

"It's not your fault," she said again.

He looked up into Sasha's eyes. She didn't sway her sight from his. It was uncomfortable for a moment, being seen so clearly. For so long, all he had felt he wanted was for someone to look at him and just see him. Now, Sasha was, and he didn't know if he was worthy to present. She placed both of her hands over his that were resting on his knees. She kept looking at him.

"It's not your fault."

He started to cry, loudly, his lungs struggling to breathe in enough air to let each sob escape. His grief tore him apart; each cry a remarkable sound of pain. Sasha cried too, quietly. She was sorry Hailey had died; she was sorry that she'd shut Melrose out. Like everyone else, she had believed him when he said he was fine. They cried together, over a sister and a friend.

Hailey had drowned alone. She had asked if anyone wanted to go swimming in the quarry down the road and over the hill, but no one said yes. She had asked everyone. Davey couldn't because he was making wine. Calliste had said no because his mother was having a good day and wanted to go outside. Sasha hadn't been in the mood; she'd just gotten into a fight with her parents and was fuming alone in her room. Hailey had harassed Melrose to come the most, but he just hadn't wanted to. He had been lying on his bed, looking blankly at his phone. He'd yelled at her to leave him alone. An hour later, bored, and feeling bad about it, he put on his swim trunks and walked the ten minutes to the quarry. She was already gone.

"I think I'm drowning," Melrose mumbled after his body couldn't possibly cry anymore. Sasha nodded quickly, wiping away tears from her own face, then placing her hands back on top of Melrose's.

"I see that. Okay? I see that," she said, her voice hushed and coarse. Melrose nodded, turning his hands over and gripping her fingers in his. They had a complicated friendship, and it was all because of Hailey.

"What's this from?" Sasha asked, pointing a little to Melrose's bruised eye. He was surprised she saw it. It had almost healed.

"My dad hit me," he said.

"What?"

"Yeah, he finally did it. Just once, though. He apologized for it a few days later. He's like me, you know? Or I'm like him. I don't know," Melrose said, brushing it off. He was happy that Bernard had finally hit him. The motion had killed a lot of the tension that had been suffocating their household for too long. Now, everything was just quiet, and Melrose felt he could live a little better for now.

"I'm sorry," Sasha mumbled. He shook his head.

"Don't be," he replied. He meant it, too. Sasha moved to sit beside him, still holding her hand on top of his knee. She rested her head on his shoulder for a while, the two of them just looking out in the woods, at the sky, into the trees. They needed a few moments to breathe deeply and calm down. If you let it, it always passed.

"You're home early, aren't you?" Melrose asked suddenly, thinking about how she shouldn't be home for another week, at least. She took a deep breath then raised her head, squeezing his hand a little. She turned to look at him.

"Yeah. I got back last night," she replied. He studied her for a moment.

"Why? What's wrong?" he asked, his eyes narrowing a little. She took another deep breath. She didn't know how to start. Her hand gripped onto Melrose's tighter.

"Calliste is back, too. Something... something really bad happened to him at the camp," she started, her face down but her eyes looking up into Melrose's face, judging his reaction to the news. She knew he almost immediately guessed what had happened. It was something he had worried about from the beginning for the smallest of his friends. He took in air sharply.

"Was there an accident?" he asked coldly.

"No, it wasn't," Sasha said, knowing he could already tell. He looked back out into the woods for a moment, trying to calm down, trying to think.

"How badly?"

"Mel...it's pretty bad," Sasha whispered. She felt his muscles tense, a new wave of energy roll throughout his entire body. God, it was so easy for him to get mad. But for this, she felt no resentment. All she wanted was for Melrose to find those boys, to hurt them the same way they'd hurt Calliste.

"How did you hear about it?" he asked.

"I just... I don't know. I just felt like something happened. And I called Adam, and he told me that something had," she said, not even sure about it herself. The morning after the light show, she'd called the Martin house, but no answer. Then, she'd called Adam's cell phone, and in a rush of emotion, he'd told her everything, all the details, every single thing he knew. She'd called while he was standing at the hospital, looking through a window into the room of his son, at something that didn't resemble his son at all. For once, he had felt something all on his own. His soul hurt.

"Where is he...?"

"He's at the hospital. They moved him here. I was going to go there today. I had to find you first though, Rose," she said. It felt nice, hearing someone call him that again. People thought he hated it, having his name shortened into something feminine, but he never minded it, not once. He was a rose – dark red, and full of thorns.

"We gotta go," Melrose replied abruptly, standing up and

wincing. Without the adrenaline, he was starting to be able to take inventory of his own injuries. Sasha took a step back, looking at him. She shook her head.

"You have to clean up first. Then we can go," she said.

He nodded.

23 – CRUCIFIX

His mother was coming to get him. She was leaving tomorrow, taking the five-hour car ride across the state to come pick up her son whom she hadn't seen for an entire summer. She'd heard some stories from Sidney and talked to Davey on the phone a little bit here and there. She was thrilled it had gone so well. Vince had never been worried. He thought it was great his son got to spend some time with his wife's family. He had always liked Sidney and Nick, even though the rest of his family had ideas about Bianchis. Vince was the rebel, and he enjoyed a little freedom now and again.

Davey was thinking about how wild it was going to be to go home, to wake up in his own room alone every morning, early. He was sitting by the open window in the attic room, kicking one foot against the old nightstand that had begun to hold quite a few of his treasures. Jimmy shook his head as he put shirts he had never worn back into his suitcase, glancing back at his cousin for a moment.

"I told you, it always comes so quickly," he said. Davey didn't reply, just let out a low sigh. He was having mixed feelings, but most of them teetered toward disappointed.

"This is up north for you, isn't it?" Davey asked suddenly, looking over at Jimmy packing all of his things into one duffel bag. He hadn't brought much and had used even less than that. He nodded, looking at his cousin with lowered eyebrows.

"Yeah? You know were we live. It's like, an hour south from your city, maybe an hour and a half," Jimmy replied, tucking the last bits of clothing into his bag, zipping it up, and then throwing himself onto his bed, his body bouncing a little as he fell.

"Right, yeah," Davey said.

"Thinking about visiting?" Jimmy teased. Davey didn't reply. He was thinking about that. He wanted to maintain whatever kind of connection this was. The freedom had been amazing; an entirely new experience for him, and it wasn't just the lake or the woods. He thought about how his mother acted so claustrophobic back home all the time. If she grew up here, he knew why.

"It's sad, I know. Listen; let's go outside or something. We can walk out to that fort we made a while ago, check up on it. C'mon," Jimmy urged, standing up and waving Davey over to the steps. He breathed in deeply and followed him down the steps and out the back door of the cottage. Karen was laying out on one of the chairs on the deck, looking a lot like her mother.

"Wanna go for a walk?" Jimmy asked, hitting the bottoms of her feet to wake her from her sun-tanning trance. She lifted her sunglasses a little, peering out at her brother and cousin. She knew what kind of walk this was going to be. Jimmy always took one last long walk through the woods the day before they left. Then, he took a long swim out in the lake. To wash the sweat off, he'd say. It was a goodbye ritual. It was nice to have Davey join in on it, even if he didn't know that was what it was.

"Yeah, I'll come. Maybe we'll see a bear out there," she teased, pushing her sunglasses up to rest on top of her head. She stretched out her body before following behind the boys down the steps and across the lawn, easily finding the trailhead. They walked through the trail quite a way, Jimmy and Karen talking about something while Davey stayed right behind them, listening a little. His hand had started to ache that morning, and he was finding it hard to concentrate on other things as the throbbing became more demanding. He hadn't unwrapped the bandage in awhile, hadn't found a reason why he'd need to. He had no idea what it looked like anymore.

"Davey! Are you listening, man?" Jimmy asked, waving his hand in front of Davey's face, breaking him away from his thoughts about pain for a minute. He shook his head to regain some ground.

"Yeah, what's up?" he asked, looking from Karen to Jimmy.

"My sister here asked you a trivial question. What was your favorite part of the summer up here? I answered for you that it must be Kate. Am I right?" Jimmy asked, being ridiculous, while Karen tried not to laugh too loudly.

"I don't know," Davey replied. He truthfully didn't. Jimmy waved his answer away in the air; as if doing so made the words evaporate. They kept walking down the trail, some of it looping rather closely to the cliff on one edge of the lake, the water crashing up on the rocks and making the loudest, most inviting sounds. That day, it just sounded dangerous.

"I just can't believe it's all over, you know?" Davey said. Karen nodded, looking back at him for a moment.

"Time always goes that fast. But, we have one more day up here," she reminded. He knew that, but what was a day? It already felt like afternoon.

"Ah, look! Still standing!" Jimmy yelled out, running up to the fort that looked amazingly sturdy but quite a bit smaller than Davey remembered it, even from a few weeks ago. Karen hadn't seen it yet, and she walked into it a little amazed at their success. So did Davey. He couldn't remember how exactly they had managed to create something that was solid, strong, and would perhaps withstand a Midwestern winter. One could hope.

"Well, this was done with some purpose," Karen said, walking out of it and looking up at her brother, who was already climbing one of the trees that made up a corner of the fort. It was an easy climb, and mostly he just wanted to look at the small clearing from a higher view. He had a lot of energy to kill. During the year while in the city, he was much quieter, got into trouble that was sometimes hard to get out of. The kids at school didn't like him very much. This, Davey knew about. Everyone had told him about it, in their own ways, not realizing the others were telling him secret details too. He had pieced all the stories together. Bad blood, Nonna would say. Davey hated that thought.

He started to climb the tree that made up the other corner of their fort. He wasn't as good as Jimmy, so it took him some time. He talked a little bit as conversation went on, but mostly, he got stuck thinking about his Nonna and all of the things that made back home, home. He ran one hand through his hair, pushing it out of his face. It had gotten long and ragged. He never brushed it anymore.

There were so many expectations within his family. For a very long time, he'd thought that they were important. If you made the right choices based on all of these rules, then good things would come to you. It was how he grew up. Outsiders made poor choices, they lived immoral lives, they didn't see the value in washing your clothes every Saturday, of cooking dinner in the kitchen every weekday, or of making sure the grass was cut evenly. Spending time with Karen and Jimmy, seeing how Sidney and Nick lived, Davey was giving that standard of living he'd been taught another look. Was that really the right way to live? He didn't know anymore. But he did know that despite not cutting their grass, not washing their clothes on a schedule, going barefoot more often than not, drinking white wine, eating leftovers straight out of the fridge cold, and not going to mass even one Sunday that whole summer, that his cousins' family was doing very well.

Church.

He reached to his neck to finger the gold crucifix his Nonna had given him. It was solid gold from Italy. His finger didn't meet the gold, just the skin around his neck. It wasn't there. He looked down quickly, his heart pounding, and searched around his neck and down his shirt. The gold chain wasn't there. Neither was the crucifix, neither was the cornicello. It was gone.

"Shit," he said, his sight going dark, his heart beating fiercely in his chest.

"What? What's wrong?" Karen asked, looking up at him from within the walls of the fort. He just shook his head, jumping down from his perch and looking all over the ground. He couldn't remember the last time he'd touched it or where he had been standing when his fingers had pressed on it tightly. His stomach felt like it had dropped, a deep-rooted anxiety spreading throughout his whole body.

"What is it? Did you lose something?" Karen asked, peering over at him as he excitedly kicked up dirt and leaves, searching. She didn't understand what the big deal was, what he could even have lost out there.

"My...my cross. The crucifix. It's not around my neck anymore," he muttered. His mind was catastrophizing everything. It felt like the worst thing he could ever have done. The one thing that he had been entrusted with to keep, and he had lost it.

"Your what?" Jimmy asked, coming down from his own tree, standing next to his sister trying to understand what was so important that he needed to find.

"My gold crucifix and the chain..." he muttered still looking around, trying to expand his search. Maybe it was down the trail or in the backyard. Maybe it had fallen off in bed. Or maybe it was at the bottom of the lake. Davey cringed at the thought; it sounded horrifying to him. The guilt inside of him rose, waking up.

"Okay, alright..." Jimmy started to say, but it wasn't enough.

"You don't understand, it's important, I need it!" Davey felt the world around him start to spin. There was no way he could lose it. It felt like a slap in the face, and the way his cousins didn't seem to understand the importance of it, didn't seem to care as much as he did, was only making everything worse in his mind. Davey hadn't felt this way in a long time, and the feelings hit him full-force after being dormant for so long.

"Dude, it can't be far. It's shiny. Calm down, we'll find it. It's just a necklace..." Jimmy tried to reason, but Davey could only afford one moment to look up at him in absolute disbelief. He couldn't believe how far down the rabbit hole he'd almost gone. Suddenly, every stupid thing he'd done the past few months hit him, and he couldn't believe he was realizing all of it shirtless, barefoot, and in a stupid grove of trees.

"It's not just a necklace. You're an idiot if you think that," he mumbled, angry. Jimmy's eyes got a little wide as he held his hands up to surrender. Karen's eyes narrowed, flashing darkly.

"Alright, I'm sorry. We'll find it," Jimmy mumbled, walking down the trail a bit to look, but he wasn't really trying to find it. Karen didn't say anything, and she didn't move to look, either. Davey barely cared. He knew he wasn't going to find it. There were two sides in his mind, and the left side had been in charge all summer, had even been winning him over. Now, in all his anxiety, he felt the right side coming back up for air. It didn't make him happy.

Davey looked up and down the trail quickly, Jimmy always staying in front of him. They made it to the backyard after a lot of searching, and still, nothing. Davey felt like he was going to boil over, but he didn't want to. Karen was judging him. She held her arms crossed and walked with the two boys, uninterested in looking for the gold cross and bull's horn. She was thinking about one word Davey had said to her brother, over and over again. They came up to the house, no luck.

Davey was shaking, but he was trying to keep it all contained until he could go somewhere alone and just let it out. He hated the way both of his cousins were looking at him, but he knew he almost deserved it. Yet at the same time, there was an overwhelming flood in his mind telling him they were wrong, they couldn't possibly understand this.

"Everything okay?" Sidney asked as the three walked into the kitchen. She could see it on every one of their faces. The last walk of the summer had not gone well. Her brows furrowed as she looked at each of them, trying to decipher what had happened. Davey couldn't even talk about it. All of the responsibility, all of the expectations, all of the rules, everything he'd been built out of was crushing him.

"Davey lost his gold cross, or something," Karen said, her voice even and sure, but her face blank of expression. Sidney nodded, slowly, evaluating her daughter's answer. She turned a bit to face the boys.

"I don't think it's lost. I just saw it. On a table or something," she mumbled, walking from out behind the kitchen island and into the makeshift living room. She stood there a moment, trying to place where she'd seen the sparkle of gold before. She turned around a few times and then remembered.

"The table by the hall. Under that creepy cross made out of old nana's broomstick," Sidney declared, turning around, walking there quickly. Sure enough, there it was, resting on the top of the table, delicately placed. Davey stared at it in disbelief. It was lying there safely, put there with intention. He looked up at the broomstick made into a cross. He remembered putting it there, days ago.

It had been weeks, actually.

"Thank you," Davey mumbled, grabbing the chain and heading outside to sit by himself on the steps of the wooden porch. He felt his face turn a bitter red. He was embarrassed, and more so, he was embarrassed by how calm he felt after finally securing the chain back around his neck, feeling the familiar placement of the crucifix and cornicello.

"Yeah, no problem," Sidney said, her voice fading a little as Davey walked out the sliding glass door. They left him alone for a long time. He sat there on the bottom step, looking out at the lake, feeling the sun burn his bare shoulders. He really did need some sunscreen or some shade. After his breathing calmed down, his heart started to beat instead of pound, the ache in his hand came back, more forceful than before. Carefully, he lifted up the gauze and peeked underneath, to see his skin a deep angry red, the cut opened once more, and shiny from infection. He re-taped the bandage, not wanting to think about it.

"Hey there, what're you doing?" Nick greeted happily as he

wandered over to Davey from the neighboring lot. Next door lived an old man, and sometimes Nick went over there to help him fix things around the house. Sometimes Nick would help him during the few weekends he came up to visit the cottage over the year, but mostly, they spent their summers together, tinkering with small home projects. Davey sighed, and Nick slowed down, growing quiet. He knew the look.

"I think I caused one of those late-summer accidents, you know, the bad ones," Davey said, not looking up at him. He sighed, but not out of disappointed.

"We all make those. And besides, they're mostly a myth. I'm sure you can fix it. Nobody's dying, right?" he asked, waiting for an answer. Davey shook his head.

"Alright, then you can fix it," he said, walking past Davey and up the steps, holding onto the railing for a little support before making it all the way up and going into the house. Davey thought about that for a long time.

He felt a sting on his feet and looked down, needing to beat away the tall grass to see the culprit. There were red ants walking through the grass, hidden by its length. Davey rolled his eyes and huffed a little, picking up his feet to set them on the wood of the steps, away from the ants. He didn't think anything else could hurt. As he held the little gold crucifix in between two fingers, he felt calm, but not happy.

24 – INAUDIBLE

She wasn't sure how to feel. Sitting next to Melrose on a hard bench in a hallway filled with hospital smells wasn't new to her. The painful curiosity was new; it wasn't something she'd had the privilege of feeling in a hospital before. She was swimming in awful thoughts. She had an answer to one of her questions. Was he alive? Yes. Was he okay? She didn't know. Sasha wanted to kill those boys. She wanted to forgive them. She wanted to curl up next to Calliste and sleep forever; she wanted to carry him out and see if he could still walk.

They sat there silently for a long time. While the clock ticked by, seconds, minutes, an hour or so, Melrose spent it all controlling his breathing and hiding his bruised hand. Over the past few years, his mind had gotten very good at playing out scenes in his head like movies. He could almost see how it had went down, how easy it must have been even though he knew Calliste had tried so hard. He had one question. He wanted to know if Calliste had even once taken a step back. Sasha spent the time thinking. What did drowning feel like?

"You can see him," Adam said suddenly, appearing from nowhere, looking weathered. Neither of them knew how he was aware they were there, but they didn't question it. Adam was not one for extra gestures or the mindfulness of censorship. He also wasn't one to hold anyone back. Sasha and Melrose were there to see their friend, so he didn't see any reason why they shouldn't or why he should prepare them. If anything, Adam was coming to terms with the realization that everyone knew more about his son than he did. Sasha and Melrose simply stood up and walked down the hall to the room, while Adam sat down on their bench and covered his face with his hands and breathed.

Calliste was always pale, blond-haired, blue-eyed. In the bed, he was shades of black and purple, his hair dull and oily, eyes red. They looked at him for a long time from the doorway, not sure what to do with what was before them.

His face was swollen, particularly his right side. He had a few stiches and tape in places his skin had split open, one gash going into his hairline, where Vaseline was used to hold the hair back away from the cut and the stiches. The other side of his face was discolored but not swollen. His left arm was in a brace of some kind, pins sticking out from where his wrist was set. He was connected to a few IV bags, and his breathing was labored. All Sasha could think about was how this was only what she could see. She knew that beneath the thin sheets and hospital gown, there had to be more bruises, more broken bones. Melrose was thinking how he was going to break a chair or punch a hole in the wall in a few seconds. Suddenly, Calliste's eyes fluttered open, but only one could stay open for longer than a moment.

He looked at them, then up at the ceiling, and then finally closed his eyes again. His breathing seemed worse now that he was awake. Melrose couldn't walk forward, but Sasha had to. She couldn't be scared of this.

"Hey, kid," she said, her voice soft. He opened his eyes again. She sat on the very edge of the side of the bed; careful not to move anything that was touching him. He seemed very delicate, as if anything that moved would tear him down. He just looked at her for a few minutes.

"I saw the Northern Lights out there," he said, voice hoarse. She took in a sharp breath, looking out the window for a minute.

There were too many things running through her mind that she couldn't process.

"Did you see them, too?"

"Yeah, yeah I did," she replied. She kept her voice even. She wasn't going to cry about this yet, not here in front of the person who was black and blue. Carefully, Calliste moved his head up a little, looking over at Melrose standing in the doorway. Sasha looked at him, too, trying to see him in the way Calliste might, not the way she did.

He was tall and solid; his black jeans dirty, his grey tee shirt even more worn out. His arms were thick, and they seemed to roll as he stood there, the muscles reacting to things that were in his head, not in front of him. Mostly, his eyes were dark, set back, shifty. They weren't blind, even under his dark hair that he kept long to cover his eyes. They sparked a little at the recognition of Calliste. Melrose was a caged animal, always needing permission to exist somewhere.

"I'm pretty cool now, right? I got into a fight," Calliste asked, looking right at his friend. It was his invitation, his acceptance of who Melrose was. He took a few steps in, standing at the edge of the hospital bed.

"Man, you lost a fight," he replied, his voice a little choked up, but trying to tease him, make things somehow okay with words and not fists. For once, Melrose was starting to see the effects that fists had.

"Ah, you think. Did you see the other guy yet?" Calliste said, trying to sit up a little but not able to move at all. Mostly, his side was hurt, the broken ribs taped up the best they could be. That, and the side of his face was pulsating. He was hoping that his sight in his right eye would go back to normal. For now, there were a few too many black spots. His voice was scratchy, but the more he talked, the more like himself he sounded.

"No, I haven't," Melrose said, looking up at the ceiling for a moment. Sasha laughed, despite herself. Calliste smiled a little, too. They both knew what he meant. There was a pause in the conversation. Sasha didn't know how to put into words what she was feeling. Melrose wanted to ask questions he didn't know if Calliste wanted to answer. Although he was beaten, broken, and bruised, Calliste felt content and safe, finally. He was home, and his friends were there. It was what he had wanted all summer.

"Mel, what are you thinking?" Calliste asked, calling him out. He got very still, his eyes shifting to Sasha for a moment. She didn't give him any kind of response. She wasn't his keeper; he had to do whatever he wanted to now.

"What do you think I'm thinking?"

"I didn't step back. Not even once," Calliste replied. It was all Melrose had wanted to know. Sasha smiled a little to herself. The lesson he'd taught all of them. A step back was permission for someone else to step forward. Melrose had meant it in terms of a fight, but maybe that was just the way Sasha had taken it at the time. He nodded a little quickly, then walked over and looked out the window for a while. Calliste looked back up at Sasha.

"I drew this picture I want you to see," he said.

"You mean for my dad to see?" she asked, teasing him.

"Well, he can. But I really did mean you," he replied. It was with his things in the closet; it had made its way back after everything had been sorted out. He wasn't sure how, but it had.

"Where's Davey?" Calliste asked after Sasha nodded that she'd look at the drawing later. He couldn't talk too much. It hurt his face, and breathing was hard. He needed to recover more before trying to do anything. Melrose looked back at them from his spot at the window, the tips of his fingers hitting his palms at different intervals.

"I think he's still up north. He's coming back soon. I haven't talked to him yet, though," Sasha said. Truthfully, she hadn't known how to talk to him about it. His summer had seemingly been the best. She also knew he worried a lot. His anxiousness was something she was well in tune with, and she wanted to see Calliste, know that he was more or less okay before she reached out to Davey, hours away.

"He's back in a day. I'll talk to him," Melrose offered, looking back out the window at the view. Sasha studied him for a moment. They'd certainly worked something out in the woods, but it was far from over.

"Were you in a fight today?" Calliste asked, his voice getting lower as the visit went on. He seemed to be getting tired.

"Uh, yeah," he replied, looking back at Calliste, noticing that he was sinking, and walked over to the other edge of the bed. He grabbed a chair and moved it over, sitting on the side where his bruises were the worst. Melrose held up his hand for Calliste to see. It was bruised and the skin on a few knuckles were cracked. His face looked discolored, too, but certainly spoke to his winning the fight. Calliste studied it for a long time, and Melrose didn't know what to think. He felt shameful about his fighting.

"Did you win?" he asked. Melrose nodded.

"If you call breaking someone's jaw winning," he replied gruffly.

"Did you really?" Calliste asked, surprised. Melrose looked down at the ground.

"Yeah, I did."

"Why?"

"He said something about Hailey," Melrose replied, looking back up at Calliste, who looked back at him sadly. He missed Hailey a lot, too. More than anyone knew. But, Calliste was tired of Hailey being the excuse for all the fighting. She had been loud but never violent. In his mind she wouldn't have liked how good her brother had gotten at knocking someone out.

"How many fights did you get in this summer?" Calliste asked, pressing on. Melrose rubbed his forehead a little, feeling shifty again, wanting to get out of this conversation, but every time he looked up at Calliste's blotted red eyes, he couldn't move.

"I don't know, a lot. We don't have to talk about this right now," he said.

"His dad finally hit him," Sasha interjected. Melrose looked up at her, his eyes flashing angrily for a moment. She shrugged. It was as if he had forgotten how the four of them operated. She felt Davey's absence, and she knew if he were here, Melrose would feel better talking about this. Those two were the most at odds, yet somehow, the closest in important ways.

"He did?" Calliste asked, waking up a little, surprised again.

"Yeah, knocked me the hell out. My mom cried about it for a week straight. But it's fine. Like I told her, I'm glad about it. You can finally *breathe* in that house," Melrose replied, thinking about his mother for a moment. She had been really upset. She hadn't talked to either of them for a few days, and that had been the worst thing to happen. Kind, gentle Daisy had shut out her own family. She'd even spent one night at her mom's house, unable to look at her husband. He'd gone over there and talked to her through the window for hours, going through his thoughts and feelings like he never had before, apologizing to her, and promising he'd apologize to their son. She came back that day, but she was hardly satisfied. Melrose, just to deal with it, had told her to stop acting like he didn't know how to take a hit, and for that, she had wanted to slap him; almost had. But stopped herself and cried about that, too. She was a mess like him.

"She wants to see you guys," Melrose added after it was quiet for too long.

"Yeah, it's been awhile," Sasha mumbled.

"Why'd he hit you?" Calliste asked, unable to let it go as easily. Melrose shrugged, thinking about it. It had just seemed natural.

"I was pushing him, and he just…he just finally snapped. It's really fine, it's not like he's going to do it again," Melrose argued. Calliste made a noise, but it was hidden by a painful cough. They both looked at him intently.

"I have a broken rib and three cracked ones," Calliste said, filling them in. Sasha just nodded, but Melrose didn't say anything. He wasn't ready to talk about that. He was still feeling the need to hit something, his hands shaking as they did anytime he felt anything.

"I'm going to be fine. I know it looks bad. It kind of was," Calliste said, looking at some far away point in the hospital room, trying to block out of the memory of that night. He was having a hard time sleeping because of the nightmares.

"I bet it was," Sasha mumbled softly. He nodded.

"But I'm going to be fine. I... I really missed you guys," Calliste said, and Sasha nodded, giving his hand a little squeeze. She wanted to hug him but didn't know if she could without hurting him. A nurse came in to check on him, breaking up their moment. She was talkative, checking his IV and making sure the pain levels were managed all right. He said yes even though they weren't. The last nurse had told him he was almost maxed out on meds. She left soon after, eyeing Melrose a little bit in a way that made him want to hide his bruised knuckles and discolored eye. He wondered if there was someone on the first floor in the ER sitting in a bed with a broken jaw.

"Are you tired?" Sasha asked, looking back at Calliste and how he was fighting to keep his eyes open. He nodded half-heartedly.

"It's all the meds. You don't have to go, though..." he said, his voice shifting a little. Sasha could hear the fear in it. She knew he was trying really hard to be okay, but looking at his ruined frame, she knew he couldn't be. Hell, she wasn't.

"Close your eyes, it'll be okay," she said, squeezing his hand again. He finally let his eyes flutter down and they stayed shut. Minutes later he was sleeping, his breathing slightly easing up. Melrose and Sasha sat there a long time, just watching him sleep, thinking about different things. She let go of his hand for a moment.

"I think you should hold his hand," she said, looking at Melrose.

"What?" he asked, confused. She looked at his shaking hands. He looked down at them, too. After a moment, he carefully brought one hand up and gently touched his fingers to Calliste's, wrapping them around. It steadied them both.

She hoped he could sleep.

25 – Contemplation

His mother hadn't even been mad about the need for stiches.

Davey had found that incredible, her quiet acceptance of the infection in his hand, the calmness around her decision to stop at a hospital on the way back home and get a doctor to clean it out and then stich it up. Seeing her for the first time in a few months felt a little different. She looked like back home, but she acted like the lake house. She and Sidney had laughed and talked for a long time, committing to one another that they would talk more often and spend much more time together. Davey thought about their promise as he stared out the car window while they drove, looking at the empty fields and short bursts of trees and billboards.

Marie had spent the night, resolving to leave in the morning. Davey had been quiet all through dinner. Karen had been cold towards him, while Jimmy just looked upset about more than just one thing. Sidney didn't press it like she normally would. Instead, she and Marie talked it up, Nick sometimes in the conversation, sometimes not. He mentioned really wanting to share a beer with Vince, like the old days.

"Do you want the radio on, if you don't want to talk?" Marie asked, breaking Davey out of his headspace. He looked over at her, not even sure what she'd asked.

"The radio? Some music to fill the silence?" she asked again.

"Doesn't matter to me," he said. She left it off. He turned back to look out the window. Saying goodbye to everyone had been surreal. Sidney and Nick had each given him a big hug, saying something that was supposed to be funny as they parted ways.

"You're welcome back anytime," Sidney had said. Davey had only nodded, not sure why the weird things that were stuck in his head kept playing in a loop, keeping him from feeling anything. He touched the crucifix on his neck a lot, nervous it wouldn't be there again, worried his mother might ask about it even though she'd be the last person to do so. It had seemed like such a big deal to Davey, but he was starting to see that there was something bigger going on, and he was upset it was there; upset he had put it there.

"It was a good time, man," Jimmy had said, giving Davey a large embrace, clapping him on the back a few times. Davey had nodded.

"It really has been," he had replied. Karen had rolled her eyes as she walked up to him, giving him a much smaller and stonier hug.

"Remember that thing we talked about? Now would be a good time to think about that," she had whispered into his ear as they hugged, then pulled away from him and took a few steps back. Davey hadn't understood it then but was starting to as he looked out the window. They had finally got on the highway; all the fields and trees seemed very far away. There were too many billboards.

The first thing Davey had said to his mom once they went to the corner gas station before even getting out of town was that his hand hurt from an old cut, and it was probably infected. She took one look at it, nodded, and drove him to an ER, where the doctor had given him a very strict lesson on how to take care of an open wound and that if something this deep were ever to happen again, he needed to get stiches that day.

"It's going to leave a bit of a scar," he had said as he threaded his needle and pulled the string through Davey's inflamed skin. He watched him sew it, unable to take his eyes away from the sight.

He knew it was going to be bigger than just a "bit of a scar". He found that fitting at the time. After all the stiches were done, he looked up to see a complacent Marie; she didn't seem to mind at all.

"Did you have a good time?" Marie asked in the car, bringing Davey's gaze up from his newly stitched hand to her eyes, trying to prod into his thoughts. She was a good listener, and Davey was usually very open with her, but this time, he didn't quite know how to express what he was thinking, what he was feeling. He took a different route.

"What happened to Nick? How did he get that limp?"

"He never told you?" she asked, her eyes forward on the road, both hands gripping the wheel. She was going much faster than the speed limit.

"No, he never said."

"Well, it happened with the four of us. We were on the boat at night, and we had been drinking a little bit too much if I'm being honest with you. And Nick jumped off the side to be funny, but he hit his leg on the boat as he went down and it broke in a few different places. Shattered, actually. It just didn't heal back up the way it should have," Marie said, thinking back to how dark of a night it had been, no moon, no stars. Davey just nodded a bit, thinking, looking forward out the windshield as Marie shifted lanes and passed up a few cars.

"Was it the end of the summer?" he asked.

"It was actually our last night there," she replied. He felt like somehow he'd known that. Marie glanced over at her only child, trying to figure out what he was thinking. She almost liked that he was keeping something from her. She found it refreshing that he'd done something he thought his mother shouldn't know. She knew he was at an age where all his decisions may not be the ones she would make for him as his mother, but as an everyman, they were all ones she'd be happy to see him stand by.

"Was it a good summer, Davey?" she asked.

"It was a good summer," he assured quickly, looking out the

window again as they sailed past city after city. He spent the rest of the time thinking about kissing Kate, building forts, getting burned and then tan, bowed legs, and Jimmy's utter honesty. The anxiety didn't leave his chest when he thought about all of those things; they seemed dangerous for some reason. He could hardly believe he had spent his summer the way he had, but a small part of him smiled when he thought about it.

His dad was waiting for him when he got home. He walked outside when he saw the car pull up and gave his wife a kiss and his son a huge hug, throwing him around a little bit like he usually did. They fooled around in the yard for a few moments, wrestling and messing around. Davey hadn't realized how much he'd missed his father. Vince was always involved with everyone; so sometimes it was hard to remember just how important he really was to his father as someone separate from the rest.

"You made it! You're home! You survived! How was it?" he asked, finally slowing down for a moment, gripping onto his son's shoulder as they met Marie at the back of the car and started unloading the few bags.

"Good, yeah. It was really good," Davey said, already in his old habits.

"What's this all about?" his father asked, pointing at the bandaged hand.

"Needed a couple of stiches, it's fine though, just an accident," Davey replied and Vince nodded, shrugging it off. He didn't worry too much, unlike his son. They brought all of the bags into the house and had a cooked lunch, one where all kinds of aunts, uncles, and cousins stopped by to say hello and snack on some of the food. Davey answered all of their questions the way he used to – with enough information so that his family was satisfied – but walked away without any real understanding of what he was thinking, feeling, or what he had really done. Vince reminded him to rest up and take a shower because his Nonna wanted to see him for dinner, jokingly adding, "She wants to make sure you're still breathing and able to cut the grass." Davey nodded. Lunch took well over an hour, and after he helped his mother clean up the dishes and put the food away, he wandered into the living room and fell into the big armchair his father normally sat in, looking out the front windows into the yard and street. Nothing had changed. It was as if the last few months hadn't even happened, but Jimmy and Karen's voices were still in his head, saying things at inopportune moments.

He noticed Melrose almost immediately as he walked up the drive from the sidewalk, and his heart skipped a beat. He jumped up from the chair and met him at the door, taking Melrose by surprise. He could see the excitement in his friend's eyes, but it looked stressed. Melrose gave him a small smile as Davey walked out the front door and stood on the porch.

"Hey," Melrose said.

"Man, you look awful," Davey commented, looking him over once he was close.

"Damn, hello to you, too," Melrose huffed, passing by him and climbing onto the brick half wall that went around the Romanos' porch, sitting on it comfortably and leaning against one of the pillars. He chose not to smoke. He thought Davey might have a heart attack. Davey instead stood around nervously, not able to sit. Melrose was used to his anxiety, and mostly, he just ignored it. It was one less thing Davey felt self-conscious about.

"How was your summer? You look a little different," Melrose said, noting the longer hair, the tan skin, and the bandaged hand.

"By your standards, I think you're the one who looks awful," he continued. Davey shrugged, hiding his bandaged hand for a moment.

"It was good, it was fine," he replied. Melrose raised an eyebrow, really wanting a cigarette, but keeping his hand away from his pocket.

"Well, which is it? Good? Or fine?"

"It was good, then it was fine," Davey mumbled, finally sitting down on the porch swing. It was uncomfortable, and he wanted to sit up on the cement, but that wasn't right.

"What happened to make it fine?" Melrose asked. He was good at playing the game. People didn't get it. The two of them seemed so different, lived such different lives, yet underlying it all were the same feelings, the same motivators. Their relationship was one of giving a hand to the other at every other turn.

"I said something stupid to my cousins," he replied. It was much more than that, but in his mind, he'd boiled it all down to that one moment, though he knew his feelings had been mounting the closer it came to the end of summer. He couldn't believe he was back, looking at the street and not a lake. He looked at Melrose. He had her eyes.

"Davey Romano said something stupid? Well, I just don't believe it," Melrose said, teasing him a little bit, pushing his hair out of his eyes. Davey watched him as he did it, looking at all the different color variations on his skin, bruises healing in various time frames.

"It was just...so different there, and nice? It was really nice. And then when I had to come back I just started getting all..." he stopped for a moment, motioning to his chest, trying to find words to explain the tightness, the pounding. Melrose nodded, acknowledging that he knew the feeling Davey was trying to describe.

"I just started feeling all weird, and I lost this for a moment, and I snapped," he said, bringing out the crucifix from under his shirt to show Melrose. His eyes widened. He knew the value behind the little gold cross, the silly little bull's horn.

"How'd you lose it?"

"I took it off and forgot."

"You took it off?"

"Yeah," Davey said. Melrose couldn't believe it, but he was almost proud of his friend. Maybe not everything he'd done that summer had stuck, but at least some of it was still in him. He needed to loosen up, get off the street more often than he did.

"Well, you got it back, man. It's fine now. Did you make up with your cousin?" Melrose asked. It was not something he was terribly experienced with, but something he knew was important. The people in his life either hated him or made excuses for him and carried on.

"Not really," Davey replied, regretful.

"Why not? That's like, your specialty," Melrose commented, and Davey rolled his eyes, looking out into the yard. His uncle's car was parked in the street, so it must have still been running. It surprised him that his uncle had done it all on his own.

"It is not," Davey said, a little annoyed. Melrose shrugged.

"I don't know about that, sir. You apologize to me all the time, for things I do and you aren't even involved in," Melrose said, still teasing him, trying to draw him out. Sometimes making him mad was a good override to his inhibitions.

"Listen, I just didn't know what to say. It was just so different out there, with them. I couldn't possibly do what I did there and get away with it here," Davey replied, waving his hands to encompass the whole street. There were always eyes on him, everywhere; they were probably watching him right now, talking to a kid who didn't look like he was from around there at all.

"Yeah? You think?" Melrose asked. Davey was quiet.

"Just think about that, all right? I know it isn't as easy as that. But just, calm down a little, loosen up. I know it isn't that easy. Just think about it," Melrose repeated, turning his own head to look out at the street, dotted with nice houses and clean-trimmed lawns. He felt the pressure too; it was everywhere.

"What did you do this summer? Sign up for cage fighting or something?" Davey asked, changing the conversation. He would think about everything, but not in that moment. He needed a change of focus.

"Pretty much," Melrose laughed. Davey waited for more.

"You guys all left me, alright? I did some stupid things. Sasha already read me the Riot Act, so you don't have to," he said. Davey perked up at the sound of that.

"The Riot Act? What *is* that?" he asked, thinking back to when he'd heard it before, over the summer. It made something stir inside him; to see his life tie in with summer and not have them stand separate.

"Just like, all the consequences of my actions. She gave me a pep talk, too, so you're off the hook for that as well," he replied. Davey thought about Sasha; he missed her a lot. She was funny and witty, and she made him feel like he didn't owe anyone anything, ever. He liked that about her.

"What kind of pep talk? Stop fighting, we all love you, register for trade school already?" Davey asked, teasing him back. Melrose smiled at that, resting his head on the pillar behind him. He thought about it for a second, and then in a moment of good faith, said, "No, more like, stop fighting, we all love you, I'm sorry your sister is dead, but it's time to move on. That kind of thing."

Davey thought about Hailey. He did a lot, mostly during mass, or whenever he was in a church. He thought about when she and Sasha were together. They had all kinds of inside jokes, secret understandings. They were so funny when they were together, always dragging everyone into some weird situation that Melrose would have to dig them out of, but it was never bad. He'd thought about her a lot out at the lake, how easily swimming came to him, and what it would be like to feel trapped by the water, taken down by it. How did it happen?

He missed her.

He wanted to miss her.

Pieces of him did, but they had never been very close. Never spent time alone. Her death had brought to life his worse anxieties, but he had lived through it. In a way, she had set him free. She had given that part of herself to him, but he felt he hardly deserved it. Every time he looked into Melrose's tortured eyes, watched Sasha grow quiet, or saw Calliste try to fit in, he felt a worse feeling than his anxiety. He felt guilt.

"Yeah, that's a good speech," Davey finally said, giving his words time to settle in the air. Melrose nodded. It had been.

"You didn't get arrested, did you?" Davey asked, a small smile on his lips.

"I didn't call you for bail, did I?" Melrose asked, playing along with his joke for a moment. Davey just shrugged.

"I missed you, man," Davey said, and Melrose nodded. As had he.

"Yeah, we all did," Melrose mumbled, starting to think about the real reason he had come to hunt Davey down before he had even had time to unpack his suitcase. Davey sensed the shift in his face, wondering what it was, what had happened. His heart started to beat hard when Melrose finally looked up at him, his face calm and serious.

"What's wrong?"

"Everyone's okay, honestly. But something happened to Calliste his last week of camp. Some guys....they messed him up pretty badly," Melrose said, trying to be calm, trying to say what had happened and nothing more. He sat on his hands to keep them from shaking. That always made Davey more nervous.

"Messed him up?" Davey asked, half not understanding, half not wanting to.

"They beat the shit out of him, man. He's at the hospital here. Will be for another day or so I think, then he can go home," Melrose said, looking at Davey who wasn't looking at him. He was so upset; his pounding heart started to make him feel taller, more solid, and he wanted to strike out. He wondered if that was how Melrose felt all the time.

"How did you find out? He's okay?" Davey asked.

"I mean, he's not okay. But he has a few cracked ribs, a broken wrist, and a swollen face. He'll be okay," Melrose replied, not looking at Davey anymore, either. He appreciated how so far, no one had come by. It was a rare occurrence at the Romano house. It was good for it to just be the two of them sitting on the porch in the shade, talking honestly. They both needed that.

"How did you find out?" Davey asked again. Melrose sighed.

"Sasha. Somehow she knew about it, felt it in the air or something. You know, typical weird Sasha shit. Anyways, she called Mr. Martin the next day, and he told her about it. She came home a week early from her grandparents' and found me," Melrose replied, going through it in his head. He hadn't questioned too much about how Sasha had known to call. It didn't really matter, he was just grateful she'd come home early and Calliste was going to be okay. Melrose knew a lot about not being okay, but still being okay.

"He's at the hospital?" Davey asked, though he knew the answer. Melrose nodded. He didn't mind repeating it.

"Yeah. You should go see him. It's kind of rough in there, but you know Calliste, cracking jokes and being an idiot, still," Melrose said, laughing a little, but mostly coughing. Davey let out a rush of air; he couldn't even believe it.

"Okay, let's go," Davey said, standing up quickly.

"Okay," Melrose replied.

Davey grabbed his shoes from inside the garage and laced them up quickly and headed down the street with Melrose. He left without telling anyone, and they were gone a long time. He missed dinner.

26 – Matters

The drive home was hard.

Every bump in the road, every turn made his side hurt, sending a sharp and sudden pain through his entire body, making his head spin. It was also hard because his father was trying very, very hard to be kind, considerate, and nurturing. It was coming off as very forced and very uncomfortable, but Calliste still appreciated the effort. He didn't want his dad to feel badly about what had happened to him; it wasn't his fault. Calliste didn't blame anyone. He didn't have it in him.

"I'm sorry, I really am trying to drive slow," Adam mumbled, upset he couldn't do this right. He was thinking a lot of things, but mostly, he couldn't possibly understand how he had failed so badly. He had failed his son; he had failed his wife. The rest didn't matter at all to him; they were the only two people in his world.

"It's fine, Dad, really. We're almost home," Calliste said through clenched teeth, as the car kept moving, hitting another unexpected bump. He was very good at not making any noise. None of his pain escaped out of his lips.

"It's far from fine," Adam mumbled, more to himself than to Calliste. They finally reached the house, and Adam helped Calliste up the steps and into the house and up to his room. All he wanted to do was lie down. His head was spinning, his side ached, and his eye was still almost swollen shut. He took a couple of pain meds before falling into bed, lying there looking up at the ceiling. It felt surreal to be home, in his big corner room with lots of windows. It was so quiet in there, so comforting. Finally, he felt so far away from it all. His bed felt so lush and soft and big; he almost felt happy.

"Are you doing alright?" Adam asked, coming back into the room to check on him one last time. Calliste nodded as best he could.

"Your mother wants to see you. But maybe…rest first," Adam said, and Calliste nodded again. He didn't think he could get back up, let alone walk to her room and talk to her. He felt bad, knowing she was mostly at the will of everyone around her, but he felt that way, too, most of the time.

"I will," he mumbled, drifting into sleep but continually waking up every few hours. His side hurt so badly, and so did his face. His wrist, for now, was held tightly together by a few pins. His mind started to drift to seeing his friends at the hospital. They had all been so nice, so normal about it. He appreciated that. Nothing had been normal for a really long time. As he kept waking up, his mind traveled back to little pieces and moments of the whole thing. He didn't remember all of it; it wasn't linear. He didn't know who had found him or how they had brought him back to camp. His first memory was of being loaded into an ambulance with Sergeant Adams yelling loudly before getting in to ride with him to the first hospital.

"It matters what you know you did!" he'd said. Calliste hadn't seen to whom, but he could have guessed as much. He felt like he saw Lukas's face somewhere but was content to never see it again. He pushed him far from his mind.

There were pieces of the ride, but he had been in and out. Every time he had opened his eyes, Sergeant Adams was looking down at him, upset. Calliste thought that the man was crying, but it didn't seem right. He didn't think that was how it should have gone, but maybe that really was what had happened.

"I know you aren't," he had said in the back of the ambulance. Calliste had wanted to back up from his words, annoyed by them, feeling like they were another punch in the face. They were supposed to be comforting, but they weren't.

"Would it matter if I was?" he'd mumbled.

"What, what did you say?" Adams had asked, leaning in towards Calliste, worried he was talking about more pain. The fact was, Adams had never seen someone with a child's face so murderously beaten. Calliste had held barely any life in him. He'd been in the meadow almost too long.

"Would it matter if I was?" he repeated, trying to pronounce the words so Adams could understand what he was saying. He sat back for a moment, looking out the back windows, thinking about it.

"No, it wouldn't," he finally said, in a meaningful way. Calliste didn't remember anything else after that. There was a lot of light at the hospital, a lot of nice voices, a lot of pain, and a lot of relief. The best was just fading into darkness, everything washing away. He could almost hear the creek again.

Calliste found himself thinking about how when he'd woken up from the surgery on his wrist, his father had been in the room, staring at him, his own eyes red. Sergeant Adams had been there, too, his hand on his shoulder, talking to him. Calliste hadn't heard much of the conversation or made a lot of sense of it, but he did remember thinking that it was funny how Adam and Adams were in the same room together. It was probably for the best. He always knew that the two of them would get along. He had fallen back asleep almost immediately. He'd made no real effort to stay awake at either hospital.

He woke up thirsty and looked over to see a glass of water on his nightstand. Carefully, trying not to upset his cracked ribs, he leaned over and reached for the glass. He sipped a little but was leaning too far back in bed and ended up choking on it, spitting it back into the cup and trying to breathe steadily for a moment to ease the pain.

"Ah," a small gasp of pain finally left his lips. It didn't matter, though. He was alone, the house was silent, and the night was dark. Putting the glass back on the nightstand, he started to think about Hailey. He'd had a crush on her from the first day he had met her, and it had only grown as they got older and became friends throughout the years. He hadn't told anyone that he liked her. Sasha would be annoyed, Melrose would have kicked his ass, and Davey would have worried about everyone else finding out. She knew, though, he thought. Sometimes, she'd hold his hand, or share a private joke, or come over to have lunch with his mom and him. He liked her; she had been a very sweet, beautiful person.

He really started to think about Hailey. It helped get his mind off the pain and bad thoughts that ruined his dreams and startled him awake. He wanted to remember her, how she had really been, not how everyone wanted to remember her as each year passed that she was not a part of. It was funny, though, because Calliste always noticed how she was still affecting things, even though she wasn't there. She was gone for the summer, forever.

Hailey hadn't liked violence, but she did enjoy confrontation. She was sharp and sarcastic and liked to call people out whenever she thought they were in the wrong. It didn't matter if it was a gas station, a grocery store, or the dog park. She was loud and messy, and you couldn't help but fall into that. He thought it was funny that Melrose fought so much on her behalf because she would never have liked that about her brother.

She had also been a risk taker, but stupidly. It drove Davey insane most of the time. She wasn't very good at anything kinesthetically, yet she took leaps that Olympians wouldn't have braved. She always thought it was funny, but it never was. She liked to put people on edge; it was something she'd picked up from her father. It didn't always go over well. If someone tried to correct her, she'd put her hands over her ears and walk away, making both of them feel stupid. He had never known why she did that or if she thought it ever led to anything good.

She and Sasha always tested the limits. They'd see how far they could go with anything, and when Sasha would stand still, Hailey would still want to peer over the edge. She was wild that way, but it was because she was curious. She had always wanted to do so much. Travel all around the world. She said often that it was her goal to go to every single country the world held within it. She didn't care if she had to go alone; she wanted to go. That was her mantra until the end.

Calliste wanted to know what she would do in this situation. Would she want to kill the boys, like Melrose did? Possibly forgive them, like Sasha? Or would she have no solid opinions about any of it, like Davey? He figured she'd have her own unique way to think about it, talk about it. She was always saying bizarre things and drawing little stars on people's arms. Her mother even had a small star tattooed on her wrist on the one-year anniversary of her death. She was tired of her daughter not drawing them anymore. He thought about that for a long time.

The day before had been good.

"Hailey!"

Sasha remembered yelling out her name to get her attention as she walked out of the woods and into the clearing, the second person to get to the old house. Hailey had always been first. Sometimes, if Sasha closed her eyes, she could still envision the smile Hailey would always flash, truly happy and excited to see her best friend, her confidant in all things. She had told Calliste those memories one late night when it was just the two of them on his rooftop, the sky covered in clouds.

They had talked for a long time before Calliste showed up, always with a nervous pace and a little red in his cheeks. His eyes sparkled around her, but her eyes did the same around him, too. Davey and Melrose used to show up together, and that day had been no exception. Melrose had that same smile on his face as Hailey, laughing about messing with some guys in the parking lot of the convenience store while Davey was inside, buying an iced tea in quarters and dimes. Davey had shaken his head at the telling of the story, and how by the end of it, they'd had to run off quickly together to avoid the guy and his friends. That was all before Melrose's antics had turned violent, his words turned vulgar.

They had talked, climbed a few trees, and sat around the empty fire pit. After awhile, they'd wandered off, heading into town, to the dollar cinema. It was their fifth time seeing *Guardians of the Galaxy*, but they mostly came for the snacks, the air-conditioning, and the cute girl who worked the popcorn machine.

Hailey had liked to mischievously throw pieces of popcorn at the heads of other patrons, then pretend it wasn't her, or worse, scold one of the boys openly as if they'd done the deed. She'd picked on Davey the most, but she always let Melrose handle those who couldn't take the joke. Davey admired her adventure, her ability to just exist and act and feel no remorse for simply taking up space. Davey felt maybe he was the only one who felt that way to begin with. Sasha thought her jokes were funny.

"Hailey, hey. Do you want some of this?" Calliste remembered whispering during the middle of the movie. She took a Snowcap from the box, nodding, and then had turned her attention back to the screen. Calliste just liked to say her name, feel her eyes focusing on only him, even for just a moment, even to just offer up some of his candy. Sometimes, she'd hold his hand lightly in the darkness of the theater. They never talked about it, but they both felt something about it.

When the movie had ended, and Melrose had finally finished talking to the girl at the popcorn machine, they had walked across town to their favorite ice cream stand. It was across the street, and Hailey had run out first.

"Jesus, Hailey!" Davey had yelled, his voice thick as a car flew by what seemed only moments after Hailey had safely made it to the other side. She'd laughed, giving him a tight hug for a moment, assuring him she was fine and safe. He kept his arm wrapped around her shoulder for a minute longer as they walked up to the line. She did it to steady him; he did it because he wanted to keep her safe.

They ordered, mint for Sasha, black cherry for Melrose, vanilla for Davey, Superman for Calliste, and double chocolate fudge for Hailey. They ate their ice cream in the field adjacent to the little stand, sitting amongst the tall grasses and talking about the up coming school year. Sasha distinctively remembered arguing about what the better notebook to have was – one-subject or five-subject. They were all so young. Sasha and Melrose had fought so hard in that debate that eventually Hailey got bored and started looking for snakes. Calliste went to help her. They were gone a long time.

"Hailey! Let's go!" Melrose had shouted, when the sun was starting to set. She came up from the hill, a small garter snake in her hands. Melrose had waved it off, afraid of the little legless creatures. She disappeared again, coming back with Calliste, and not the snake. They all trampled through the field to a trail that led to the old house again once more. It always seemed like they'd start their days there and finish them there, too.

They started a fire, Davey building it up with Calliste's help, Hailey cheering them on. It was roaring and ready for s'mores by the time the sky was orange, the sun all but disappeared below the horizon. They ate their last sugary meal while telling ghost stories and pointing out constellations. Hailey was almost as good as Calliste, but he always knew at least one more than she did.

It was late before they all headed home; sure they'd see each other again soon. Hailey had gotten off her stump, stretching high enough for everyone to hear her back crack before she was ready to walk home with her brother.

No one had looked back.

The day before had been good, but it was the day after that consumed everyone's minds, stealing away the good thoughts. The day before wasn't something anyone had remembered, but there were many days after that no one could forget. Everyone remembered the day Sasha had disappeared for hours upon hours, her parents calling around asking for her, their minds racing with the unimaginable. It had been storming so heavily all day. The boys were the ones to find her, dripping wet from the rain, cold and curled up on Hailey's place by the fire pit. She wailed the whole way home as Melrose carried her. He remembered Frank thanking them quietly while Vivienne was upstairs with Sasha, trying to warm up her daughter and dry her tears.

They remembered the day Melrose broke his hand punching holes into the sides of the old wooden house. He wouldn't stop, and he couldn't see. All that he felt surrounding him was white noise and red vision. Davey had to get physical with him. The three of them sat around in the emergency room with him, hearing him curse as the doctors reset his hand and put a cast on. They'd watched as the tension in that room started to grow between Melrose and his father, and they watched as Daisy shook and grew small, quiet.

They remembered the day Davey had a panic attack that lasted for hours. It had seemingly come out of nowhere; growing out of the quietness that now bounded their group. It was hard to listen to him gasp for air and try to keep his body from trembling uncontrollably. They'd each sat with him, held his hands in theirs, tried to get him to breathe slower, calm down, see that the world wasn't actually spinning out of control. It hadn't worked. After awhile, Calliste had gone to get Marie, and they all listened as her soft voice calmed her son and brought him out of a panic he couldn't escape alone.

They'd watched the sparkle die from Calliste's eyes as he watched them and stayed silent. Sasha didn't have it in her to talk about it, so they started to watch sunsets silently. Davey couldn't focus, so he had pushed away anything that made him feel he had to. Melrose was too angry to care about what the small, blond kid wanted. Together, they had let Hailey slip away in their own ways. And for that, they paid the price.

The day before had been good, but two years of grief had washed it away.

He started to cry, alone in his bed, all bruised and bandaged, hurting. Everything hurt. He had yet to cry about it, yet to feel anything about it. In the meadow, he had been scared. In the hospital, he had wanted to let it all go. Here at home, he just wanted to be quiet and not make waves, but he couldn't. He hurt, he was hurt, there were things that happened that hurt very deeply, and he was beginning to feel them all at once.

His face throbbed, his side ached. His missed Hailey. He felt terribly about his mother, about her stroke, about how she was living in a quiet house. He loved his father but hated how mechanically he looked at everything. He hated how Jack Turner had ruined him because he thought being gay was weak. And Calliste hated how the one place at camp that he had thought would be his sanctuary turned out to be the worst place for him to ever be. It hurt, and he cried for a long time about all of it before finally fading to sleep.

It was almost noon before he woke up again. For the first time, he'd slept deeply and soundly, and with the light streaming in through the windows, he felt better. A lot better, almost happy, almost content, and almost safe. He got out of bed and immediately went to the bathroom and showered. It was his first real shower in quite a few days, and even though it took a long time and a bit of maneuvering with the cast, he managed to make it work and felt better than ever after drying off and putting on clean clothes that had never left his house. His body ached, but it was slowly not hurting anymore. He took a few pain meds and went downstairs to eat something. It was almost two in the afternoon.

"You look better, feeling alright?" Adam asked, coming down from his office when he heard the sounds of kitchen cabinets opening and closing. Calliste nodded, both of his eyes open for the first time.

"Yeah, I slept well and took a shower, basically back to new," he said, trying to be light. Adam nodded, making a small sound in his throat as he watched his son try to fry eggs with one hand. He didn't offer to help; he knew he wanted to do it on his own. He would if things were normal. Adam was trying to bring things back to normal, but to a time before the house had gotten quiet. It was what he had resolved was best after having to face a horrible reality alone in his office, both his wife and his son crying quietly to themselves. He hadn't made the best choices. Now, he was going to.

"If you're all set, I'm going to finish up some work in my office. Catch up on some things from the past few days," his father said, looking at him genuinely as he spoke. Calliste nodded, sure of himself.

"Yeah, please do. I've got this. I'll let you know if I start burning the house down or something," he replied and Adam let out a little chuckle that time.

"I would hope so. Okay…" he said, trailing off a little.

"I love you, kid. You know that?" Calliste didn't say anything for a moment, frozen in place; letting those words sink into his skin. He wanted them to stay there forever. He hadn't heard them in a long time.

"I know. You, too," Calliste said, his voice soft and quiet. Adam didn't say anything, just nodded and walked slowly up the staircase back to his office. Calliste made his eggs with those words in mind the entire time.

As soon as he had finished eating, he heard a timid knock on the door. It was the standard two loud knocks and one softer, yet this time it was more like two soft knocks and one almost nonexistent.

"Hey," Calliste greeted, opening up the door to see Sasha standing there, wearing her loose green cotton pants and a cropped white tee, her black hair braided back in the most intricate design he'd seen yet. She seemed surprised to see him at the door, but smiled warmly a few moments after.

"You're up! Walking around! How're you feeling?" she asked, walking in as he ushered her, following him into the kitchen. He still walked slowly, but he walked.

"Not terrible," he replied, setting his dish in the sink. She looked around a little bit, trying to see if anything had changed over the summer. It hadn't. She looked at him; he might have been taller than she was now.

"I see you showered. That's a relief," she teased, and he rolled his eyes at her.

"Sorry I was so offensive to be around," he replied, sitting down at the counter next to her while she stood, simply leaning against the granite.

"I mean, it was almost getting to be unbearable," she said.

"Yeah, my dad threatened to hose me off in the yard last night when I finally got back," he replied and she laughed lightly at the thought of that. She walked over to his fridge and peered into it, settling for an apple to munch on. She turned back to look at Calliste, hopping up on the counter and sitting on it, leaning against the side of the fridge.

"So, how are you doing? For real, though," she said, looking at him intently.

"I'm getting a lot better, honestly," he replied.

"I see that," she said, looking him over.

"But how are you?" she asked, moving her hand up to her head and tapping the side of it with one finger. He looked away from her for a moment, thinking about it. Last night had been a hard time, but with the morning, things were better. He just had to go through it sometimes.

"Better, yeah. It's a process, I guess," he said softly, thinking about it, thinking about what it would take.

"If you ever want to talk about anything, you know I'm around," she said, and something about that struck him. She was always around. Even when he had felt so alone out at camp, so far away from everyone, the distance hadn't meant that he didn't have friends, didn't have people to write to, talk to. He realized he had been isolating himself more than anyone else had been.

"It was weird, being away from the three of you for so long," he finally said, trying to put into words what he was feeling. She nodded. She'd thought she'd needed space from them, time to think, time to grow and do something new. There was nothing wrong with doing something new, but she hadn't needed distance from them to do that.

"I know what you mean. I thought I needed space, but that's not at all what I was after in the end," she said, contemplating her last night there, on the beach with Gillian. She didn't regret that at all. She still owed Gillian a phone call.

"Did you have a good summer?" he asked. She nodded.

"For the most part, yes. It was a different perspective, that's for sure," she replied, smiling a little bit. It made Calliste happy to see her thinking about something fondly. He certainly hoped everyone had something good to think back to from the last few months.

"Hey, I have to go up and see my mom for a bit. You can just hang out if you want," he said and she nodded.

"Of course, no problem. Tell her I say hello," she said, glancing up at the steps that went up into the house. Sometimes Alice wanted company, other times she didn't. It just depended on the day, like so many other things. He walked up the steps slowly and crept up to her door, pressing on it a little bit before knocking. He was surprised to see light. The window shades were up.

"Hey, Mom," he greeted quietly, walking in carefully. She was sitting in her armchair in the corner of the room, just looking outside at the bright sun warming up their backyard. She looked up slowly at her son and then stayed quiet for a really long time. She was thinking about a lot of things, trying to connect them all in her mind. The bruises, the cast, his face, his eyes. All of it was so different than the Calliste who had said goodbye to her at the beginning of the summer. Though, she had little grasp on how quickly or slowly time passed.

"Are you okay?" she asked, her voice getting a little choked up. He nodded, sitting on the edge of the bed, keeping a distance between them.

"I really am," he said.

"And you're back now, for good?" she asked. He nodded again. She looked upset.

"Your father and I talked a long time about…all of it," she said, waving her arms to the big empty space in the room, a place where she could envision the way that her son's summer had turned out, like a play with an imaginary cast. He just nodded again. He felt like she wanted to talk more so he stayed quiet, letting her have the time that she needed to form her words coherently. His discolored skin said all it needed to.

"I am so sorry this happened," she whispered.

"Don't blame yourself," Calliste said, reading her mind, knowing exactly what her thoughts were when it came to things like this. She was always upset that she couldn't be around more, couldn't talk more, and make choices to be a part of things.

"I'm back now, and I'm good, okay? And this...this is okay. It's just something to work through, to get through. I don't know. I'm talking to Sasha, to Melrose. To Davey. Okay? So I'll be fine," he said, trying to assure her. She thought about his friends a lot.

"I'm here for you, too, okay? I love you," she said, her eyes staring intently at him. Her speech was too slow for her mind, which was still always racing.

"I know, I love you, too," he said. For a moment, they were both quiet, thinking about things, looking out the window. His mother sighed after awhile. He looked up at her, and she thought about what she wanted to say before she did.

"It seems like a beautiful day outside," she said.

"It is," Calliste replied, looking back out, seeing the sun shine brightly over the woods that were far off in the distance.

"Sasha's here. Do you want to go outside?" he asked, cautiously, not imposing anything on her or sounding too anxious about it. She thought about it, wondering if she really felt like she wanted to. She did, though. She'd been thinking about it all day. She missed feeling the grass and smelling the flowers.

"Yeah, that would be nice," she said. Calliste moved slowly but deliberately. He stood up, helping her stand with both hands, and staying close to her as they walked out of the room, down the hall, and down the staircase. Sasha was sitting at the counter, looking through an old magazine at the table in the kitchen. She looked up quickly at the noise and gave the two of them a warm smile.

"Are we going out?" she asked, and Calliste nodded. Sasha

moved slowly but deliberately. She walked to the living room and unlocked the sliding glass door, opening it up wide and setting up some chairs on the grass in time for Calliste and Alice to make their way out and into the lawn. She sat down quickly and took a moment to look around before she said anything about it.

"This is nice, thank you," she said quietly. The three of them sat outside for a while, looking out at it all. It wasn't so scary when they were together. Nothing bad was going to happen to Alice, no one was coming for Calliste, and for Sasha, she just reveled in the fact that there were more people out there in the world who cared about her then just Hailey.

"Sasha, how was your summer? Didn't you go to your grandparents' place?" Alice asked her after some quiet and acclimating. She hadn't been outside in awhile.

"It was really nice, for the most part. They have a house by the ocean, so I spent a lot of time there. It was…a different perspective I guess. I'm glad to be home, though," she replied. Alice nodded. She was happy everyone was home, too. They sat out there for a long time, talking a little but about nothing too serious. Eventually, Adam came out with cut-up apple slices and caramel sauce, and that was their dinner out there on the lawn. He was trying, too. The Martin household was full of people who were trying but never quite making it high enough to count. Maybe it would be different in the fall.

Alice got tired as the sun started to set so Adam helped her back inside to sit in his office with him while he finished working. Sasha and Calliste raided the freezer for ice cream and went up to his bedroom and then like old times, climbed out his bedroom window and sat on the roof, watching the sunset and eating ice cream with two spoons.

"I'm glad you came over today," Calliste said, his face colored orange from the heavy sun that was painting the sky a variety of deep, bright colors. It made his bruises look far away, and Sasha liked the contrast.

"Well, I'm glad you're back," she said, taking a bite of the ice cream.

"Is Melrose going to be alright? Davey told me you talked to him," Calliste said, looking over at her, trying to gauge her reaction. He knew it had always been her responsibility to clean up after the Bartlett kids, but looking at her, he saw how hard that was. She did a lot, for everyone.

"I don't know. I think he's okay, for now. I did talk to him. He just... I don't know, nobody tells him he's good, you know?" she said, fumbling for words. Calliste knew exactly what she meant and exactly how Melrose worked. The only thing was, nobody seemed to listen to anything unless Sasha yelled it.

"I think we can do that," he said, and she hugged her knees, hopeful.

"Have you seen Davey yet?" he asked her. She shook her head.

"No, I haven't. Maybe tomorrow," she said.

"He's kind of weird. Rose said he took off his cross for awhile at the lake, and now he's having some kind of existential crisis about it," Calliste said, laughing a little. It still hurt his ribs a bit, but it was more of an ache instead of a sharp pain. Sasha looked over at him, an eyebrow arched.

"Is that a direct quote?"

"Yeah, pretty much. Davey didn't look happy to have it summed up like that, but I don't think Rose cared too much," Calliste replied, helping himself to some of the ice cream before it turned into a melted puddle. It was pretty hot out on the roof, but it didn't bother him to sweat up there. It was nice to sit, eat something cold, and watch the sunset. It was nice to know exactly how it would go down, what the colors would be and how they would layer upon one another.

"I don't know about that. Melrose and Davey are like this, more than either of us realize," she said, crossing her fingers in front of his face to show him just how tight they were. Calliste shrugged, already knowing. Sasha had said it before.

"Always at odds, yet the two that need each other the most? I think you mumbled that when you were drunk once," Calliste teased as Sasha rolled her eyes, laughing at the memory of a night that only came in slices.

"Oh, whatever," she said.

"We should all hang out tomorrow, at the old house?" Calliste said, his voice getting quiet. Sasha nodded. She wanted that more than anything. They quietly watched the sunset as it went the rest of the way down, just thinking about their own things for a while. When the sun left, the moon and stars came out, and they lay down on their backs and looked up at the constellations, talking about them a little here and there. It was a beautiful, clear night.

"Do you remember that day... the day before..." Calliste started to say, but found himself trailing off, not exactly sure how to bring it up or how to describe it. Sasha turned her head to look at him, studying his face for a moment, then turned her gaze back to the night sky before answering him.

"Yeah, I remember the day before it all," she replied. She really did, it had come back to her that summer, slowly and in pieces, but sitting on the roof with Calliste that night, she could have sworn it played like a movie in her mind.

"Do you remember the last thing she said that night?" Calliste asked.

"I don't, no," Sasha replied. They were quiet for a long time after that, trying to think of what it might be. Both thought they might know, but didn't have the gumption to talk about it anymore after that.

"Thanks for helping get my mom out of the house today," Calliste said, breaking the silence, pushing through the moment.

"Always," she said. They looked into the sky longer, thinking about the same thing for the rest of the night.

27 – UNITED

"*Come si potrebbe perdere la cena!*" Nonna shouted as Davey walked in the backdoor of her house. He'd never really been the object of her anger, though he certainly wasn't a stranger to it. He just took a deep breath in, piecing a few of her words together to understand what she was saying. She mumbled some other words under her breath, but he tried to push those aside. He just stood in her kitchen while she sat at the table rolling meatballs.

"I know I missed dinner. I'm really sorry about that. My friend got hurt, though, he was at the hospital, I had to go see him," he said. She rolled her eyes, focusing on the food in front of her. That was what she always did, turned her attention to the food.

"That friend of yours who's always fighting? I knew he was trouble," she mumbled, about to go on, but Davey stopped her.

"No. Calliste. Some guys beat him up really badly, actually," he said, trying to make her feel a little uncomfortable for jumping to conclusions. She only mumbled in Italian a little longer, thinking about his strange group of friends. She wished he would spend more time with his cousins on their street. They were good people who she could control. She didn't like not having the final say.

"Well, that's too bad. But, you don't leave people waiting. You should tell them. It's only the right, responsible thing to do. Good men tell the women in their lives what they are doing," she said, and as she talked, Davey scrunched his eyes together, rubbing his temple. He was tired of hearing about these things. He was picturing Jimmy listening to this conversation, or Karen, or Kate. It was ridiculous. They'd take a stand.

"Nonna, I'm sorry I kept you waiting, but I just didn't have time to tell anyone what was going on. It wasn't that kind of situation," Davey said. He was making her angry by continually giving her reasons for his actions instead of just going along with whatever she said, like he used to. She glared up at him, narrowing her own eyes.

"Just who do you think you are? One of those Bianchi? I knew going out there all summer was a bad idea, Marie should have known better and Vince, of all people..." she said, but Davey shook his head again, stopping her from saying another word about either of his parents, or his cousins she refused to acknowledge.

"Really, they aren't bad people. They are just people. I had a really good time out there; I learned a lot. And my mom's really good, too, and she tries to make everyone happy around here. And my dad loves her, okay? He has for like, twenty years. This is just the way that everything is," he said. His voice didn't grow loud, but he said his words with conviction. Nonna didn't say anything to him; she looked down at her meatballs, rolling them more vigorously than before. The backdoor slammed in that moment, some of the younger cousins sneaking in for treats. Her expression immediately changed as she hugged her youngest grandchildren and walked them over to her candy jar. She didn't look at Davey, but for some reason, it was a relief. He wanted her to be mad at him for a while, to understand that he wasn't perfect. The weight of being the best was too much.

"*Ciao,*" he said quietly, walking out the back door, his goodbye lost in the chattering voices of his cousins as they snacked on some chocolate. He walked across the lawn and down the road back to his house, touching his crucifix a little. He decided to call Jimmy, see if he wanted to hang out again one last time before school started. They weren't as far as they had seemed before.

Sasha was sitting in the living room, a neutral zone of the house. Her parents were both looking at her, trying to decide if they should be serious or more lighthearted.

"Are you upset about something?" her father asked, looking at her. She shook her head. It wasn't that, not exactly.

"Sad about something? Or happy?" her mother asked. There had been a lot going on the first week Sasha had been home. Both of her parents had given her some distance as she worked out what she had to with her friends. Sasha shook her head again because it wasn't that, not exactly.

"Oh no, are you pregnant?" Vivienne asked, looking at her daughter. Sasha laughed out loud. While that might have been her mother's path out of the life up at the point by the ocean, it wasn't Sasha's.

"No, not possible with who I was kissing," Sasha replied, and her mother nodded, assured. Her father laughed a little at both of the girls in his life; he reveled in them. They gave her a few more moments to think things over, and finally, she started talking.

"Listen, I don't know what I'm feeling. I just…I miss Hailey, and I thought that maybe if I went away from this place, I wouldn't as much, but that's not how it works. And I know I don't talk about it, and I know you guys give me space and all that, but I'm realizing I hate big houses. And I missed everyone a lot while I was out there. And I just…I wish you guys would be able to feed the chickens," she said, all in a rush. Again, her words didn't come out like she had wanted. They sounded a little more blunt and abstract than what was in her head, but it was really hard to transfer emotions into words that other people would understand.

"You didn't have a good time?" her mother asked.

"I did, but that's not the point. Everything is still the same here," she replied, a little exasperated. She was like her parents in that way; it was tiring trying to talk about how she felt. She would just rather not do it at all. Her parents looked at her for a moment, their beautiful little creation. She wasn't as finished as they thought. Everyone was unfinished.

"I know living with us is hard sometimes. I kind of raised you like a sister instead of a daughter," Vivienne started, thinking about it. She'd wanted such a different life for Sasha than what her parents had given her, but she was seeing there was a middle ground to be found. A little stability was needed, it was wanted, and it was all anyone ever looked for in life. Some stability, a little place to stand and brave the waves.

"It's okay. I'm just feeling…washed up, I guess," Sasha replied.

"Well, we can do better. We're here for you, love. Really, even when I'm painting, or your mom is writing, it's always about you, kid. I'm sorry it doesn't feel that way, but we can all work to make sure you do," Frank said, stepping into the conversation a little more. Sasha's eyes were a little teary, but she quickly blinked.

"Well, thanks," she replied. Her parents nodded, looking at her.

"Let's go feed the chickens," Vivienne said, holding out her hand to her daughter.

Daisy wasn't cooking meals like she used to, but no one dared say anything about it. Instead, Bernard and Melrose ate their food in silence, thanking her for every meal she made for them with a quiet murmuring and soft eyes. They were being so quiet for her; they thought it was something she wanted. They figured she was soft and quiet. It was a sunny summer day, at yet another silent lunch, when Daisy felt so imprisoned, so alone that she broke a glass in the sink, just to see if anyone could hear it. No one looked up. She looked back at them, exasperated, something deep inside of her growing and reaching up for the surface, needing air.

"My daughter is dead," she said.

They both looked up, eyes wide. She nodded. Finally, they were looking at her.

"I'm not alone in that, you understand that, don't you?" she asked, her hands on her sides, dripping water and soap onto the floor from the sink. She was so tired of washing the dishes. Bernard stood up, immediately trying to soothe her, make things quiet again. They thought that was what she needed.

"No, shut up. Knock it off. You two get to be loud, noisy, hit things. Hit people, even. What about me? I'm just locked up in this house, washing dishes in this sink? God, I can't stand it anymore. We've all had enough time with it. She's... she's gone. Okay? Can we work on that together now, please? Please?" she begged, her voice strung out and choked up at the end. They just looked at her, neither of them knowing quite what to do. Daisy had always felt so different to them, unlike anyone in the house, the neighborhood. But she wasn't so different. She had grown up there, chosen to stay there, just like them.

"You need to talk more," she said, pointing at Bernard.

"We talk," he said. She rolled her eyes, tears already falling from them.

"No, I talk to you, and you say nothing back. I might as well be talking to the wall, but I didn't marry the wall, now did I?" she asked. He shook his head, still standing by the counter. He was a big man, so tall and broad. But Daisy, in that moment, looked bigger than he did. Melrose hadn't seen his parents like this in a long time.

"And you, since when did you get to start making all the choices around here? Huh? What's going on with you, what are you thinking? What are you feeling? What do you want to do now, I mean. You graduated a few months ago. Why didn't we ever talk about that?" Daisy asked, looking from Melrose to Bernard, then back at her son again. He was sitting in the back corner of the table, his food only half-finished. His dark hair was still covering most of his eyes, but as she was talking, he had begun to tilt his head back to look at her more clearly. She wanted an answer from one of them, but they were both still so stunned by how many words were being spoken aloud at one time, with such conviction, and such love.

"Well? It's been two years. Okay? Can we talk now? Please?" she asked. Something strange was happening to Bernard. Melrose noticed it first. His face was turning red, but it wasn't out of anger. His eyes were narrowing, but they weren't mad. And his lips were quivering, but not in the way they usually did when he was about to shout. Daisy noticed it, too, and she let it happen. She walked up to him and wrapped her arms around him, and at first he tentatively hugged her back, then with more force grabbed her up and held her tightly to his chest. He wept.

Melrose sat at the table, watching his parents cry and hold each other, and he knew that was the conversation she had wanted so badly. He thought about Hailey, if she were sitting here, watching this. She'd probably laugh, say something to make fun of the moment, but deep down, she'd be happy about it. She had liked these kinds of moments. He knew how it felt. They could hold each other up now, maybe. He smiled softly, even though his eyes were blurry, too.

He was feeling a lot better. There were still things that were sore, that ached. But the bruises were lighter, his eyes opened fully again, and the pain in his side wasn't so bad that now he could laugh without immediately regretting it. They hadn't taken anything away from him that he couldn't gain back.

It was weird, but in a way, the incident had pushed Adam out of his world of tangible predictability and statistics and had thrust him back into the reality his son and wife lived in. What had happened to Calliste had shocked him, woken him up. He realized that perhaps, the lack of poetry had nearly killed his son. He was trying to talk more to both Alice and Calliste. They tried to be in rooms with the curtains open. The three of them together made Alice feel like she could open up the windows again and appreciate what was just outside the walls of her very pretty house.

They spent some time together, avoiding the different rooms the house offered and instead coming together in the living room with the big windows. Adam tried to cook again, something he had always been very good at even though he didn't do it often. And they talked, they kept talking, they didn't stop trying to connect again, find out where each of them began and stopped, and appreciating all the space in between. Calliste's French was a little rusty, but he tried to talk to his mother in the language she loved best, and it helped to bring her back up to the surface. She'd lost a lot, but they didn't have to stop trying to find different avenues to get to the same places.

They were eating dinner one evening, talking. Adam had made a roast and a variety of sides, and they were eating slowly to enjoy it. Alice wanted to go outside afterwards, enjoy some ice cream in the grass with the setting sun.

"You guys should, but I told everyone I'd meet them tonight," Calliste said, as he helped his dad with the dishes. He looked over at his mom, but she didn't seem upset.

"Go ahead, go. Have fun, okay? Tell your friends I said hello," she said, smiling a little bit and thinking about all of them. She was so proud her son had the friends he did. She was so happy something like the four of them existed.

"Are you sure? Really?" he asked, looking up at his father, still always anticipating some kind of sharp words or directions. Adam shrugged instead.

"Go ahead," he said, his voice quiet, his eyes focused on the pan he was hand drying with a dishcloth. It wasn't in his plans, but he was trying to mind less. Because like Alice said, if something good was going to happen, why stand in the way?

"I'll see you guys later," Calliste said, touching his dad's arm softly with his elbow, then walking over to his mother and giving her a light hug and kiss on the cheek before walking out the back sliding door and into the yard and then into the woods, following the trail. Alice watched him walk so easily, disappearing into the trees.

He walked slowly to the old *Chateau* enjoying his own woods for the first time all summer. They seemed more forgiving, more inclusive than the other woods he had spent time in during the hottest days of the year. He also knew how much better the destination was than a secret meadow that was hardly a secret.

"Finally, the kid makes it!" Melrose yelled out from his perch on the old roof. It had still not caved in, standing strong all summer long, waiting for them to come back.

"I'm still impressed that this is your land, and you make it here last every single time," Melrose said, looking down at Calliste as he came to stand right beneath the porch, shielding his eyes from the sun so he could look up at his friend. Melrose looked a little different to him, but he wasn't sure why. Sasha laughed, sitting up on the tree next to Davey. Maybe it was the lack of a cigarette or that he could see his eyes.

"Are you admitting that I'm an impressive person?" Calliste teased, and Melrose rolled his eyes as he slid down to the edge of the rooftop and then jumped to the ground, landing perfectly. Normally, he'd throw Calliste over his shoulder or something, toss him around a little, but the bruises were still there, even as they faded and turned yellow. He couldn't ignore that.

Sasha and Davey made their way down the tree, hopping down less athletically than Melrose had. They'd been talking about school – their senior year. It was starting in just about a week, and they weren't sure how they felt about it. It didn't seem like the kind of ending their summers had intended for them.

"Are we going to start this fire or what?" Calliste asked, looking at the fire pit with a little excitement. He'd missed all of this so much. Melrose noticed.

"I don't know, call the Boy Scout over here," Melrose said, waving Davey over.

"Literally, I was never a Boy Scout," he replied, coming over and getting ready to start the fire anyway. Sasha laughed as Melrose shrugged, not caring about specifics.

"Couldn't have fooled me, buddy," he replied, punching him lightly in the shoulder, but helping to toss some wood into the fire pit and laughing when Davey yelled at him about the correct way to stack the wood and how all the loose kindling and paper really needed to be in the center.

"Have any of you seen a better fire than a Davey Romano fire? I mean, really. All summer, I was hanging out around these little dinky things that some drunk asshole was making. Hardly comparable," Melrose said, waving his arms around as the flame in the center was growing, about to consume the wood and become a great fire.

"And here I thought your summer was going to be a quest for sobriety," Davey muttered between breaths into the fire, giving it oxygen to live. Melrose huffed a little, knowing that Davey was teasing him.

"Well, if so, the quest for sobriety is littered with an awful lot of beer cans and liquor and trap music that people really like dancing to, if you can call what they're doing dancing," Melrose said. He didn't want to admit it to anyone, but more than anything, he wanted a beer in his hand in that moment. He tried to shake off the thought, but it was planted firmly in his being.

"How do people dance at the parties Melrose Bartlett attends?" Davey asked, throwing back a little bit of his own joke at him. Melrose stood up.

"Allow me to demonstrate," he said, and with that, started to move around obnoxiously, attempting to recreate all the dance moves that he'd seen that summer. He had Sasha and Calliste almost rolling on the ground, they were laughing so hard.

"Doesn't look too bad to me," Davey replied, finally sitting up as the fire started to take care of itself, growing big and strong. Davey was proud of it. Melrose laughed, walking over to Davey, trying to get him to dance. His face turned red, and he was a little awkward, but after a moment, started to shake his body in time with whatever Melrose was doing. Sasha clapped out a beat.

"There we go, there's the enthusiasm I was looking for!" Melrose said, pointing to Sasha as if she was in a crowd, and he was pulling her up onstage. They kept it up for a few more minutes, before both of them settled down and sat on some of the logs around the fire. The sun was setting above, the sky darkening in hues of reds and oranges. It was something all of them focused on, some more than others, but nevertheless, they all, from time to time, looked up to the sky.

"So, what did a Sasha Raskova summer look like?" Melrose asked, looking up at her a little coyly. Her letters had been vague. They all focused on her, curious, and she blushed a little with the attention.

"Nothing, really," she said, and Melrose let out a roar.

"Oh, no, that's not all you're going to say about it," he objected, and she laughed, waving her hands in front of everyone to settle down.

"Well, Grandma Ann bought me some new clothes that cost more than I could ever admit. My grandfather is a bit of a racist and an elitist... Um, I spent a lot of time at the beach. I like whiskey. The ocean is nice. And.... oh, I made out with a girl named Gillian a few times," she said, and the boys laughed wildly.

"No shit?" Melrose said. She smiled, shaking her head.

"No shit. It was pretty great," she replied. Melrose smiled at her. She was a lot of things to him, to everyone. Davey just shook his head.

"You know what the Catholics have to say about all that," he replied. Sasha laughed, looking at her friend, then at his gold chain.

"Yeah, and what do you have to say about it?"

"I hope you didn't leave her hanging, that would be rude," he replied. She nodded. He was made from some of the best things, and used it right.

"I didn't. We talk," she said, holding up her phone.

"Getting some scandalous messages on that thing?" Davey asked.

"Oh yeah. Very detailed," Sasha replied. Melrose let out a howl, and Sasha laughed lightly at it. The sun had set some more; it was getting dark in the woods around them, but they had a Davey Romano fire in front of all four of them, and it kept everything very bright.

"Davey?" Sasha asked, looking up at him, pulling her eyes away from the intensity of the flames that often locked her attention. He looked up but didn't say anything. Melrose talked for him.

"Davey is having what is commonly referred to as an existential crisis, and also he told his old lady to…" he started, but Davey punched him in the shoulder with more force than he originally intended. Melrose just smiled at that.

"I kissed a girl this summer, too. Her name was Kate."

"And, get this, everyone, that's *all* he knows about her. No biographies or family histories. Doubtful she's Italian. My god, do we know if she's even Catholic?" Melrose joked, looking over at Davey, who was trying not to laugh at how outrageously honest the whole thing was. His friends really knew him.

"You caught me. I was living wild this summer," Davey replied.

"I mean, anyone could see that. Look at this hair," Melrose said, running his hands through Davey's thick brown hair that was the longest it had ever been in his life. He liked it, though, and no one in his house had asked him to cut it. He whacked Melrose's hand out of his hair, smoothing it back down.

"Watch out, this guy is going to try to get you to do a Mohawk with it next," Calliste said to Davey, eyeing Melrose. Sasha giggled.

"I remember helping you gel your hair up in middle school," she said, looking at Melrose. He threw his head back just thinking about it, a little embarrassed.

"It looked alright. I was the coolest kid in middle school that you ever saw," he replied.

"I think we're all just surprised you don't have more facial piercings," Davey said, elbowing his friend.

"Hey, I'm not the only one who remembers the lip piercing, am I?" Calliste asked and Melrose tried to shush him. Sasha shook her head.

"No, you certainty are not. I was there when he stuck the needle in," she replied. Davey looked nauseous for a moment, and Melrose huffed.

"I can't win with you idiots," he mumbled, and they each laughed a little as they shook their heads. There were a few moments of quiet between them as the fire changed colors, and they sat closer to each other. They started thinking.

"Are things different?" Calliste asked, breaking the silence.

"No," Melrose said, almost immediately. He was leaning forward, resting his elbows on his knees. He didn't want to think about that, but it was getting easier.

"I think they are. But I don't think it's a bad thing. We'll always have this," Sasha said, spinning her hand in a circle to encompass them all.

"I don't know, but it's okay," Davey replied. Calliste nodded. He hadn't expected anything less. He felt different, but things were always the same out at the old house in the woods, around the fire that was now sending bits of hot embers into the sky, floating up until they vanished.

"What really happened this summer?" Calliste asked. He didn't want to be the only one anymore. He hated that his bruises were so plain on his face. He wished he could hide like Melrose did, or cover things up, like Davey, or be so beautiful that nobody suspected anything, like Sasha.

"I lost my crucifix and blamed my cousin. But I didn't actually lose it. I had taken it off. And I missed dinner at my Nonna's, and I wasn't sorry about it," Davey said, having wanted to throw that off his chest and into the fire for a long time. It was hard, changing, becoming something different, and being something different than what everyone around you thought you were.

"I tried to run away from you guys, my parents. I just... I really miss Hailey, and I just feel sometimes that... I could blow away. I don't know how to talk about it. I just thought I wanted to go somewhere different, but it wasn't actually what I wanted," Sasha said. Davey nodded at her, understanding. It was quiet for a long minute after that, but finally, Melrose spoke up.

"I got into every fight I could this summer. And I broke a guy's jaw. And my dad finally hit me, too. You already know that shit," Melrose said. Sasha shook her head.

"Yeah, we know that. What else, Rose?" she asked.

It was quiet.

"I felt like I let my sister die," Melrose said.

Again, it was quiet. They thought about that, sitting out by the fire, one log empty like it had been for two years now. It seemed to be the encompassing thing. Everything constantly reminded each of them that she was gone, and it affected them all in different ways. It was time to move forward with it, instead of walking around directionless, exploring all of the grief it had caused. It was just time.

"You didn't."

"I know," he said. That was good. They all knew. They let it be quiet for a little bit longer, looking at the fire, watching it burn steadily. The embers in the sky were beautiful, dancing up into the dark sky to the stars and the moon, all the constellations and shooting stars, the meteors, and the lights. There was so much to take in.

"I had a crush on your sister for a long time," Calliste said, just throwing the words out there. He wanted that to be the thing to happen to him that summer. He felt it changed what everyone thought they knew about the beating. The misconceptions didn't bother him, but he thought they should know the truth, maybe now, at least. Melrose choked on a laugh he was trying to suppress.

"I bet you did," he said softly, looking at Calliste, smiling a little.

"She probably liked you back," he said. Sasha squeezed his shoulders, and Davey just looked into the fire, thinking about it. It was out now – what all four of them had done that summer. It took a moment for each of them to take that in, too.

"I registered for trade school. Electrical classes," Melrose said, shifting everything. Sasha smiled at him. That sounded about right to her. It was something he needed.

"Senior year is going to be weird for us," Davey said. He was going to miss seeing Melrose around the halls. It would be okay, though. The three of them would do all right, and Melrose was going to do great things alone for a little while, the one who wouldn't be left behind.

"You'll be just fine, straight A's," Melrose replied, ruffing up Davey's hair again. He couldn't help it; it was so inviting. Davey smiled lightly, letting it happen.

"Is all the s'more stuff gone?" Calliste asked.

"Well, the raccoons got into the cooler this summer, but, since I am now a responsible adult who brings home a paycheck..." Melrose trailed off, running into the old house to grab his grocery bags of marshmallows and chocolate and graham crackers. Out of tradition, Sasha laid out the graham crackers on her legs, Calliste handed her chocolate as she put the marshmallows that Davey and Melrose cooked between the two and passed them out. They made more then they could eat, but always left a few out for the animals or whatever else might want one.

"I see you guys didn't lose your touch," Sasha said, eating her second one.

"Of course not, it's a true talent, and talents never die," Davey said, carefully roasting one more. Melrose was happily eating a third one. It was helping distract him from the urge he felt inside that was begging for a beer, or a taste of liquor. He didn't need it. He wanted some, but knew he didn't need any.

Calliste ate his slowly, looking up at the sky, watching the embers disappear into the vast darkness with all the pinpoints of light shining down. No one could ever make him not enjoy looking up at the sky. He looked at a couple of the constellations he knew, watched as the moon seemed to get bigger and smaller as the smoke of the fire changed its shape as it went up.

"Another one?" Davey asked, handing him one, breaking Calliste from his thoughts. He shook his head; he'd had enough. Not knowing where to put it, they started a stack on the empty log around the fire of the s'mores they couldn't eat.

They looked up at the stars together, for once. And that was the best part of it all, despite everything, there they were, together, looking up at the same thing, and feeling the same thing about it.

"Was that a shooting star?"

"Yeah, it was."

ABOUT THE AUTHOR

Allison Astorino is the author of both *The Wood Stains* and *Duct Tape*. She currently lives in Michigan with her family, and works at a small farm where she has a one-eyed sheep named Sox. She is a student at the University of Michigan – Dearborn, studying English Literature with a minor in Psychology.

Made in the USA
Monee, IL
03 February 2021